To Peter,
With My
Warmest Best Wishes.

Ted Stowell

Back to the Tamar
*Country Tales from Early Post-War Days*

Also by Ted Sherrell:

*Kingdom of Cain*
*The Lonely and the Lost*
*Milltown*
*A Bitter Wind from off the Moor*
*Nor the Years Condemn*
*Point of Order, Mr Chairman*
*And the Days Grow Short*
*Fire and the Phoenix*
*The Cutting of Mary Park. . . and Other Devonshire Tales*
*Looking Towards the Tamar – More Tales of Devonshire Life*

# Back to the Tamar

## Country Tales from Early Post-War Days

# Ted Sherrell

UNITED WRITERS
Cornwall

UNITED WRITERS PUBLICATIONS LTD
Ailsa, Castle Gate, Penzance, Cornwall.

British Library Cataloguing in Publication Data:
A catalogue record for this book is
available from the British Library.

ISBN 9781852001636

Printed in Great Britain by
United Writers Publications Ltd
Cornwall.

To my beloved Ann,
the rock upon which I have built my life
and
to my much loved family –
we mutually are *semper fidelis*.

# Contents

# I

# The Old 'Oss

Arthur Dixon moved, a touch stiffly, to the forge, then operating the ancient but capacious bellows, excited the heaped coals from glow to dancing flame. Although this had been done in pursuance of his trade, his four 'guests' were nonetheless most appreciative.

It was November; there was a cold, damp wind bustling up from the Tamar, one which promised to get colder – and produce rain. On such a day the smithy was the coziest business place in the village, especially when he was boosting the heat to mould shoes for the next mighty beast to be shod.

Some of those availing themselves of his hospitality had a home every bit as snug (although there were many who did not), but they often had no desire to spend long winter days within such confines – and many a spouse was of like mind. So, with no work to go to, most of Arthur's visitors tended either to be retired or unemployed.

The old, cobweb strewn, almost cave-like blacksmith shop had an allure, not least of which was the general affability of the blacksmith, who was usually tolerant, even welcoming of such guests. Their numbers tended to vary from day to day, ebbing and flowing from, say, a couple to, on occasions, half a dozen (as many as eight had been counted there, though that was exceedingly rare). They were drawn from a pool of about a dozen, virtually all fellows who had been born and bred in the parish and had rarely, if ever, left it for any period – save for those who had fought for King and Country in the First World War. All though, had been far too old for the second global conflict which had been won some five years previously. Tales from the Great War abounded – some terrifying, most gory, the occasional one funny – and even though the blacksmith had heard them many times in the past (indeed almost word for word in many instances) he still enjoyed their telling as he hammered away, nailing heavy metal shoes to the capacious hooves of a mammoth shire.

A couple of fellows, most days, went over the top at the Somme – and still survived – whilst another had survived the horrors of Gallipoli; the privations of a German prisoner of war camp had been endured, a wizened old retired carpenter had rubbed shoulders with Lawrence of Arabia when fighting the brutal Turks, whilst another – a 'ladies man' – swore he had met the real 'Mademoiselle from Armentières', although in what capacity he never said.

Arthur's favourite, though, was George Spencer who had spent 25 years in the Royal Navy, having fought at Jutland. Such affection was spurred not so much by the old sailor's amiability (although assuredly he was amongst the most affable of men) but more due to the fact that after a quarter century of imbibing the senior service daily rum ration, the old matelot had retained a powerful taste for the liquor, and had never been known (in public at least) to be without an ample hip flask, a portion of which always found its way into the blacksmith's cup if Spencer was warming himself before the forge.

Most of the others were also generous, as appreciating his hospitality, they ensured he was supplied with cigarettes on a regular basis. Being a virtual chain smoker, this was a much needed and appreciated bonus as far as the blacksmith was concerned, and was provided with reasonable constancy throughout the average day. Not that anybody would be there dawn to dusk, but they came and went, staying anything from half an hour to an entire morning or afternoon, as reasonable access to the warmth of the forge could not be gained if there were more than six – possibly seven if the weather wasn't bitter – at any given time.

Thus attendance during the winter months (clearly the principal period of the blacksmith's popularity) tended to be self-regulating. And, generally speaking, Arthur Dixon was happy enough having them around, being a tolerably sociable chap, interested in village news, gossip and rumour – and happy, of course, to have the bulk of his considerable tobacco intake supplied free of charge, not to mention the rum.

Alfie Tremain finished tying the blacksmith's final customer of the day into the ancient, battered, soot shrouded shoeing stall, then moved rapidly to the forge to warm an ageing body chilled by the rawness of the late autumn day.

Dixon eyed the megalithic black and white beast which stood, apparently placidly, in the stall. His was a lingering look, pregnant with suspicion, perhaps even hostility. For he and Farmer Martin's mature shire were enemies of long standing; he had shod Prince for many a year, and knew the animal to be somewhat schizophrenic. For the magnificent creature – much loved by the farmer and his wife – by reputation the most placid, amenable equine it was possible to behold despite his vast power and strength, and an asset upon the land it would be almost impossible to replace adequately, changed character in dramatic, almost alarming fashion, when he became aware his long standing adversary, the village blacksmith, was going to affix fresh footwear. Even now, before the shoeing had begun, the beast – over a ton in weight – was stamping his hooves and laying his ears down close to his head, sound signs of trouble to come.

Dixon though, was more than a match. Whilst, like Prince, he was essentially easy going, evidence of another side to his character was displayed in the hue of his human 'mane' – a vivid ginger. As regulars at his forge would readily inform anybody willing to listen, the slightly built blacksmith, turning the scales at no more than ten stone, had the courage of a lion, the solid strength of granite and the temper, when provoked, of the devil. Prince never failed to invoke all three character traits in the man; but the old horse had not ever succeeded in defeating his perceived tormentor, never yet leaving his workshop with fewer

11

than the requisite four shoes firmly, efficiently and freshly attached to his capacious hooves.

About to do battle, Arthur spat on his hands, picked up his grimy, ancient work tray holding tools, shoes and nails, then moved towards the horse's rear. His audience, including Alfie Tremain, the highly experienced horseman who had delivered the beast, leant forward expectantly. They had seen this confrontation in the past and anticipated a riveting show to end the day.

As the blacksmith bent over to pick up Prince's left back leg, the old horse immediately lashed out. Arthur, though, was well out of the line of fire – he had been at the shoeing game for over forty years, starting as a twelve-year-old apprentice before the outbreak of the First World War – and had never yet been caught in any serious fashion by the flailing hooves of an unruly horse, and assuredly he had known a few, though none, he had to concede, worse than this ill-tempered beast of Farmer Martin's. As the hoof returned to its original position, the blacksmith grabbed it, thrust it between his bony knees, picked up the flat lever designed to prize the old worn shoes from the soft bone of the hoof – and began to swear.

It was an idiosyncrasy of the man that whilst he rarely used an expletive in all other aspects of his life (and assuredly never at home when in the company of his devout wife Molly, who had long been a Sunday school teacher in the Congregational Chapel), his language when shoeing was often 'colourful' – and when dealing with the 'hard cases' of the equine world, crimson.

"Old Arthur's in form today," said the ex-sailor to the fellow sitting next to him, Jack Barton, who had retired a few years earlier following the best part of a lifetime working for Devon County Council as a ganger on the roads. He nodded, then taking his pipe from his mouth briefly, verbally agreed.

"He is that, boy," he grinned broadly. "When Arthur's in form like this, he can swear for ten minutes and not use the same word twice."

Dixon had started with the words: "Stand still you..." then proceeded to a diatribe of invective, which was, in a perverse way, quite awesome – as were his skills, tenacity, strength and sheer gut courage. For despite the constant thrashing about of the old shire, the piston like movements from his hooves, not once was Prince able to shake himself loose from the clam-like grip of the man he saw as his oppressor – an unfair view by the equine of the human as in reality this master craftsman and essentially humane fellow, did not, nor ever would, cause any pain to Prince or to any other of the multitude of horses of all sizes, shapes and strengths that came his way in the line of duty and making his living.

At the end of this fierce, protracted session, his intention, in accordance with his regular practice, was to leave the shire as fit and well as when he had entered the smithy, but with the benefit and comfort of four freshly and stoutly shod hooves which, being pristine, would afford the still hardworking Prince greater protection plus a firmer footing. The operation was nearing its close; the blacksmith lifted the right back hoof – the sole one remaining to be shod – proceeded to douse the beast with a shower of abuse, then recommenced his hammering. Two more nails remained to hit their target then his tiresome task would be completed, he mused to himself as he reached towards his work basket to pick up the sturdy, sharp spikes.

A few years ago he almost relished his jousts with Prince, but now in his fifties he found the challenge infinitely more exacting – although his equine adversary apparently did not. Not, mind you, that he had any intention of walking away from it – not in the near future, at least. Horses such as this, though (and Harry Martin's turbulent Prince was by no means unique, although he was the blacksmith's most exacting foe), held for him a declining attraction; an elderly, docile mare, of which there were a reasonable supply available, made his working life so much more pleasant and his living easier. For he could charge no more for fighting the war of attrition that was the shoeing of Prince, than he could when slipping shoes on some sleepy old horse who did nothing in the shoeing stall except contentedly munch hay. They all had four hooves and that was what the farmers paid for – if one took twice as long to sort out, and demanded the strength and energy of a heavyweight boxer, then such were just the 'slings and arrows' of his profession.

13

Putting one of the nails into his mouth for easy availability, then holding the other above one of the small holes in the thick, still hottish metal curve, he raised his lumpy hammer to beat it into place – but was not destined to swing it downwards; for suddenly major mayhem ensued as before their eyes an event of calamity unfolded – with rapidity – and one which none of those gathered in the smithy, including the blacksmith himself, had ever before witnessed. A drama which all would expect, and assuredly hope, never to see again.

Alarmingly, Prince emitted a sound which chilled all in the warm forge – a wail, almost a scream, and deafeningly loud. More followed with a rapidity and drama which stunned even the hardened blacksmith. The old horse was seized by a spasm which appeared to thrust him upwards – indeed, so powerful was it, all four hooves cleared the ground (or so it seemed to the shocked spectators – and certainly a view they were all to give afterwards).

Such force there had been in this seizure that even Arthur Dixon was unable to retain a grip, the hoof flying from his hands, along with the hammer, causing him to stagger backwards, doing well to retain his balance. It was as well he had moved from the line of fire, for the great shire, after the apparent rising, fell back onto his hooves before tottering towards the ground like a mighty felled oak. Seeing what was happening, the blacksmith's sense of personal danger overcame his shock sufficiently for him to stumble the few paces to the rear, which would take him from harm's way, before the beast hit the cobbled floor.

For several seconds – some said it was as long as half a minute – there was a flailing of Prince's trunk-like legs before one by one they fell still save for just a few twitches. All was silence, the spectators to the dramatic happening rendered speechless by what they had seen. For none of them had witnessed anything remotely similar throughout their long lives. Even Rollo Wilkins, who had handled hundreds of horses on both the Somme and at Ypres (amongst many battlefields) and, in consequence, had witnessed unspeakable carnage of both equine and human, had never seen a beast taken by such a seizure, or fit, before.

The first to react – and then only after a protracted pause – was

Alfie Tremain, the realisation suddenly sweeping over him that Prince was in his charge, so as the animal had been struck down by a seizure which could prove, or had proved, terminal, it was he who would have to explain matters to the boss. And fair and amiable though Harry Martin was, and had ever been during the thirty plus years Alfie had been in his employ, it would be no easy task to explain any mishap (seemingly a most major one) that had befallen his best shire – which Prince still was although well into his twenties in terms of age. And it would be even harder if he was confronted with the 'missus'. She was a kind, generous, compassionate lady, but a touch over sentimental for a farmer's wife. She certainly doted on all three of the heavy horses at Downside Farm.

Slowly, apprehensively, almost fearfully he eased towards the prostrate horse, looking like a beached whale – and lying very still. How moribund, however, he could not be sure, as with it being gone half past four on a deteriorating mid-November afternoon, the light was fast fading, the still dancing flame from the forge doing little to neutralise the gloom. Momentarily he stood beside the massive mound that was Prince's belly, then shuffled up to the head, where he knelt. Instantly he noticed the eyes were open, but unblinking. He felt the neck, searching for a pulse, then moved his right hand close to an eye to see if there was any reaction. He remained kneeling for what to the others seemed an eternity: to the blacksmith especially, he sensing that a major calamity had occurred, something exceedingly rare in his well regulated workshop where his mastery of his craft was acknowledged and respected by the farmers and horse owners of the parish.

Slowly Alfie got to his feet, dragged his gaze from the prostrate Prince and looked in bewildered fashion in the direction of the proprietor. There was shock, disbelief and alarm within his tone when at last he spoke, "The old 'oss – 'ee's dead, Arthur; or so it seems to me. You have a look."

The blacksmith, still stunned by the drama, was slow to move, but not so Rollo Wilkins.

The old soldier and horseman got up from his rough seat by the forge and strode over to the prostrate beast with both urgency and sense of purpose. Whilst he, like the others, had no real idea as to what had assailed Prince, when it came to ascertaining whether or not he was dead his judgement would be as sound as any vet's. Deciding if horses were dead – men as well come to that – was something he had become most adept at between 1914 and 18. He lent over the horse's head, put his gnarled fingers onto his neck, cast his eyes over the prostrate body, stood up, glanced firstly at Alfie, then at Arthur – and shook his head: "Dead as a stone," he opined. His pronouncement was accepted by all without query; a man of his knowledge and experience would make no mistake over an issue like this.

The blacksmith's face was ashen, his voice soft virtually to the point of being inaudible. "Dead – I can't believe it, dead? The 'oss is dead? Really, I can't believe it. Forty years and more I've been at this game and I've never had such a thing happen before. I've had some old 'osses in here, a fair bit older than this; some frail ones too – some even sick – that had probably died soon after being shod, but I've never had one drop dead like this, in the middle of being shod. Never – never."

Alfie Tremain began to get a grip of himself, albeit slowly. The realisation came to him that the horse he had brought to be shod was now just a large portion of cat or dog meat lying on the cobbled floor of the blacksmith's forge and something would need to be done. Clearly as it was he who was in charge of the beast, it was he who had to take responsibility and action, Arthur Dixon being in such a state of shock (somewhat surprising, he mused, when considering the man's vast experience and, generally, level-headed temperament). Firstly it was clear to him that the owner of the animal – his employer – would have to be told, and with urgency, as the corpse could not long lay where it was at present.

"I'll have to get hold of Farmer Martin, boy," said he in the direction of the blacksmith. "He's got to know – it's his 'oss; and he'll have to get hold of the knackers to come and pick Prince up, although seeing the time I don't suppose he'll be able to get here 'til the morning; he's got to come from the other side of Tavistock. 'Tis a bit late for me to walk back to the farm to tell him, so I'd best phone."

He reached into a trouser pocket and produced a shilling and a half penny. He shook his head, then gazed at Dixon. "All I've got is a bob and a half penny, boy. I need tuppence for the phone box – you got tuppence there?"

Awareness returning at last to the blacksmith, he nodded, then reached into his pocket, and pulled from it a jumble of coins. Slowly he selected two pennies and handed them to the horseman.

"Thanks, boy," said Alfie. "I'll nip up to the phone box – I'll not be long."

With that he was out of the small side door and on his way to the red box just one hundred yards up the hill. He was followed almost immediately by the spectators, all shaken, to greater or lesser extent, by what they had seen, and all feeling that their presence was not what their host would have wanted at that time. Dixon was not long on his own, though, for the horseman was prompt in his returning.

"What did Harry say?" The words hurtled from the blacksmith's lips before Tremain had closed the door behind him. "I bet he's shocked – and upset."

"Well, yes, of course he is – both, very much so. I mean, like all of us; none of us would ever have thought that any such thing could happen, would we? – You said yourself, Arthur, it's the first time in your life you've ever experienced such a thing, and if it's never happened to you before when you think of just how many 'osses you've handled in your life – thousands for certain – then clearly it's something that hardly anybody anywhere would have witnessed. Anyway," he continued, getting to what he saw as being the main issue at present, "like I said earlier, it's too late to get Don Coleman here tonight with his old lorry to pick the 'oss up, but the boss'll make sure he comes first thing in the morning so you can carry on with your business. That be all right?"

The final words were spoken in pursuit of basic courtesy, for in reality there was nothing other which could be done, in the very short term, to remove Prince from the premises, save if it was possible to recruit the strength of a posse of men from somewhere to drag the beast out to the edge of the road – and clearly, being late afternoon and now almost dark, it was not.

The blacksmith nodded, his sensibilities still in shock over what had happened. "Yes, that's all right, Alfie – of course it is. I'll be here before half past seven in the morning – I'll see you then, or a bit after." He raised an arm in a weary farewell to the farm worker, but his gaze remained riveted to the so still horse laying before him. He would recover from the shock of this dramatic event, being a man of much resilience – but it would not be this day.

Alfie Tremain acknowledged the farewell, then took his leave.

The following morning saw Alfie trudging through the gateway into Downside Farm dead on 7.30am. A good timekeeper was Alfie, even though he had to walk three quarters of a mile from his cottage in the village and had journeyed into a buffeting head-on wind bringing regular squalls of icy rain and hail. It would take more than this, more than a bit of unfriendly, winter weather, to interfere with his customary precision in terms of arriving at work.

He made his way to the wooden packing shed – largely redundant during the late autumn and winter months with no flowers or fruit to be sent to market – waving to Herbie Parsons on his way, he having just appeared at the shippen door as he passed.

Herbie, a fellow in his early thirties, had worked for the Martins ever since being demobbed from the army in 1945, continuing employment interrupted by his wartime service, he having come to Downside on leaving school in the 1930s. Enjoying working with the bovine, he relished being in charge of the farm's smallish herd of South Devons. ("The only 'proper' cow is a brown one," was Harry Martin's maxim – also that of both his father and grandfather, who had, with Harry, farmed Downside for over a century. Mind you, back in those earlier times, anything other than a brown cow would have been a major rarity in Devon.)

With two young children to bring up, Herbie was glad of the extra income it brought him; for he started an hour earlier than both Alfie and 'Dead Eye' Dawkins, the third workman on the farm (so nicknamed because of his expertise as a marksman in the

home guard), and finished an hour later, the demands of milking
both mornings and evenings making such extra time essential.

Farmer Martin often gave a hand with the daily task of
milking, mainly mornings and at weekends, but the bulk of it,
plus the wide ranging husbandry involved in caring for the
valuable creatures, especially in winter when they spent so much
of their time indoors, was done by the cowman.

Such overtime was augmented even more during the summer
when, along with Alfie and Dead Eye, Herbie would often start at
six in the morning and, on occasions – when the weather
demanded – work until ten at night. That truly was harvest time
for all at Downside, with the sizeable acreage of strawberries
requiring intensive picking, especially in the morning, to be in
time to be dispatched from the local railway station to markets
throughout the land. Often evenings were set aside for saving hay
– hard, unrelenting work if the sun was hot, which of course,
usually it was, such being needed to make decent forage in the
first place.

There was, though, reward (albeit, hard earned) for the farm's
loyal staff – many hours of overtime pay being both a timely and
necessary boost to their incomes, enabling them to put money by
as some shelter against the 'rainy days' of life.

After passing Herbie, Alfie then went into the snug packing
shed, which apart from its horticultural use, doubled as the place
where the three men had their 'crib' and dinner. It was a touch
decrepit, but possessed comfortable chairs – although old and
somewhat threadbare – and during the cold winter days was
surprisingly cosy. From the bag slung over his shoulder, he took
a large pasty made the previous day by his wife Queenie (who
also did service at Downside during the daffodil and soft fruit
seasons, being a picker of all such crops at remarkable speed),
hung the bag up onto a nail, then trudged from the shed to the
kitchen door, some thirty yards away. Knocking loudly, he
opened the door and entered without being bidden as had been
his habit over the decades.

The farmer was pouring himself a cup of tea from the
capacious enamel pot sitting atop the massive black range which

dominated the far side of the big kitchen. He glanced up from his task, greeted the newcomer with a brisk "Morning, Alfie," told him to help himself to a mugful from the pot, went to the long, plain kitchen table, helped himself to milk and four spoonfuls of sugar, then sat down at the table facing the back door.

The workman who had replied, "Morning, Farmer," then "thanks," had put his pasty on a work surface close to the range for the 'missus' to put into the oven for warming later that morning – as was the routine two or three times a week during the winter. He poured his tea, copied his employer's routine exactly in terms of milk and sugar, then sat down opposite him. Such had been the routine for many a long year, summer and winter – a cup of good, sweet, strong tea at the start of the working day.

Alfie glanced at Farmer Martin, awaiting his instructions regarding the morning's work and, on this occasion, his reaction to the calamity at the forge the previous afternoon. The farmer looked weary, and distracted; all was not well with him. Momentarily he rubbed his eyes, then picked up his cup; he seemed once more back in the present.

"Sorry, boy," said he. "I'm a bit tired – been a busy morning already. I got up half past five, got the cows in and made a start on the milking before Herbie got here. I want to get it all over and done with as soon as possible, 'cause we'll need his help this morning – Dead Eye's too, when he comes."

There was a modicum of irritation in his voice when he spoke the last five words; for middle-aged man though he was, Dead Eye had never been a good timekeeper and throughout the year the number of days he arrived at work on the dot would probably be in single figures. He was, though, a hardworking, experienced and knowledgeable fellow, especially on the hedge building and horticultural side; in fact, the farmer would often say there was not a man in the parish with a wider knowledge of the strawberry plant, and of how to get the most out of it.

Alfie Tremain grinned at the reference to his colleague, drank a goodly amount of his tea, then eyed his employer. "What's on, Boss?" asked he, a touch of urgency in his tone – it appeared to him that something was afoot well apart from the usual routine, and he had little doubt it was connected to Prince's untimely death.

The farmer again appeared a touch distracted, but was soon back in control of himself. "I want you to harness up Rosebud, boy, and put her in the big wagon. We'll need Daniel as well – again, fully harnessed. If your could do that as soon as you've finished your tea, we can be round at Arthur Dixon's forge by about a quarter past eight. You take the wagon, of course, and Dead Eye can bring Daniel. I'll bring Herbie in the van."

It was a few seconds before the horseman gathered his thoughts; he was bemused. "But what are we going to the forge for?" he stuttered at last. When he had been told to harness the mare for the wagon, he had assumed it would be to bring in a load of hay from the rick in the nearby field, dwindling stocks in the forage barn needing replenishment.

The farmer now appeared more embarrassed than distracted. "It's, well – it's to bring back Prince; to bring him home to Downside."

Alfie looked even more bemused: "Bring him home, Farmer? You mean – well, can't Don Coleman collect him? I thought that was the arrangement; that Don would call around to the forge first thing this morning to haul him on board his truck. Something wrong with him, is there? I mean, Don'll usually turn out most times as far as I know. I've heard he's turned out on Christmas Day before now if it's really urgent."

"Yes, yes, reckon that's true, Alfie," agreed Harry Martin. "I've always found him very obliging, I have to say. This time, though, he's not coming because I've not asked him to. I've not phoned him at all. No, me and the missus had a chat about it last night and decided we didn't want old Prince to end up in the knacker's yard. He's been here ever since he was very young – probably no more than two years old, which is some twenty-five years now. He's part of the place, Alfie – so – so – so this should be his final resting place. That's why we'll need the wagon and both the other 'osses – a big beast like him'll take a fair bit of hauling up into it. Still, with those two and the four of us as well; we should be able to manage. It's a pity Graham isn't here – we could do with his strength."

21

The reference was to the Martins' son, a burly young man, six feet tall and some fourteen stones in weight, who was at present in hospital having his appendix removed, but who had, since being at home working with his father after leaving school, proved himself invaluable, especially when problems arose the solving of which required good old fashioned brawn. Not that the young man lacked intelligence as well; the opposite was, in fact, the case, for despite his youth the general consensus was that there was a 'wise head on his shoulders'. Certainly the general opinion was that he would be an adequate successor to his father when the time came.

"Yes, you're right," agreed the horseman, "Graham would be a brave help. Still, we'll manage, I dare say. There'll be us and the 'osses – and you may depend there'll be a few about the forge to see old Prince being taken away. They can make themselves useful and get onto the end of a rope."

An expression of positivity, almost enlightenment flitted across the farmer's face – "Yes, yes, you're right, boy. I'd not thought of that. A good idea – let them earn their keep for once. They spend enough time cluttering up Arthur's forge; good thinking. Perhaps you'll get Dead Eye to go into the barn and get some ropes – three or four, I should think. And there's a couple of old doors there as well – they'll be needed to put up against the back of the wagon, then hopefully we'll be able to pull the old 'oss up them and onto the floor of it. Won't be easy, mind you, but we'll do it, I fancy."

Alfie nodded, got up from the table, put the mug into the kitchen sink, went to the back door to exit himself, then looked back in the direction of his employer to ascertain information which he thought might have been volunteered already. "When we get old Prince back here, what are we going to do with him?"

The farmer looked a trifle sheepish; certainly, he took a few seconds to answer. "Well, boy, well – we – we thought the best thing to do would be to bring him back to Downside, take him down to the meadow in front of the house, take him right to the bottom and then, well – then we'll have to bury him."

Upon his employee, the final two words had the stunning

effect the farmer had anticipated, thus had not voiced until it was unavoidable.

"Bury him?" Alfie's tone was a mixture of incredulity, shock, even alarm. "What, bury old Prince, down in the meadow?" So astonished was the horseman, he merely stated exactly what he had just been told – possibly to ascertain that he had not misunderstood what Farmer Martin had said. Certainly the plan was so extraordinary it would have been simple to misinterpret; indeed, he hoped he had got it wrong and that the mighty old 'oss was not to be planted deep into Downside's rich soil. He had, though, not misheard.

"Yes – yes, obviously, boy. There's not much else we could do with him once we get him back here, is there?" Harry Martin pointed out, reasonably.

The farm worker had to concede that, true, there was no alternative – the animal could not, clearly, be left in the middle of a field to rot. This, though, did nothing to assuage his shock – then his concerns, especially those of a practical nature.

"But I mean – well, it'll take days to dig a pit big and deep enough to hold Prince. I mean – look at the size of him, it'll be a massive job and it'll need – well it'll need all of us to give a hand to dig anything that size. And it'll take a long time – days, perhaps two or three. And – well, boss, there's plenty else to do this time of the year, what with looking after the stock, bringing in the hay, straw, turnips and such like. It's up to you, of course – you're the boss," he added hastily – and accurately – "but it'll not be easy to do it all – and even harder if rough weather comes in, which could be the case by the feel and look of it."

"Quite right, Alfie, it'll be a major job to do it," agreed the farmer. "We'll all help though, the four of us, whenever there's nothing else crucial to do. Herbie with the milking and so forth, and you with all the horse work – draying things around and the like – won't be able to be at it more than the odd hour or two, but Dead Eye and me'll be able to put a fair bit of time to the digging. As long as the weather doesn't turn too rough and wet, it's surprising how quickly we'll make some progress. At least there's not any ploughing or tilling to do at present."

The horseman nodded. The farmer had made a decision, he had received his orders – so there was no more to be said, except to accede. "Righto – I'll go and harness the 'osses, and get the gear you want us to take. I'll tell Dead Eye – I reckon he'll be here by now."

Closing the back door behind him, he was confronted by Dead Eye Dawkins who, having deposited his dinner bag in the packing shed, was hastening to the kitchen to receive his own orders.

"Morning, Alfie," he grunted. "Bit behind," he added, somewhat superfluously. "The old scrumpy's lying a bit heavy this morning."

Such was not a rare occurrence, the middle-aged worker being a keen imbiber of the rough cider found in the barrel behind the bar at the Tamar View Inn, or from any other source for that matter. Harry Martin also often got in a goodly supply for himself and all at the farm, being a keen life-long scrumpy drinker, although this tended to be more in the summer months when the powerful apple based brew was deemed essential to the slaking of the thirst of hot men and women picking fruit and saving hay or corn.

The words 'lying a bit heavy' indicated to Alfie that Dead Eye had drunk too much the night before – he had been known to, often. Still, he reasoned, that was Dawkins' business, not his. So with no more ado, the horseman quickly outlined their immediate orders, and hastened towards the stables, the sore-headed fellow worker following in his wake.

"You say we've got to harness up the 'osses to go and fetch Prince from Arthur Dixon's; why? What's the old 'oss still doing there? I thought you took him there to be shod yesterday afternoon – why's he still there? And why does it take all of us, and the other 'osses to bring him home?"

Alfie suddenly stopped, then turned around and looked at his companion: " 'Course, you won't know about it, Dead Eye, will you? – I'd forgotten that. You'd have gone home yesterday before the boss would have been able to tell you. The fact is, Prince is dead; had a fit or seizure or some such thing when Arthur was shoeing him – dropped like a stone; terrible sight – I certainly hope I never see anything like it again. Anyway, it was too late to do anything about it then so we've got to go round there now and sort things out before Arthur has his first 'oss to shoe."

Dead Eye followed the horseman into the stables, silenced temporarily by his shock at the news of the demise of a venerable old animal whose service at Downside exceeded even his own twenty plus years. Although not a horseman by choice, Dead Eye did quite a bit of work with them when needed, and was very competent. He had an innate respect, if not affection, for the shires, which provided the power at Downside, there being no tractor. A few minutes in which both men busied themselves were to pass before Dead Eye spoke again. "Never expected that, boy," said he, with a shake of his head – stating the obvious, "must have shook you up."

Tremain nodded. "Yes, it did, I have to say. Not much does, really, but that – that was different. I've never seen anything like that before – nor's Arthur; and when you think of the thousands of 'osses that have been through his hands. Shook him up a fair bit – Arthur – and it takes a lot to do that. In fact, he couldn't credit it, couldn't really understand what was going on – he was sort of frozen to the spot."

"Good 'oss, Prince – take some replacing. And he'll have to be replaced, and soon. Can't go on long with just two 'osses." Dead Eye spoke the words as a statement rather than an opinion.

"No, no, you're right. It's probably all right 'til after Christmas, but the boss'll have to get a decent 'oss in soon. Mind you, perhaps he'll not be looking for one – perhaps he'll go the way of most other farms in the area and have a tractor. It makes sense, boy; it's very much the coming thing. I know Farmer Martin likes his 'osses and has always said he'd never have a tractor on Downside, but things have moved on fast since the war – too fast. Change, change, change everywhere; and folk changing with it, of course. No, the time's coming, sadly, when Farmer Martin will have to change as well – and turn his back on 'osses. It won't suit me, of course; I hate the thought of it. I've handled 'osses all my life and I want nothing to do with any engines. But it's coming, and there's nothing we can do to stop it."

Dead Eye shook his head. "No Alfie, it's not going to happen

b

here, not in our time here, anyway. Yes, there's a lot in what you say – change is going on; too much of it, too quick, a lot of it no help to anybody. But Harry Martin's the sort of man who when he makes up his mind to something doesn't change very fast. He's always set his face against tractors – always reckons 'osses are every bit as strong, are easier to manoeuvre and do far less damage with their feet than tractor tyres do – and I reckon he's right. No, there'll be no tractor here in the next ten years at least – and if we're spared, you'll see I'm right."

The horseman was not prepared to abandon his argument: "You forget one thing, Dead Eye – Graham."

"Well, what about him? He always seems happy enough handling 'osses." Dead Eye Dawkins was never quick to back out of an argument, especially when he was convinced he was right – which was often.

"Perhaps he is, on the whole, but he's a young man – only twenty or just over. I'd lay any amount of bets that he'd be even happier handling a tractor. I mean, it's only natural he would – tractors and modern machinery are the future. In many parts of the country you'll hardly find a working 'oss – or so I'm told. In fact, in many parts of even Devon you'll not find many, that's what they say, anyway. And another thing is 'tis getting ever harder to buy an 'oss, especially a young one. They're not being bred like they were before the war – not being bred as they were at the end of the war for that matter. It's the modern age boy – progress, they call it." Briefly he stopped, then grinned. "Tell you what, Dead Eye; I said I'd lay a bet on it, and I will – ten bob says there'll be no more new 'osses brought to Downside and poor old Prince'll be replaced with a tractor instead."

His companion took but a second to accept the challenge – "You're on, boy. Ten bob it is – and I look forward to collecting. Still," said he, moving forward – well aware that once again he had been late getting to work, and being essentially a conscientious man, feeling a touch guilty about it – "I suppose we'd better be getting on, especially if we've got to go right off to Arthur's forge." He went just a handful of steps then stopped again. "I've just had a thought – something which should have occurred to me before now; don't know why it hasn't, really – though I'm not at my best this morning." Mind you, Dead Eye was never at his best at such an hour, even when stone cold sober, although he was, of course, much worse after a gutful of scrumpy the previous evening. "What I'm asking is, why are we all going to Arthur Dixon's forge to bring the old 'oss back? Don Coleman'll do that, surely. The winch he's got on that truck of his would pull a battleship out of the water, so he'll have no problem with old Prince. I mean, Arthur'll be there so I don't see he needs anybody from Downside there at all. And he'll take the beast direct to his knacker's yard. If we bring him back here, then all that'll happen will be that Don'll have to come here and load Prince up. 'Tis all daft, boy – everybody's running around mazed like, when 'tis all straightforward really."

"Well, the thing is, Don Coleman's not going to pick him up at all – he's not been called, and he's not going to be either. We're going there to load Prince upon the wagon – then – then – well, then we're going to bring him back to Downside." He hesitated briefly, still astounded at the news he was imparting.

"I know that, but why? I mean, what are we going to do with him when we get him back here?"

The horseman looked directly ahead of himself when giving the reply – he knew his expression would betray his feelings on the matter; a combination of shock, bemusement, exasperation, and even a touch of anger. "Take him down to the lower meadow and bury him."

"Bury him? Did you say, bury him?" There was no need for Dead Eye to repeat the question as he had no real doubt he had heard correctly the first time. The news though, was scarcely credible. "But – but – but, it'll take 'til Christmas to bury him – he's massive, Prince is; it'll be like burying a bus. Think of the size the pit'll need to be – who's going to dig it?" The shock of the news was now seasoned with the reality that heavy, exhausting labour would be needed to excavate with pick and shovel enough heavy, wet Devon earth to make a pit of sufficient capacity to accommodate the gargantuan corpse.

"All of us – boss as well; or so he says. Mind you, to be fair to him, if he says he's going to help, then help he will." The horseman had worked for Harry Martin long enough to know that what the farmer stated as intention, invariably was what he did.

"But why, Alfie? Why are we going to bury the 'oss? I reckon we've both known a few 'osses drop dead over the years – you especially, as you've always worked with them – but when it happens the knacker man gets called out and he hauls them away; they don't charge for it as far as I know, but they're pleased to do it 'cause the body of a beast that size is always worth a few bob – it's their living. Although it would be tough, there's plenty of meat on old Prince. Feed a brave few dogs and cats he would. Come to that, in the war he would have fed us as well – perhaps even as recent as two or three years back," he added, with some accuracy. "So why, for God's sake, are we going to slog our guts out and bury him?"

The horseman shrugged his shoulders. "Missus, I fancy," said he. "I don't know for certain, but he said he and the missus had talked it over and, because old Prince had been part of Downside for so long, his last resting place should be here. They didn't want him to end up in the knacker's yard. He made it sound as if they decided it together, but it's what she wants, you can depend on that. The boss can be a hard man sometimes, but he always gives ground to the missus. If she wants things done in a certain way, then that's the way they'll be done. It's always been like that and always will be. Sentimental is the missus – the boss isn't; tough as old boots he is, he'd have had Don Coleman take the old 'oss away, but missus won't have it – that's it in a nutshell."

Dead Eye shook his head in weary fashion. "Towny," said he; the single word, as spoken, was meant more as an explanation for her conduct than a condemnation. The farm worker's thinking being that because she had not been born and bred in a rural community, there was about her that which so often afflicted folk, women especially, of such a background – sentimentality and a failure to recognise the harsh realities of the farming world, indeed, of the natural world also.

Sarah Martin had certainly been born in a town (albeit a small one) – nearby Tavistock – and whilst that, being a market town, was far more in tune with a rural, farming area like the Peninsula than was Plymouth, the blitzed conglomerate some ten miles to the south, it was still in many aspects somewhat sheltered from the rawness of life in the open countryside and the harsher, more basic ways of a village community, the survival of which was majorly dependant on the prosperity of the farms and smallholdings surrounding it. She had been married to Harry for over thirty years, she having met her future husband at a dance in Tavistock Town Hall – a life altering moment for them both as it had been truly 'love at first sight'. They were wed within six months and had lived together in an atmosphere of mutual respect, devotion and trust.

Whilst not an assertive person, her influence over her husband had been profound. Always a good farmer, as had been his father before him, Harry Martin, a strong minded man, could be a touch hasty, possibly even a little irrational, in both decision and action. Sarah though, right from the beginning, had been a steadying, curbing influence of considerable power, and rarely during their married life had he ever taken any action or made any decision of note contrary to her wishes or advice.

Rapidly she had become a much respected member of the village and farming community and now, in middle age, was a long serving member of the Women's Institute, the flower show committee, the Mother's Union and the church choir, her gentle outgoing personality and sharp intellect making her an asset to the first three, whilst her strong soprano voice made her invaluable to the last.

Sarah had always, as well, been most highly regarded by those who worked at Downside, all having, over the years – indeed, the decades – felt the benefits of her kindness and consideration, none more so than Herbie Parsons. A few years earlier, when his first child was born, his wife, Dora, had been struck down within days of the birth by a very severe attack of 'flu, leaving her husband trying to cope with the newly born child, basic home duties and, of course, his livelihood as stockman on Downside. Some help was provided by Herbie's family, but Dora, being an orphan, had none to call upon. Sarah, though, was magnificent, baking food such as pasties, cakes, sausage rolls and suchlike for the workman, making broth and soup to temp the frail appetite of his sickly wife, and going around regularly to their home in the village. There she tidied, helped with the baby, collected the dirty linen – which she took back to the farm to wash and iron – and, generally, lifted the spirits of the unwell, somewhat depressed young mother. Neither Dora nor Herbie would ever forget what the 'missus' had done, never forget her immense thoughtfulness, compassion and practical help.

Alfie and Dead Eye, likewise, had received nothing but generosity and consideration from her over the very many years they had worked at Downside. She appeared ever mindful of the hard, physical and skilled work they did, of the adverse conditions in which, often, they had to perform their tasks – in terms of both weather and terrain – and of the fact that, like their employers, there were times they would have their own personal problems and challenges to confront. Added to this was her culinary expertise, especially during the summer months. It was a long established custom that when the workmen stayed on in the evenings for either haymaking or to continue fruit picking, farmers' wives provided tea. Sarah's were such that many found it none too easy returning to work afterwards, so laden were their bellies – filled with an array of savoury and sweet foods which, whilst basically simple, were always cooked to perfection and flavoursome to a level which would satisfy a gourmet. Assuredly, no supper was ever required when they arrived home.

"She is a lovely lady," Dead Eye had once stated to someone in the village and, if he and the others were frank, one of the principle reasons why none of them had ever sought employment elsewhere. There were a few farmers in the parish who paid a higher hourly rate, but none, they knew full well, would give them the quality of working life and benevolent ambience to be found at Downside. So, the unspoken word amongst the trio of employees was that, daft though the idea of burying the old 'oss clearly was, unnecessary hard work though it would bring their way, if that was what the missus wanted – then, fair enough, it would be done without question or complaint.

Reaching the stables, the two men speedily harnessed the brace of burly shires, then led them out into the yard murmuring to them in encouraging fashion as they went. Dead Eye hitched Daniel to a rail then proceeded to one of the squat, ancient granite-built barns to fetch the ropes and other paraphernalia needed for the morning's stiff challenge, whilst Alfie backed Rosebud between the shafts of the wagon.

Within a few minutes, men, horses and capacious carriage were in the yard with the equipment lodged aboard. They were joined by the farmer and the cowman.

Harry looked about him, saw everything appeared to be in order, then gave his instructions. "Right, Alfie, Dead Eye, if you'll go on with the 'osses and wagon, me and Herbie'll put the churns out for the lorry. Soon as that's done, we'll follow on in the van."

The two men nodded their understanding of the instructions and briskly moved away across the yard towards the road, whilst, with equal alacrity, Harry and Herbie went towards the dairy to load the collection of large metallic milk containers on to the low level trolley they used to take them the one hundred yards, or so, to the platform constructed by the parish road, built adjacent to the farm gate. Within the hour the lorry from the dairy on the far side of Tavistock would call, as it did daily with remarkable consistency throughout the year, to haul the rich cream-laden milk to the plant to be pasteurised, bottled then dispatched to milkmen around the area (especially Plymouth). The following morning they would be placed upon countless doorsteps. Fortunately Downside was some two thirds the way around the driver's daily collection route, so the time the churns needed to be in place for loading was the best part of an hour and a half later than that needed for farms located at the commencement of the collection.

Within twenty minutes, the two shires, with their escorts, had arrived at the forge, to be joined, in little more than a minute, by their employer and Herbie Parsons, the farmer parking the somewhat battered old Commer van just past the door leading into Dixon's sanctuary.

The blacksmith was busy giving life to the fire in preparation for the work which would commence as soon as Prince was removed. He looked exceedingly surprised to note that no fewer than four had arrived from Downside Farm to assist with the removal of the corpse which dominated his workshop.

"What's on?" asked he. "I never expected you to come mob handed, Harry."

His tone was a touch sharp (the presence of a very big equine body lying within his forge had upset his routine, exceedingly). He regretted it, instantly, only too well aware that the beast, apparently healthy, had died in his care – literally in his hands – a fraught happening which made him, conscientious man that essentially he was, feel just a touch guilty, though in reality, he had been around long enough to know that it was just wretched luck for all concerned, including himself.

"What I mean is, old Don with all his gear could just hitch the cable to the old 'oss's hind legs, then pull him out of the forge and up into his truck – the body'll pass through the double doors, no doubt about that." His tone was somewhat more conciliatory. "I reckon you've all got enough to do at Downside without having to do the knackerman's job as well."

"He won't be coming," replied the farmer.

"Why not? He bad or something? It'll be unusual if he is – fit as a fiddle is Don. I've never known him let anybody down, ever."

"No, he's not bad – I've not sent for him, that's why he's not here, and why the rest of us are. Graham would be here as well if it wasn't for his appendix – we could definitely do with his strength."

"Strength – what do you mean, strength?" The conversation puzzled the blacksmith, he essentially being a most logical thinker.

"The strength to help get the old 'oss up onto the wagon there so we can take him home." The farmer's reply was given in tones which suggested he saw nothing unusual in such a course – although, in truth, the opposite was the case.

The blacksmith's voice, however, unlike Harry Martin's,

suddenly rose an octave. "Take him home – what, the old 'oss, take him home? But why? What do you want him home for? What are you going to do with him when you've got him there."

"Bury him," came the simple response from the farmer; his three workmen maintaining total silence, and, with some effort, dead pan expressions.

"Bury him?" By his shocked tone, there would appear to have been no news which could have shaken the blacksmith as greatly as this. For a few seconds he appeared immobilised, then once again he spluttered the brace of words – "Bury him?" He shook his head; looked away from the farmer towards the whale-like corpse, then back at Martin again. "But – but look at the size of him, Harry – I mean, well, I mean, look at the size of him," he spluttered, almost incoherently. "He's – he's – he's almost the size of the *Ark Royal*!" – He could be prone to a touch of exaggeration could Arthur. – "It'll take you a week to dig the pit – I mean, just think how big it'll need to be, and deep."

Harry Martin nodded. "Oh yes, it'll take a fair pit, boy," said he (understatement tended to be the farmer's habit, rather than the opposite), "and a brave bit of digging; and it'll certainly take us a day or two. But there's the four of us, and we'll all put our time to it between doing the other work that's got to be done, of course. One thing this time of the year, though, it's mainly looking after the stock – nothing much to do on the land, no sewing or reaping, ploughing or drilling. That's the one good thing about winter. No, we'll get it done, all right, then dear old Prince will be laying in the earth he's worked for so long – just as it should be."

The last sentence had originally come from his Sarah, almost word for word, on the previous evening, and after she had spoken the words, he knew there could be no other disposal of the old 'oss than to plant him in Devonshire – and Downside – soil.

The blacksmith was about to launch a further broadside as to the insanity of the plan but abruptly thought better of it. Rather, he shrugged his shoulders, and said, correctly, "Well, this is a matter for you, boy – none of my business, really," then proceeded to open the double doors to facilitate the removal of the moribund 'guest', the presence of whom was disrupting his business.

"You'd better bring Daniel round, Dead Eye," instructed his employer. "We'll stand him a few feet behind Prince, fix a couple of ropes to his hind legs, attach them to the 'oss's harness, then he can pull the body out of the forge to the back of the wagon. I would think he can do it on his own, but if he can't then you'll have to take Rosebud out of the shafts, Alfie, so that she can pull as well."

Dead Eye began to bring the young shire forward but was stopped by the blacksmith: "I wouldn't do that, boy," he rasped, some urgency in his tone. "A young 'oss like that could well play up – they don't like death, horses don't. He'll know old Prince is dead before he gets within twenty paces of him – he'll sense it. He could turn awkward; I've seen it happen. No, I don't think you'll be able to use him to pull the old 'oss out – big, young, strong 'oss like that, anything could happen."

Alfie Tremain nodded in agreement. "Yes, you're right, Arthur. I should have thought about that – like you I've been around 'osses all my life. I'm not sure Rosebud'll like it either. She's older than Daniel, mind you, with a far more placid nature, but I don't doubt she'll sense the old 'oss is dead, and she could play up a bit. And when you think of it, it's bound to upset her, isn't it? After all, they've stood side by side in that stable for years – worked side by side, as well, pulling the plough and suchlike. Just think how we'd feel."

The farmer did so, and agreed, "No, you're right, both of you. Clearly there's no way we can use them to pull Prince out of the forge. We'll just have to do it ourselves." He looked about him, noting the accuracy of Alfie's prediction that there would be an audience for the removal of the equine corpse. Four were in attendance despite it being an earlyish hour on a stormy, raw winter morning, three of whom had witnessed Prince's dramatic and untimely demise the previous day. "I reckon you chaps'll give us a hand to pull the old 'oss out and up onto the wagon won't you?"

There was assent, unanimous, to the request – although a couple were well into their seventies and not built in such a way as to promise great physical strength. It was a most rare event, though, and assuredly something they would be able to hold court on over their scrumpy and beer in the Tamar View Inn that evening – and for many more thereafter, probably.

The farmer was about to organise the fixing of ropes to the beast when another thought struck him: "If it'll frighten the 'osses pulling him out of the forge, then old Rosebud'll not be too happy pulling the wagon back to Downside, will she?"

The blacksmith agreed, and quickly voiced a possible solution. "She certainly won't be happy if she sees Prince dragged up onto the wagon, but if you take her and Daniel round to the yard behind the forge and tether them there – then bring them back when he's been loaded, and covered with that tarpaulin I see you've brought with you, then it should be all right. Hopefully, they'll not know he's aboard; and Rosebud being an oldish 'oss, and quiet, helps a fair bit."

Knowing there was not a man living in West Devon who knew more about horses than Arthur Dixon, the farmer took his advice without demur. Thus, the shires were led to the yard around the back out of harm's and vision's way, ropes were attached to their stricken former workmate – and the pulling began. The sinews of the motley gang who gave strength to the ropes were perplexed to maximum extent, and there was much grunting, groaning and swearing, especially from the blacksmith, who nonetheless avoided (not easily) stating that the entire exercise of taking the corpse back to the farm was madness, he still feeling, as the animal had died in his care, he had no moral right to make criticism of its disposal.

Painfully slowly, the old 'oss was eased – inch by grudging inch – out of the forge and then, even more slowly and laboriously, up the improvised ramp and onto the floor of the spacious wagon. At last, the body stored safely aboard, the ropes were released and the tarpaulin employed in shrouding the mighty body (big though the sheet was, it was only just sufficient to hide the corpse from view). Alfie and Dead Eye retreated to the yard to collect the shires, whilst Harry thanked the forge regulars who had helped upon the ropes; their assistance, whilst not dramatic, being possibly the subtle difference between success and failure. "I'm obliged to you chaps," said he. "There'll be a pint or two of scrumpy for you all when next you're out Downside way – just look in when you're passing." It was, he was sure, an offer which would be taken up, and without major delay, as the cider made on the farm by generations of the Martin family had ever been at the highest levels of both taste and potency.

There was general thanks all round, then the Prince funeral party were left to make their way, sedately, back to Downside, whilst the blacksmith was free to start his day's shoeing, and his regulars were able, following their unexpected exertions, to warm themselves before the forge; although one of the number decided to return home as his breakfast was a priority, the energy he had used so early in the day needing replacing with the fuel of a fry-up.

On getting back to the farm, Harry Martin told his men to return the two horses to their stables – briefly in Rosebud's case – then take a belated, but much needed and deserved 'crib' break; he included himself in this.

Having consumed sufficient to sustain themselves until their dinner-time pasties, they all returned to the disposal of the old 'oss. The spot chosen for his final resting place was the meadow – a permanent pasture which lay down in front of the farmhouse.

Rosebud slowly but steadily pulled the wagon with its macabre cargo down across the field to a far corner, the old mare still apparently unaware of the cargo hidden under the tarpaulin. Once arriving at a spot some twenty yards from the bottom hedge, Alfie unharnessed Rosebud from the shaft, leaving her to move away to crop the meagre winter grass of the meadow, then joined the other three to give assistance to pull on the ropes attached to Prince's hooves in order to remove his carcass from the wagon down onto the ground, and his final resting place.

It was another task which involved hard graft – albeit a touch easier than the loading – but was accomplished without complication, Prince lying on the cold, wet turf.

Alfie disturbed Rosebud in her grass gathering pursuit, returned her to her engine-like duties between the shafts, then went about his regular winter task of fetching hay from a partially used rick in a nearby field. He would ferry it to the large barn attached to the shippen, a task which, by the time he had used the big hay knife to cut large chunks of the compacted hay from the big, brick shaped rick, would fill the rest of the morning.

Herbie also took his leave, returning to the shippen to cleanse it of the dung-laden straw which remained following the cows' overnight occupancy of their stalls – which happened during the winter months – afterwards replenishing it with fresh straw. His task then was to fill their feeding troughs with turnips, mangolds, cattle cake and hay in preparation for when they were brought back in from the field, mid-afternoon, for the second milking of the day, to be followed by their cosy night sheltered from winter cold and storm.

Thus Dead Eye and the farmer remained alone to prepare for the gargantuan dig.

Firstly, the dimensions of the grave had to be marked out. Harry Martin, well aware that Dead Eye had impeccable judgment in matters requiring accuracy and precision, and not just in his ability to aim a rifle expertly, gave over the lead and awaited the workman's instructions. The sharp featured, somewhat gnarled – but exceedingly fit – fellow (he put his general good health down to his regular, often copious, scrumpy imbibing – "No healthier drink," as he would say), was not long in assessing the size of plot needed to accommodate the body, his employer pushing short wooden stakes into the sodden turf in accordance with his instructions. The task having been completed to Dead Eye's satisfaction, they stood back and cast their eyes over the plot bounded by the stakes.

"That's going to be a master pit, you know," said Dead Eye with some understatement.

The farmer nodded, silenced temporarily by the cold realisation of what was going to be required. "It is that, boy," he replied at last, "and it's going to take some digging." He shook his head slowly and lapsed again into silence. Quickly, though, he rallied. "Well, it's got to be done, Dead Eye. The poor old devil can't be left laying there for long – the blasted foxes will soon be at him, and he'll soon start to stink as well, even though it's wintertime. I've a few things to see to this morning, and I need you to grind up some oats for Rosebud and Daniel before dinner, so we'll make a start on the digging this afternoon – all of us to start with, although Herbie'll have to go and get on with the cows and the milking about threeish. Still, we should be able to make our mark before half past four, or so – it'll be too dark after that."

Dead Eye nodded, then went about his business, as did the farmer, both aware that a mammoth task – one which in reality, had been avoidable (though nobody was ever going to say such a thing) – lay before them.

The weather, whilst breezy, was dry as they began the job, though there was much cloud about suggesting the light would be failing quite early – possibly just after four o'clock. The quartet, armed with spades, shovels and picks, began to dig, and by the time Herbie left to attend to the milking herd, a sizeable heap of freshly dug soil lay around the rim of the capacious, rectangular grave. This, though, had been the easy bit; for just prior to the abandonment of work at ten minutes past four, due to the gathering darkness, they found they had removed all the soft, rich topsoil and were confronted with a mixture of shillet, clay and rocks: Pickaxes and hand diggers would be the order of the day from then on – and progress would be infinitely slower.

"Still, we've not done bad," stated the farmer with some satisfaction, as they trudged back up the meadow to the farmyard. "Thank you for your efforts; it's not been easy – and tomorrow it'll be even harder, of course, with all that shillet and stones. But with a bit of luck, if we can have a full day at it, we might be able to plant poor old Prince before dark – or the morning after, at the latest. It's down to the weather, of course – everything always is," he added, with the wry wisdom of a man who had spent his life clawing a living from the land, sometimes thanks to, very often despite, the vagaries of the West Devon climate.

The weather the following day was benign, and the farmer and his team were able to have a full day hewing the ever stonier and heavier soil from the deepening pit. Their progress though, was slower than he had hoped despite Herculean, exhausting efforts from them all. And even though they were able to work until half past four – the light being better – the job had still not been finished. The farmer opined, however, that a couple of hours hard graft in the morning would see the pit deep enough for the old 'oss to be buried, and the entire, protracted business should be over by dinner-time.

It was to be, however, a case of the 'best laid schemes of mice and men', as a south westerly gale coming in off the Atlantic and sweeping up the Tamar in the early hours produced a vile day of lashing rain, turbulent winds and a rawness which would not aid the health of anybody working outdoors for long. Further work that day on the pit was clearly out of the question.

The following morning, though, whilst still windy, produced weak winter sunshine; thus, the farmer was confident their macabre, exhausting task would be completed. The early morning winter day routine completed and crib consumed, the quartet proceeded to the bottom of the meadow, their tools over their shoulders eager to remove the relatively modest amounts of stone and soil remaining, then to bury the old 'oss still laying beside the pit shrouded in a tarpaulin. The mission was to complete the mighty exercise before returning to the farm to consume their dinner-time pasties.

Arriving at the pit they halted almost in unison and gazed into it, all still clinging onto the implements they needed to finish the job. To say they were shocked would have been an understatement – stunned, possibly, would have been more apt. For they were not gazing down into a deepish crater, but at a freshly dug pool! The old 'oss's grave was full of water, a situation summed up, after many seconds of shocked silence, by Dead Eye:

"There's enough water in there to end a drought."

The farmer nodded his agreement, sighed, shook his head then scratched it. He was confused, frustrated and perplexed – feelings and emotions rare in a level-headed, clear and logical thinking man who usually saw the way ahead quite clearly.

"I must say, I never foresaw this," said he, still shaking his head. "Granted there's been a brave bit of rain – any amount, I suppose, when you think of it, but it never entered my head that the pit would fill up like this. Come to that, I never thought of water going in at all. 'Course, it's down the bottom of the field, so there's bound to be a bit of a run off, but I never would have thought there could ever have been enough to fill it up. Anyway, the question is as to what we do now?"

"Empty it, I suppose," replied the horseman, simply. "Although it'll be a fair caper to get that lot out – hard work without doubt, and it'll take a long time."

"Days, it'll take," commented Dead Eye. "Then I doubt we'll do it – hit a spring, that's what we've done. I never thought of it properly, although I should have. The other night when we were last down here, just as we finished, I fancied it was getting just a bit wet down the bottom of the pit. The trouble was that the light was failing that fast it was impossible to see what was happening. I bet we'd already hit a spring and all the rain on the past day or two has really got it going – rainwater alone would never have filled a pit like this." The words were spoken with the quiet confidence and authority of a man who had worked over thirty years on the land and knew its ways better than most.

Harry Martin knew this, and suspected that he was right. "If that's the case, then it'll fill almost as fast as we empty it – a total waste of time and energy it'll be," said he, "and I'm very much afraid that is the case. I reckon Dead Eye's right – we've hit a spring. So, the question is – what do we do now? We can't dig another pit, that's for sure. Even if the weather stays reasonably dry – and the forecast says the opposite – it would still take us a couple more days. Poor old Prince can't wait that long, even though it's coldish, he's beginning to stink already, so he's got to go underground today."

"But there's no way he can, is there," stated Herbie Parsons, simply. "It's just impossible for us to dig another pit in a day – look how long it took us to dig this one."

"You're right, boy," agreed his employer, "no way at all – it's clear." He again shook his head, in highly exasperated fashion. "Sorry gents, despite all the efforts you've put in over the past few days – and they've been appreciated, let me say that, by both the missus and myself – despite everything we've done, there's only one thing that can be done now – I'll have to phone the knackerman to come and take him away. What a caper, eh? What a game."

No comment came from the other three, although all were stunned by the upsetting, and highly unexpected, turn of events.

"I'll go back to the house and phone Don Coleman. Hopefully he'll be able to pick up Prince fairly soon – he needs to go today, that's for sure. Missus'll be upset the poor old 'oss can't be laid to rest here, but she'll know there's no other way."

They all knew that this was so, for Sarah Martin, whilst being a most thoughtful, compassionate person was essentially realistic and pragmatic. Crucially – being the wife of a farmer – she was not burdened with the curse of complete over-sentimentality. Harry returned to the house to make the call whilst the other three busied themselves about the yard; Herbie and Alfie in the shippen, Dead Eye sorting out the tools he would need to repair an ever-widening gap which was blighting a hedge in the field adjoining the meadow, and was to be his task once the old 'oss had been disposed of. He, in particular, worked with alacrity and a sense of purpose; a master at hedging (the best Harry Martin had known at Downside, and as good as any in the parish) it was a task he enjoyed and from which he derived much satisfaction. Certainly his work was there displayed for all on the farm to see for decades to come – anything Dead Eye put up remained there for a lifetime thereafter.

Harry spoke to the knackerman's wife and was told that her husband was out and about picking up various dead beasts. She expected him back for his midday meal and was confident he would not be late as it was lamb that day and Don, being a man who liked his food (indeed, seeing his corpulent frame, there had come from the quick-witted Dead Eye Dawkins the observation that "Old Don probably eats most of the beasts he picks up") would be home on time unless something most unexpected and exceptional intervened. She would pass on the message, and he, having, to her knowledge, no other collections that afternoon, would surely be along after his repast – somewhere around three o'clock, she would suggest.

Don Coleman was ever a reliable man in terms of both time and honesty, the former being displayed admirably, he arriving in Downside's yard at ten minutes to three. He and the farmer chatted briefly then both climbed upon the knackerman's old but sturdy truck. Slowly Coleman drove it down across the soft ground of the meadow to the tarpaulined bulk at the bottom.

The three farm workers carried on with their usual work, Dead Eye having proceeded to the other field to begin his satisfying task of filling the gap. It was agreed that none would be needed to help load Prince aboard, as the heavy winch on the back of the truck would be more than adequate to drag up the shire – "Pull up an elephant this beauty would," as Don Coleman had stated proudly on many occasions; and it had never yet been found wanting. Nor was it on this occasion. For the knackerman backed his lorry to within a few yards of Prince, deftly attached the winch to his back legs, and then slowly but inexorably pulled the old creature up into the high-sided vehicle. The winch was disconnected, the rear barrier bolted back into position, and both men got into the cab to drive back to the yard.

The engine was started, first gear was engaged and the back wheels began to move – ever faster – but the heavily laden truck moved not an inch. Rather the rear wheels dug themselves, ever deeper, into the rich and sodden Devon soil. Both men alighted from the cab, went to the rear of the truck, saw the tyres deeply embedded in the ground and simultaneously scratched their heads.

"I know it's soft," commented Coleman, "but I never expected this to happen. 'Course, the old 'oss is a brave weight – as big an 'oss as I've had aboard in a long time – but I've known bigger and heavier over the years. I can't understand it. True, the ground's brave and soft but for the truck to sink right down to the axle – well, well, this is a right caper and no mistake, a right caper," he repeated, bemusement etched upon his face.

"It is that, boy," agreed the farmer. "But we've got to try to pull it out – although it won't be easy, especially with Prince aboard."

"It'll be impossible with the 'oss aboard," stated the knackerman, authoritatively. "And it won't be easy if somehow we're able to pull him off, either. We need a tractor, Harry, that's what we need – and I fancy you've still not got one, have you?"

"No, and we don't need one, not for this," Martin asserted. "I've two first class 'osses here who, I reckon, will be able to pull your truck out – and with Prince aboard. A tractor would never do it – it would just sink down like the lorry has in this soft turf. 'Osses though, don't have tyres – they've got hooves and they don't sink very easily. I'll give Dead Eye a shout – he's hedging in the next field, and Alfie's working up in the barn. They'll fetch Rosebud and Daniel, bring them down with some ropes, tie them to the front axle of the lorry and I bet that sturdy pair will have you out of there in no time at all."

"Never, boy, never," said Coleman with some vehemence. "There's no way they'll pull out a load like this. In fact, I'll go further and say there's no way they'll pull the lorry out even if we get Prince off – although," he added, "I'd dearly love to see them do it; it would surely make life easier if they could. But they won't – it's just not possible, two 'osses can never move a load like this, even though they're big and strong."

"Tell you what, Don – I'll bet a quid that they'll pull your truck out, and with Prince aboard." The farmer knew what the answer would be, as Don Colman had long been a betting man, something which fitted nicely with his favourite leisure pursuit – horse racing. He was a regular attender of most of the local point to points and also frequently travelled a little further afield to the race courses at Exeter and Newton Abbot where he was a staunch friend to the bookies.

"You're on, boy," came the instant reply, the two men slapping right hands to seal the deal. With that, the farmer hastened up the meadow in the direction of the yard, along the way shouting over the hedge to an unappreciative Dead Eye (he hated being interrupted when in the process of bringing his expertise to the rebuilding of a Devon hedge) that Daniel was needed urgently to help pull the truck out of the soft ground. Grumbling to himself, the farm worker moved off to do as he had been bid.

Approaching the stables, the farmer espied Alfie, told him of what had transpired and what was planned, then went with him, closely followed by Dead Eye, into the stables and helped harness up the horses. Gathering some heavy, think ropes, they returned at a pace to the bottom of the meadow.

The two workmen, made aware by their employer of the bet that had been made, hastened to tie the ropes to the front axle of the lorry. Knowing that Harry Martin was the kind of man who would share his winnings with them should he win the bet, their maximum assistance was guaranteed.

The thick ties firmly and strategically placed, the two returned to the horses, Alfie taking control of Rosebud and Dead Eye, Daniel. Then, in unison, they coaxed the mighty pair forward. The ropes tightened, then stretched. The men and the farmer cajoled, exhorted and willed the mighty, straining beasts onward.

The lorry, almost imperceptibly at first, then inch by precious inch, began to move forward, the back wheels climbing slowly, so very slowly, out of the deep ruts. After a couple of minutes, the tyres were on slightly firmer ground – albeit still very soft and, in consequence, not a sound foundation for the heavy lorry and load which stood upon it.

The shires did not cease their labours, however. Led ever onwards, they maintained a sustained pull upon the lorry, with Don Coleman now assisting by starting the engine and engaging bottom gear. This was continued right up across the meadow and then onto the solid cobbles of the yard. The ropes slackened and were removed, then the horses were led off to their stables, leaving in their wake a delighted farmer and a stunned knackerman shaking his head in amazement.

"Well, boy," said he, "I've never been one to underestimate the strength of 'osses, but I never dreamt that pair could ever have pulled that kind of weight in a sodden field like that. Dear me – dear me." He continued to shake his head, then reached, with a somewhat grubby hand, into his back pocket, produced a wad of pound notes, peeled one off, handed it the farmer, and said, with total honesty, "It's almost worth having to pay up just to have been able to witness those two 'osses do that – never seen anything like that before, and never will again; wonderful. Well, see you again, Harry." With that, he climbed into the cab, started the engine, gave a wave, then moved the truck across the yard and onto the road, the equine cargo safely aboard.

Briskly, the farmer walked to the stables to thank Alfie and Dead Eye for their efforts. "Well done, the pair of you – good effort, that. Don Coleman can scarcely believe what he saw."

"Don't thank us – the 'osses did the work," retorted Alfie Tremain.

"Well, yes, that's true," the farmer granted, "but you know how to get the best out of them. And at their best, there's still nothing to touch them. Tractors have got their place, yes – but not around here, in my view. Up in Norfolk, places like that where it's flat, certainly – ideal, but in Devon, with our hills, and our rain making the ground so wet. No, all they do is cut up the ground, make a mess and generally don't do things any quicker: I know there's several in this parish that have bought a tractor since the war, but there'll still be a place for 'osses for many a year yet. And I'll say this, there'll not be a tractor on Downside as long as I've a say in it – and as long as they still breed 'osses, of course. I hear tell there's far fewer being bred now than there was even five years ago. Still, hopefully there'll still be enough about to last me my time. What Graham does when he takes over will be up to him, naturally. Anyway, I've got to nip into the village in a minute to get something for the missus from the grocer's. Whilst I'm there I'll put Don Coleman's quid behind the bar of the Tamar View for you two – and Herbie, of course – to have a drink or two tonight." With that, he was through the stable door and making for the battered van which was to convey him to errands in the village, the thanks of the two workmen ringing in his ears.

As the van sped out of the yard, Dead Eye looked at Alfie and said, "What was that you said about there not being any more 'osses bought – that poor old Prince would be replaced with a tractor. Well whether Graham likes it or not, I don't reckon there'll be a tractor at Downside for a few years yet – as I said a few days back."

"No – I fancy you're right," agreed the horseman. "I really did think though, that Farmer Martin might well have thought it was time for a change; and I still think he could well have given serious thought to getting a tractor – partly for Graham's sake – if it had not been for the knackerman getting stuck this afternoon."

"Yes, old Don Coleman's worked wonders today without really knowing it – or meaning to, him getting stuck with his truck, and old Rosebud and Daniel pulling him out..."

"With the old 'oss aboard," interjected Alfie.

"Yes – with all his weight as well. Master effort by those two 'osses. Mind you, it's done a favour for Don in the long run – he'll have the carcase of another 'oss to carry away one day; he wouldn't be needed to haul off a dead tractor."

The horseman grinned. "Yes – true enough, boy. Anyway, I'd better get on and feed the pair – they've earned it all right."

"Yes, they have that," agreed Dead Eye Dawkins. "They've certainly done me a couple of favours today."

"How do you mean, favours?" asked Alfie.

"Well they've got me a nice lot of free drinks in the pub tonight – and they've earned me ten bob?"

"Ten bob?"

"Yes – our bet, Alfie. You remember, don't you? The other morning when we were getting ready to go over to the forge to bring back Prince, you were saying Farmer Martin would replace Prince with a tractor. I bet you ten bob he wouldn't – and you took me on. So you owe me ten bob, boy."

For a few seconds the horseman looked totally bemused. He then shook his head, and said simply, "I forgot about that, you know, with everything that's been going on. Totally forgot. Pay you on pay day, all right?"

"Yes – yes, boy, that'll be a proper job. There'll be a pint or two more for you in the Tamar View on Saturday night.

# II

# The Barber

Hard working man though unquestionably he was, there was one
avenue along which Harry Martin was indolent – shaving. Not
that he was in any way a slovenly man. Granted, as a farmer he
rarely dressed in smart fashion unless going out, but his working
clothes were relatively clean considering the nature of his work,
whilst he himself was never shy of applying soap and water to his
person, summer or winter. He did, though, detest the necessity to
regularly scrape the stubble from his chin, seeing it as being
amongst the greatest of time wasters.

He would happily have grown a beard, pointing out to his wife
Sarah that clearly God had meant men to do just that as he caused
them to grow hair on their chins, and it was intended for it to
remain there – after all, there was no mention of razors in the
Bible.

Sarah, though, being a women who maintained high personal
standards (even when busy doing somewhat dirty jobs on the
farm, she always looked remarkably neat and tidy), expected her
husband to do likewise; and whilst he was very much his 'own
man', never afraid to stand by what he believed in, or thought was
right, in his marriage he rarely went against the wishes of his
spouse. This was not so much the pursuit of an easy life, but more
the realisation – one which had come to him early in their married
life – that she was a lady of rare perception and common sense,
usually right about most things.

Thus did he, with reluctance – when she gave him a certain disapproving look, usually at the breakfast table after milking – on occasions fetch his razor and shaving soap when the meal was done, and scrape, joylessly, the worst of the blackness from his jaw. This, though, probably was the routine in respect of fewer than half of his shaves. More often than not, he took the easy and lazy way out and got somebody else to do it; that someone being Lawrence (known universally as Lol) Parnell, who had been the village barber for almost forty years, learning his trade from his father (who had set up the business in the 1890s) then taking over from him when he retired.

Parnell Senior had been no master of his craft, and his son was in the same mould. Never a man to waste too much energy sharpening scissors or cut-throat razors, and in the hair cutting field never one to follow fashion or fad (indeed, oblivious to such frivolities), a short back and sides was not so much his speciality as his sole product, and the fact he did not do even this particularly neatly in no way discouraged his clients, which constituted most of the males of the parish.

It had been a trend in post-war years, mind you, one which was increasing, for many of the younger fellows to use the regular trains to Tavistock – some even to Plymouth – to avail themselves of the services of barbers with flair and mastery of more than one basic style, but there remained more than sufficient older men to keep Lol in business. Some of these might well have forsaken him, to avail themselves of more professional services (and less painful ones, Lol's eternally blunt scissors often bringing moisture to the eyes of even the most stalwart as they gripped the arms of his barber's chair) had he not possessed one quality well beyond the scope of anybody else in the area, possibly in all of Devon – he was ridiculously cheap.

Before the war his prices had been lower than those of anybody in Tavistock, and he had not put them up since, even though it was his constant moan that he would have to work until the grim reaper came as he would never be able to afford to retire. There was possibly something in this, but it was clear his living expenses were low, as he dwelt in the cottage left him by his parents, and never having married he had no dependants. So whilst, no doubt, he was in no position to retire – still being seven years short of his old age pension – it was unlikely he would do so even if he could afford to, he enjoying very considerably the camaraderie, friendship and involvement of those who came in and out of his ancient and decidedly unkempt premises.

It was a drizzly, quite windy November morning – a mildish south-westerly sweeping up the Tamar – that Sarah fixed her husband with that 'look' which only a grizzled chin could bring about and, realising it had been three days since he had last shaved (and being a paleish complexion, with darkish hair he needed really to shave daily – and would have had to had he worked at something where personal appearance was important) he knew that the blade of a razor would need to make contact with his jaw before the day was out. Still, it worked out quite well, for he had to go into the village that morning to get a couple of things from the grocer's and a loaf of bread from Des Mullin's shop, he, the baker, not due to call on the farm on his twice weekly mobile round for a couple more days. These shops being not more than a hundred yards from the barber's, he would park the old van in the main street and spend ten minutes in Lol's chair, hearing news, gossip, scandal and assorted nonsense – and have his chin soaped, lathered and scraped.

Within an hour of his deciding to patronise Lol Parnell, he was closing the door of his battered old Austin van behind him and strolling uncharacteristically unhurriedly towards the alleyway which led to Lol's 'salon' – though such a name imbued it with an ambience scarcely matched by its battered reality.

As he entered the alley he mused, as was usually the case, that it was a trip, albeit no more than fifty or sixty yards, which needed to be done in daylight – thus, in these short days, one to be travelled before four o'clock when the light began to fail (earlier on a murky day such as this).

There was no lighting of any kind, the alleyway and yard into which it led, that had received no maintenance for generations, was strewn with moss covered cobble stones, displaced by time and abuse over the decades, the holes they had left behind being just that, holes into which the unwary could step and turn an ankle

c

(if really unlucky, break one); whilst other obstructions proliferated, not least the large part of a high wall skirting a small nearby garden having collapsed many years previously, causing a major heap of stones and debris.

Lol's establishment was not the only building to which the alley and yard gave access – there were two lock up stores, a workshop used regularly by Alfie Duncan a sign writer and decorator, and, most surprisingly, two small cottages, both occupied by elderly folk, who had no other means of access.

Who actually owned the entrance and the yard, Harry had not the slightest notion, but he was perpetually astonished that it was permitted to remain in such a deplorable state. Not that he had ever heard of anybody having a major accident there – remarkably – though he had been told of the occasional stumble and, more seriously, a couple of sprained ankles.

Picking his way slowly and carefully across the yard, he opened the paint starved, weather ravaged door and entered Lol Parnell's barbershop. Glancing to his left as he entered, he saw a half dozen customers seated amidst the musty gloom (Lol's only sported one light, a naked one hundred watt bulb immediately above the barber's chair, to the right), said briskly, "Morning, gents," and received muttered replies.

To call these fellows customers was, technically, correct, as they did all from time to time avail themselves of Lol's cheap services – possibly a shave a couple of times a week and a haircut once a month, but seated where they were, none of them were in the market for either a chin to be scraped or head to be shorn that morning. Had they been, they would have been sitting on the decrepit chairs to the right of the door, only in view to Harry after he had closed the door behind him. As was very often the case, these were empty, the only occupants of that area being the short, slightly tubby, balding figure of the barber himself, and a client who was just arising from the chair, wiping his chin with a somewhat grubby towel.

"You're next on, Harry," grunted the barber – in slightly morose fashion, which was unlike him, he in reality being amongst the most affable of men.

There was, though, about the entire gathering an air of gloom, which was unusual. Indeed, it had long been a paradox that the ancient, cobwebbed, dingy barber's salon, which was akin to something out of Dickens (indeed, had probably not altered since the time of the great writer), was generally a place of conviviality and bonhomie. The constant posse of men, generally older and retired, whose numbers usually fluctuated from about a quartet to seven or even eight, drawn from a pool of about a dozen or so (always far more during the winter months, when the snug, scruffy comfort of Lol's was most attractive) usually kept up a fairly constant backdrop of chatter about football, the fortunes of the village side (usually good) and those of Plymouth Argyle (usually bad), politics local and national, plus gossip and scandal (invariably local), repartee and conversation which the barber enjoyed. Thus the presence of these men, only occasionally customers, was always welcomed by him – so much, in fact, that he always provided a copy of the *Western Morning News* and, on some cold winter days, if there were only three or four present, he would make a brew for them all, and for any customer he actually had in the chair.

As he closed the door behind him, Harry saw that Lol's freshly shaved customer was Clarence Langton, the undertaker. Clearly the tall, lean Clarence, who was essentially a carpenter, but who had taken care of the Peninsula's corpses for some twenty years, had an imminent funeral, for he was similar to Harry, in that he was no great lover of shaving. Having a wife more tolerant of grizzled chins than did the farmer, he would often grow the stubble to the point of being a beard if there was a fair gap between interments, but always saw it as professional etiquette, and essential respect for the deceased and their family, to be completely clean shaven when leading the funeral procession.

"Who is it, Clarence?" asked the farmer.

"Old Queenie Clark," said he, knowing exactly to what the farmer was referring. "Congregational chapel this afternoon, two o'clock. Eighty-seven she was, so she didn't do bad. Well known, of course – lived in the parish all her life, so it'll be a fair funeral. Might not fill the chapel, but it won't be far off." The undertaker raised a hand in farewell, then departed, leaving Harry to take his place in the chair.

Without a word, the barber applied shaving soap to Harry's skin, then worked it up into a lather. He picked up a cut-throat razor, drew it up and down lethargically against a very well worn leather strap a few times to make its edge keener (very much a cosmetic exercise, as Lol had performed a like ritual before every shave since time began, never seemingly increasing the sharpness of the ancient blade), then proceeded to remove the soap – and some of the stubble – from the farmer's jaw, still maintaining his silence.

Harry's bemusement at the silence all around him, not just from the barber, but also amongst the audience in the back, rapidly turned to annoyance – and if unhappy, he was always a man to let it be known.

"What the hell's going on, Lol?" he rasped. "You've not said a word, nor's anybody else here for that matter, which is pretty rare. I mean, there's usually a few tales doing rounds, but today, not a whisper. Is it me? Have I upset somebody or something? If I have, then tell me. Then again, if it's nart to do with me, then tell me that. But say something, for God's sake."

The barber, suddenly, was overwhelmed with contrition. "Oh Harry, I'm sorry, boy – truly I am," said he, shaking his head almost violently. "I should have told you, clearly I should, I've told these fellows" – he indicated the silent ranks at the back of the shop, "and that'll be the reason, I reckon, why they're so quiet. Fact is, boy, my days here are numbered – very much so, as well. A few weeks and that'll be it. I've had notice to quit, Harry – or, in effect at any rate. Here, take a look at this letter. It was there in the post when I got home last night. I could scarce believe it – still can't. You read it, boy. I've let these fellows see it – that's why they're so quiet. After all, they're going to be thrown out too."

He stopped scraping, reached forward to a shelf in front of him, picked up a folded sheet of paper and handed it to his customer.

"You read that, boy – notice to quit that is, in effect, anyway."

The farmer scanned the letter quite quickly. It was from a firm of Tavistock based solicitors, and, for a lawyer, was reasonably brief. He handed it back to the barber, then leant his head back to enable Lol to finish removing the soap from his chin, which he proceeded to do.

"I see, Lol – so these premises are leasehold, with you paying an annual rent."

"They all are round the small yard outside – yet I'm the only one to have a letter like this. I checked that this morning. I'm not sure about the two lockups, mind you, but Archie Duncan over in his workshop has heard nothing, nor have they in the cottages. Just me, and what that lawyer says in the letter – 'deplorable state' of my premises. Did you ever hear such nonsense, boy? Granted, it could do with a bit of tidying up in here, the odd lick of paint perhaps, but it's not in bad order, is it Harry." The words were not put as a question, rather a statement.

"Well, Lol, well – it could, to be fair, probably do with a bit of attention."

The words did not flow from the farmer, as he had no desire to further upset this lovely man, part of the fabric of the parish, who clearly was deeply distressed over the situation in which he found himself. Yet the reality was that the entire building seemed to be held together by the cobwebs, some seemingly as thick as ropes, that had abounded for generations. All around was decay, not just in furnishings and accessories, but also the fabric of the building, with loose, indeed, missing slates on the roof, and water coming in around the two small, exceedingly grimy windows when the rain came from the 'wrong direction'. No, the premises were in an appalling state – inevitable, Harry mused to himself, when considering nothing had, in his recollection, ever been done in terms of repair, or for that matter, basic cleaning and tidying. A veteran sweeping brush whose bristles could, with some ease, be counted was occasionally pushed by the barber around his immediate working area to gather together the assorted hair of his clients, but that was about it.

"I mean, boy – well, you've not done too much to it in the past

– past – past few years, have you," stuttered the farmer, using the
words 'years' when he, if honest, should have said 'decades'.

"Well, I've done what I could, Harry," he wailed, "but I
haven't the money to do a lot. I mean, I don't charge very much
for shaves or haircuts – never have. As long as I can make a
living, as long as I've got enough to put a bit of grub on the table,
a shirt on my back and pay the rent on this place, that's all I ask.
But see what they're saying in the letter; the shop here – the
premises – have got to be restored to a 'standard' of repair and
maintenance in accordance with the requirements of a surveyor
who will call and inspect the premises. Failure to do so, means
that according to the lease agreement – and I've never ever seen
that, though I suppose father must have had one at some time or
other, but that probably goes back to before the turn of the century
– well, it means I forfeit the lease with immediate effect. So I'll
be out for certain. It could be before Christmas; almost certainly
will be, in fact. Even without a surveyor looking at it, I know full
well I couldn't afford to put things right. Stopping the rain
coming in round the window alone will cost a fair bit – and the
place needs a bit of paint, that I do know. And if a surveyor looks
at it, he's going to say I need to spend a fortune on the roof –
perhaps even have a new one altogether. No boy, as it stands, it's
the end of me. And what I'll do to make a living, I've no idea. My
needs are few, true, but nobody can live off nothing – and that's
exactly what I have, nothing. I'm still about seven years short of
my pension, and have very few savings – and I've not the faintest
idea where I could get a job at my age, certainly not as a barber,
and that's all I know. I've never spent a working day in my life
doing anything different. But it's more than that…" Tears were
welling in the man's eyes now, as his distress became very
apparent. "No, it's far more than that – it's life itself, to me at any
rate. I've no family, no real hobbies or great interests of any kind
– my work is my life, this barbershop, you chaps who come in for
your shaves and haircuts, or who come in just to sit and chat, and
to read the paper…" He indicated the half dozen at the back of the
shop with a sweep of an arm. "That will be gone, all of it – all of
you. And you'll miss it, I know that – all of you."

### The Barber

Harry Martin glanced towards the back of the musty salon, saw the faces of those sitting there in rare silence, all looking as if they had been told of a death in the family, realised the instinct which had swept over him as soon as he had entered a quarter of an hour earlier, that all was not well, was assuredly on the right track (although things were, he had to concede, much worse than he thought at the time). He glanced up at the barber who had just placed the razor back on the shelf in front of the chair. "You're right, Lol – I can't argue about that, nobody would. You're part of the fabric of this village, you and this shop, and the way you play host to us all – even if we aren't customers – although I suppose we all are at some time or other. As for myself, I hate the thought that I might in the future have to shave myself, quite apart from the fact I'd miss the chat, the news, the gossip I get when I come in here once or twice a week. As for the chaps at the back there and the other regulars, no wonder they look so upset. I mean what are they going to do if they can't come in here, especially in the winter. Reckon they'll have to spend days on end home with the missus. Mind you, that'll probably upset the ladies as much as the men." He smiled a touch ruefully after saying that, for it was known that many a wife of the village was very please to have, in the village, such refuges as Lol's and Arthur Dixon's blacksmith shop, which would host, for many hours of the week, indolent retired menfolk who otherwise would merely litter the tidy homes.

Getting up from the chair, the farmer dried his damp chin in the solitary towel provided by the barber, handed over the paltry fee for the service just rendered, then posed the question which, strangely, had only just come to mind. "What's this all about, Lol? Why suddenly, after all these years – these decades – have you had such a letter as this, such a demand – ultimatum in fact, what's happened to bring this about?"

The barber looked somewhat surprised at the question and, by his tone when he answered, clearly was. "Well, old Albert died, that's what happened, boy – you know that, surely. He passed on and his daughter Amy inherited. Ninety-one, he was – died just over a year ago – you must remember that, Harry. Big funeral –

well known and liked man, Albert; church was full to overflowing."

"Yes, yes I remember that, Lol – remember it well. I was there, but like a fool, I forgot that he owned this place here. He always owned it, did he – and his father before him?"

"Yes, this and all the others around the yard – and the yard itself. Yet, as I said just now, I'm the only one to have a letter like this – the only one they want out – or Amy wants out, to be more accurate.

"But why should she want you to go, Lol – you've done nothing to offend her, have you? I mean I can't imagine you ever offending anybody. Frankly, I doubt there's anybody in the parish easier to get along with than you." The farmer spoke the words aware there were none he could speak which would ever be truer or more sincere.

"Well, I pay very little rent, to be fair. In fact, I've not had a rent increase for over twenty years, and I remember even then, when I did have one, it was only a small one. Here now, five years after the Second World War, I don't pay a great deal more than poor old father back before the First World War. Dear old Albert never worried too much about money. Amy married back in the first war, as I recall, and Albert's wife, Ada – a nice lady – died reasonably young in the early twenties. After that, all Albert seemed to worry about was having enough to keep him in grub and whisky. Back before the war, he owned quite a bit of property about the village but sold it off over the years, all except these premises around the yard, and that tiny cottage he ended up living and dying in. He let that get in a fair old state and it's only got one bedroom, so Amy wouldn't have got much when she sold it; and I heard months ago, what with his drinking and living to a great age, he left virtually nothing. In fact, when the funeral was paid for, I believe there was nothing left at all. If he hadn't died when he did, he might well have had to sell off these buildings and the cottages around the yard, just to live. Not that he would have got much, as everything is leased out so anybody buying all or any part of it takes over sitting tenants, who cannot be moved as long as they keep paying the rent – except, of course, if they go along

56

the route Amy's using with me – saying I've not kept the place repaired to the standard I should have, so triggering a clause which says she can terminate the lease. Typical of Amy, that. How good, kindly folk such as Albert and his missus could have bred a daughter like Amy I really do not know. Selfish, greedy and, in many ways, downright nasty – that's what she is and always has been, even as a girl. Good looking, mind you, I remember that – always had plenty of local lads chasing her; luckily for them, though, none of them caught her. Des Blanchard was the one who did, of course; an officer in the army in the First World War, as you know. Lieutenant when she first met him, but ended up a major, of course. Pity from his point of view – and hers – he didn't stay in uniform forever. I fancy he had a few bob when she married him, but there's not been much there in recent times."

"No, no, I know that much, although I don't know him that well – didn't know him, I should say. I mean, it couldn't have been more than three months after Albert went, that he died. Cancer wasn't it?"

"Yes – stomach, I think. Nice chap, really. He used to come in here for the odd shave and haircut. He had two problems, though – he was no great shakes at making money, and he was married to a woman who demanded he did just that. She was forever pushing him into schemes, business enterprises and suchlike for which he just was not suited – or that's the impression I got, partly from him, but mainly from the tales that came my way from folk sitting in the chair. That's the thing with this job, boy, it's amazing what people tell you when they're laying back with their faces lathered and you're scraping away at their chin. It's not always accurate, mind you – and sometimes it's not true at all. But it is usually, or, at least, there's an element of truth to it. Whatever, in a sense Amy's been unlucky; she was born into a comfortable well off family – Albert was certainly worth a bit fifty years ago – and married a fellow who seemed to be going places. Sadly, from her point of view, her father spent the last forty or so years of his life deposing of his assets, whilst her husband, once he'd left the army, was a failure in business terms at any rate. I heard that when he died, Amy had to use part of the money she got from an insurance policy on his life to pay for the funeral. The sad thing is, that folk should feel sorry for her. After all, she lost her father and her husband within just a few months of each other, something which should bring sympathy, should make people want to help her, befriend her and suchlike. I mean, she's got no kids of her own, no brothers or sisters, no close family at all. I doubt that many do, though. I certainly don't, and that's nothing to do with her throwing me out, either, 'cause I've never had any time for her, ever. As I said, all her life she's been self, self, self; she's never attempted to help anybody else or to make friends. And she is now paying the price, in a way. To my knowledge, she's moved houses at least four times in the past ten years, the last couple of times here in the parish – and always downwards. I know that before the war they lived in a lovely house in Down Road, Tavistock – all quality places there. Yet just six months before Des died, they moved into that small semi-detached place here, just off Tavy Street – run down place that had been empty for a couple of years since dear old Daisy Drew passed away. They wouldn't have paid much for it, but even then they struggled to find the money – or that's the story I heard anyway, and I fancy it's true, 'cause I heard it from a young fellow whose sister works for the agents in Tavistock who were selling it. He reckoned, according to her, that Amy and Des had to mortgage themselves up to the neck to get hold of it, even though it was up for sale at a bargain price because it was in such a poor state. And you can be sure her financial position hasn't improved any. Not working, and inheriting just that tiny cottage from her father which wouldn't have been worth much – she's desperate for money. That's why she's turned her attention in my direction. She sees my shop here as being, well, perhaps a touch less well maintained than the cottages or the lock ups..." He avoided Harry Martin's eyes when saying these words, ones which he knew were an understatement of mammoth proportions.

The other premises in the ownership of the unloved Amy Blanchard being kept by the tenants in a decent condition, meant that certainly she would find it difficult to terminate the lease of any on the grounds of the premises being in an unacceptable state of repair.

"Still, Lol, while I can see she has options for this shop if she gets you out, I don't see them at being such that there'll be much in it for her," said Harry, thoughtfully. "All right, she is, no doubt, fairly confident there's no way you'll be able to afford to do even a part of what a surveyor will state needs to be done to this place but I don't see there's any way she'll be able to afford it either. I mean, where's she going to get the money to do major repairs to the roof, say, being hard up the way she is. She'll get you out, have the place on her hands, but will not be able to do what will need to be done, so will have it empty with no income from it at all. So she'll be worse off than she is now. As it is now, she's getting some rent from it, small though it is. I can't see where she's coming from – unless she's just motivated by spite in some way."

"Spite wouldn't be beyond her, boy, that's for sure," agreed the barber, "but I don't think that's anything to do with this situation. I mean, she's no real argument with me personally – she hardly knows me. No, I've been thinking about it – as you can imagine, I've thought about nothing else since opening the letter last evening. I didn't sleep all night, not even for a minute. No, I've been thinking about it, all right, and I fancy her plan is a simple one – but clever, nonetheless; certainly one where she cannot fail to gain no matter what action I take. I mean, let's say for instance, I could somehow raise the money that would be needed to do whatever the surveyor says I have to do; there is no way, of course, and Amy will suspect that's the case – but she cannot be sure. But for argument's sake, let's say I did just that; well she would be a winner, for she will have had both the quality and value of the premises raised considerably, and so would be able to raise my rent – very considerably. So her income would increase very healthily from her point of view. If I couldn't afford to pay such a rental, then I'd be given notice to quit, and she would have back in her direct control a building which she could sell at a decent price, or let out to somebody with the means to pay the sort of rent she'll be looking for. And she'd find somebody, you can be fairly sure of that; there's nearly always somebody who comes along in such circumstances – with more money than good sense. And if, as will be the case – which she well knows is by far the most likely – I hand back the keys and walk away, then she takes back the premises as they are, and does the very minimum when it comes to renovations and repairs. She'd have the inside cleaned and given a coat of paint, and possibly the woodwork outside painted, then rent it out again; she'd not worry about the roof or windows. By the time any new tenant found out about this, a lease would be signed and they would find that if they weren't happy with the condition of the building, then a clause in the lease would say they have to pay to put things right – not Amy. And they'll be paying a lot more rent than I am, you can be sure of that. No, she's got it worked out has Amy, no doubt about that, boy. And she's certainly got the beating of me I'm afraid. As I said earlier, it's the end of the road for me, after a lifetime in this trade, and in this shop." He stopped, as tears welled in his eyes, then shook his head. "End of the road, boy, end of the road," he repeated.

"There must be something that can be done, Lol – somebody who can help. We can't see you turned out of here – we just can't; and not only for your sake, either – but for ours," said Harry with raw candour. "I mean, as I said just now, what will any of us here now – half the village, in fact; what will we do if we can't come in to Lol's for a shave, haircut, a moan, to hear the news and the gossip – or just to chew the fat. Something has to be done – and, clearly, right away."

As he was saying the words he was aware they seemed futile – vague statements of hope, rather than intent, with no basis in reality.

"I had Reg Perkins in the chair first thing this morning for a shave. He said the same thing," grunted the barber. "He's a regular like yourself, but I could see he had no idea as to any way out of it – and sharp man is Reg in matters like that. After all, he's worked for the district council and been clerk to the parish for decades. There's not many around who could spot a loophole like he probably could. But sitting there this morning, he had to admit I was, in his words, 'in a weakish position'; and he's right, of course. In fact, that's an understatement – I'm in an impossible position. I'm done for – there's no way out. He said he'd give it some further thought and see if there was some way I could beat Amy, but there isn't, and we all know it if we're honest. It's the end of the road – by Christmas I'll close the door on this barber-shop for the very last time after, what, well over sixty years."

For several seconds Harry Martin stood gazing into space, saying not a word. There was, he knew, not much he could mouth, beyond vague platitudes, which would not help Lol Parnell in any way. The barber needed a practical solution to the problems which confronted him in mammoth fashion – ones which would, unless solved, and exceedingly quickly, bring about what he had just stated in such a melancholy, defeatist way, the end of his lifetime's work, and, worse, that of his entire purpose in life.

"Well, Lol, I'd better be off – things to do as always." He turned towards the door, raised his hand in acknowledgement of the sombre crew sitting at the back of the shop then looked, as he reached the door, in the barber's direction. Not sure what to say, he lapsed into banalities – inadvertently – saying in the general direction of the dejected figure stood there by the chair in his once white smock, "Don't worry too much, boy – things could yet work out all right. All's not lost. We're all with you in this – and it could be a solution will be found. Reg Perkins could come up with something; certainly if anybody can, then it's him. Knows his way around, does Reg."

For the rest of the day, busy though he was, Harry found himself thinking of the barber's predicament, puzzling as to whether there was any way out of it. The thought of Lol Parnell closing down for all time, after he and his father would have been there for the lifetime of virtually all in the parish, was too bitter to contemplate. Quite apart from the fact one of the parish 'institutions' would disappear, he would have to shave himself at all times, a dreadful thought. Yet despite turning things over in his mind almost incessantly, there seemed no solution. Certainly the barber had done nothing to help his cause, the premises in which he carried out his business being truly in a deplorable state.

That evening at tea he stated his intention of going to the pub. "If I get there about half past seven," he explained to Sarah, "I'll almost certainly catch Reg Perkins; a creature of habit is Reg. Most weekday evenings you'll catch him in the Tamar View between about a quarter past seven and half past eight. I want to talk to him about Lol Parnell, and the pickle he's in – as I described to you at dinner-time, maid. I don't know if anything can be done to keep him in business – I doubt it, but we've got to try. For sure there's nobody in the parish who knows his way around such things as well as Reg. He's the only hope Lol's got, I fancy. It could be – probably is, in fact – he's already given it a lot of thought. He told Lol this morning he would do, and Reg is a man of his word. I just want to know if there's anything he's come up with – or if me or anybody else can help in any way. It would be awful to see old Lol go out of business after all these years – tragic, almost."

"Well, he's brought it upon himself, Harry, as far as I can see," stated Sarah in unsympathetic tones. "I've never been in his barbershop, but you've always said just how rundown it is – dirty too. Certainly from the outside it looks a disgrace. No, I've no sympathy with him I'm afraid – it's his own fault."

Her husband shrugged his shoulders in acquiescence. "Yes, yes, basically you're right, maid; but it'll still be a great shame if he has to close down. I must say that I'd miss him, but there's a lot of old chaps who would miss him more – winter times it's a second home for a lot of them. Some live on their own – widowers, bachelors and the like – and often an hour or two in Lol's is all the company they see all day. So if it can be kept open then it'll please a lot of folk – even though it could be argued that, as you say, any calamity that comes his way is of his own making." He spoke the final words to appease his wife who had never really approved of Lol – the lamentable state of his premises and the haven he provided for many men whom, despite her husband's sympathy for them, she felt could be doing something a little more useful in life than sitting gossiping and smoking in Lol's hovel. Nobody in the village was more imbued with the traditional 'protestant work ethic' than Sarah Martin.

At just prior to 7:30 that evening, Harry entered the bar of the Tamar View Inn, accompanied by son Graham whose intention was a couple of pints and a few games of darts – "to keep me hand in," as he put it, being a member of the pub's darts team.

Casting his eyes around the rather drab bar (not in the same league as Lol's barbershop, of course, but in real need of the paint the premises, in and out, had not seen since before the war) the farmer espied the parish clerk sitting alone in a far corner sipping a stout; except for Scotch, the man's favourite tipple. Perkins looked up, and Harry caught is eye – "Same again, Reg?" A question answered with a thumbs up sign from the corner.

A stout and a pint of half and half ordered and received from the affable landlord, Billy Baldwin (who retained a sizeable and reasonably contented clientele despite the deficiencies of the premises), and Harry joined the ageing council officer at his table. Pleasantries rapidly exchanged, and drinks partially quaffed, the farmer hastened to the main reason for his visit. "I hear you were just about the first customer in Lol Parnell's chair this morning, Reg. That's what he told me, anyway – I got there about half past ten. In a right state, is Lol. Reckons it's all over for him – reckons he'll be out by Christmas. It'll be a sad day for all if he is, of course. He says he talked to you about it – any way out for him do you think? Any way he can get round what the solicitors are saying in the letter?"

The parish clerk placed his glass on the table, then shook his head, gravely. "I doubt it, boy – I doubt it very much. The letter was straight to the point – unusual for a solicitor in many ways – and poor old Lol hasn't got a decent card in his hand. Mind you, it's his own fault to a large extent, Harry, isn't it? The state of that place is almost beyond words. I mean, if you get rid of the cobwebs the whole place would probably collapse. He's been there decades, and his father before him, of course, and I don't remember even a single brush load of paint ever being put on. No, Amy Blanchard holds the whip hand without doubt, and she'll not hold back; she's not a kindly, sympathetic women at the best of times, Amy – in fact, she's probably as selfish a person as you'd ever meet – and these, for her, are not the best of times. She's got her back to the wall – which means she'll be totally ruthless. I mean her father, Albert, who had a few bob back along, lived too long and squandered a lot, so left her virtually nothing, whilst her husband, Des Blanchard, in effect did likewise. Granted he passed on well before his time, but everything he turned his hand to after he left the army turned to dust. Nice chap was Des – a gentleman basically, far too good and decent for Amy if truth be told – but one of those fellows who prosper in uniform and in the military world where everything is organised for them and life runs on rails, but who tend to get lost in civvy street where generally you're on your own. When he died it's no secret he left Amy not much short of penniless – not something she'll be happy about. To be fair, mind you, it's not something any of us would be too keen over. Anyway, she'll fight like a lioness to keep afloat, and nobody can blame her for that – so she'll try to capitalise on the few assets she's got – and virtually all of them, except for the little cottage where she's living now, are in that cluster around the yard. I reckon she'd love to sell off the two cottages there – although more likely she'd like to sell one and live in the other – it's better than that hovel of a place she's living in at present, but there's no way she can get the folk out that are living in them, not at present. Both cottages are well looked after, the tenants keeping them neat and tidy and in a reasonable state of repair. Lol's, though – we all know the state of Lol's, I mean to say, there's no court judge in the land who would stop her throwing him out if ever he contested it. Not that he will – it would be a waste of money, and he'd be the first to realise it. No, as most have said, sad though it certainly is – and I'll miss him, most certainly I will, 'cause he's given me a couple of shaves most weeks for donkey's years – no, sad though it is, it is his own fault, and frankly I doubt if there's anything that can be done." He stopped talking, emptied his glass of stout – then for a few seconds, looked exceedingly thoughtful, gazing at the far wall of the bar.

"You're looking thoughtful, boy," muttered the farmer, before taking a long draught from his own drink before returning it to the table. "Have you had a moment of inspiration or suchlike?" This was unlikely, Harry well knew, but he was also well aware that Perkins was a canny man well versed with the vagaries of human nature, who had lived in the parish all his life – his only period away being in the service of the King in the Great War, the scars of which he could carry to the grave – who knew the people, the way of life and, thanks to his involvement with councils both local and district, what was happening in the community well beyond the knowledge of most others, even those of long residence and great age. Certainly if there was one person throughout the Peninsula who could see a way that the much loved, though indolent, Lol Parnell, could be extracted from the calamity which confronted him – and, to a degree, his loyal customers and supporters (especially those who enjoyed his hospitality) also – then it was the parish clerk.

Reg smiled gently, then shook his head. "I doubt it, Harry," said he. "There have been one or two ideas playing around my head, though, which might be worth a look at – but I fancy it's highly unlikely, very highly, in fact, they'll lead anywhere. But the situation for Lol is so grim, it's probably worth looking at anything and everything, no matter how unlikely. So that's what I'll do – but I fancy poor old Lol will fulfill what he expects – he'll be out by Christmas. It certainly won't be a happy one for him. Still, I'd better be off, boy – missus'll wonder where I am." He struggled to his feet, leaning heavily upon the stick held in his right hand, wished the farmer a brisk "Good night," then hobbled slowly – and still painfully, even though the wound had been inflicted some thirty-five years previously – towards the door and out into the damp, Devonshire night.

Almost three weeks passed before Harry Martin trudged across the 'minefield' that was the cobbled yard leading to Lol's shop for a shave – probably his longest absence from the old barber's chair in twenty years. Not that he had suddenly developed an enthusiasm for shaving himself; he hated it as much as ever, but he felt that standing in his own house scraping his chin was marginally better than enduring the funeral-like pall which he knew would be engulfing Lol's. However, one morning at breakfast, with his spouse glaring malevolently at his stubbled chin, he decided he would show a bit of character – and support the beleaguered barber whose spirits, according to his horseman, Alfie Tremain, were exceedingly low.

Alfie had dropped in late on the previous afternoon, on his way home from work, for a haircut and had found the atmosphere morgue like, even though there were a quartet of Lol's regular attendees sitting at the back. The barber himself said virtually nothing (or so it was reported by the horseman to his employer in the farm kitchen early that morning when, in accordance with custom, he sipped a cup of tea prior to receiving his orders for the morning); and he was looking as down and defeated as any human being could. About the only thing he had said to Alfie was that the haircut was the last he would ever give him, as he foresaw himself shutting up shop by the yuletide which was only three weeks away. Hearing Alfie's melancholy talk, the farmer felt that he had to show just a little support for old Lol, if only for old time's sake – make him feel he was not forgotten or forsaken by all his long standing customers and friends (and most folk were both). For sure, there would be few opportunities in the future to sit in the old chair.

Thus it was that following breakfast that morning, he got in the old van and took himself off to the village. After getting a couple of items in the grocer's following instructions from Sarah, he arrived at the door of Lol's salon, summoned his resolve to face the gloom which awaited, opened it and quickly went inside, pleased to be out of the chill morning air, the eternal warmth of the shop enveloping him most pleasurably. This, though, was not the sole thing which swept over him. No sooner had he closed the door behind him, than he was aware of chatter and laughter coming from his left – indeed, a loud guffaw rent the musty, rusty air. Five or six of the regulars were, clearly, in good spirits – a couple of them raising hands in acknowledgment of the farmer. He looked to his right and caught the eye of the barber just as he was looking up from studying, and scraping the chin of 'Tadpole' Drake, so nicknamed because of the somewhat bulging eyes (though not as bad as in his youth when he had acquired the name) that gave him a slight frog-like appearance.

"Hello, Harry;" the barber's greeting was warm, his face wreathed in smiles. "I'm almost done – you're next on then."

The farmer looked bemused – some morgue, this; clearly

something had happened, something dramatic and exceedingly positive – more, something joyous. "You're looking happy, Lol – and everybody else here for that matter; you must have had news, and it must have been good."

"More than good, Harry – wonderful news, the best; the like of which I never thought was possible. When I got home last night, I found a letter waiting for me." He stopped his shaving for a few seconds, reached to the shelf in front of the chair, picked up a folded sheet of paper and handed it to the farmer. "Read it, Harry – it's from Amy Blanchard's solicitor; she's had a change of heart. I don't know why; certainly it's not like her. If she's got the knife in, she's the sort of woman who'll usually twist it. But not this time, to give her her due. No, she says I can stay here – through her solicitor, that is – I don't have to do the place up or anything. Certainly there won't be a surveyor looking around or any nonsense like that. He says I should tidy the place up a bit – though why I really don't know. I can't see anything wrong with it, can you?"

Fortunately he carried on talking before anybody had to fabricate an answer which wouldn't upset him too much. Certainly it would have been impossible to state the truth and not upset him.

"There's no rush to do that, though. Nobody's going to come and inspect it. Perhaps I'll do it in the spring if I've got time. The only disappointing thing is that she's going to raise my rent here – by about fifty percent, would you believe. I didn't expect that, but it's something I'll have to accept. The only way I'll be able to pay is to put my prices up – something, as you know, I've not done since before the war."

The farmer still smiled broadly. "Good news, Lol – yes, great news in fact, and for us all as well. None of us here – right though the village, for that matter – could imagine life without you and the shop here. Heavens man, we'd miss this place every bit as much as we'd miss the pub if it closed down." After saying the somewhat dramatic words, he pondered them as he felt he had somewhat overstated, but realised that in effect, he had not – the cosy, shabbily comfortable barbershop, with its amiable host, set

67

in the centre of the village where one could sit for a large part of the day and spend not a penny, in convivial company, keeping in touch with the world (especially local), eschewing loneliness and isolation, was a facility possibly found nowhere else in the country and, arguably, one to treasure. With these warming thoughts, he sat down and waited for Lol to finish shaving Tadpole Drake.

That evening found Harry Martin again entering the bar of the Tamar View at just after 7.15pm. Espying Reg Perkins sitting in his usual place in the corner – alone – he ordered a stout and a pint of half and half, paid, then carried them over to the man whom, he felt sure, must have been instrumental in getting the, generally, hard hearted, self centred Amy Blanchard to change her mind regarding Lol Parnell and his calamity of a barbershop. It could be the parish clerk would tell him nothing – he was not obliged to. Indeed, it could be he had nothing whatsoever to do with it, but the farmer would take some convincing of that. With his lifelong involvement in the parish, his vast experiences as a council official on two authorities, his considerable intelligence, quick mind and a gift for shrewdness – conspiracy, in fact – when the need arose, he was probably the sole person on the Peninsula who could have brought about such a dramatic change on the part of the lady. And to have achieved such, he must have employed powerful – perhaps nefarious – means. The farmer delivered the drinks to the table on the far corner, was thanked by the parish clerk, general pleasantries were exchanged – then Harry moved the subject on to the saving of the barbershop from closure. "Good news about Lol, Reg. The best, in fact. Totally unexpected as well."

"Yes – yes, 'tis that. I was in his chair this morning – early on as I usually am. He told me about it then, showed me the letter. Good news, really – after all, old Lol and his shop would be greatly missed. It's hard to imagine the village without it – even though it's an eyesore; a disgrace, in fact."

"Yes – true. It's a surprise, though, isn't it, that Amy Blanchard changed her mind the way she did – climbed down, in fact. Bizarre, to be honest. A woman of her character giving ground like that – makes no sense, Reg – no sense at all. I reckon somebody leant on her. Which is, I fancy, the right words to use;" as he said these last half dozen, he riveted his gaze upon his companion.

"Why would anybody do that, boy?"

"Well, to save Lol and his shop – as you said just now, Reg, they'd be greatly missed. Both have been there so long – and Lol's father before that, of course; they'd be a terrible loss."

"True enough, Harry – and I'm pleased she's had a change of heart, though why she did I really don't know." He shrugged in dismissive manner as he said the final words.

The farmer though – a persistent man when in the mood – was determined to know more (if there was more to know) so decided to push it a little further.

"Well, Reg, I'm being a bit pushy here – and I have to admit it's none of my business; but I reckon you do know, and I reckon that because I fancy with your knowledge of council matters, parish affairs, local folk and the law, you're the only one who could have brought up things, perhaps legal or council issues, that could have forced her hand. Am I not right?"

Harry said the last four words with a steely softness which, clearly, put the parish clerk in the 'dock' in a sense. He either had to plead guilty or otherwise. He chose the former. Firstly he smiled, then again shrugged his shoulders.

"Oh well, I can tell you, Harry, 'cause it will go no further." He looked in hard fashion at his drinking companion after saying the words, and was assured instantly and honestly by Harry Martin, that indeed anything told him would never be passed on. "Yes, I did have a bit to do with it, boy – a fair bit to be honest. You probably wouldn't know, even though like me you've lived in the parish all your life; come to that, it's unlikely many in the parish would know of it, 'cause basically, it's a private matter. The fact is that Amy and me go back a very, very long time. She was my first love, Harry. The best looking girl in the parish she was – and by quite a bit. Her character was the same, mind you, looking back – selfish, greedy, callous in a way, but I was only a lad, really, and her looks turned my head. Anyway, we became

engaged to be married – June 1914. My mother and father
weren't happy mind you, even though she came from a good
family – Albert and her mother Emma were nice people – and
there was a few bob there then as well, although it had all gone
by the end as we all know, poor old Albert having moved most of
it out. Still, that was the situation that summer – and, of course,
you know what happened less than two months later: the First
World War broke out. Well, although a lot of fellows joined up
right away I had no intention of joining them unless I was called
up – which, no doubt, I would have been sometime, but probably
not for a year or two. And, as you'll remember, we thought it
would be over by Christmas anyway. Amy, though, instead of
being pleased I wasn't going off to war, wanted me to join up –
kept on to me, day in, day out. 'Make me proud of you, Reg',
she'd say, or 'you'll look so handsome in uniform', and things
such as that. Well, I was only just twenty, didn't know that much
about the world or life, and was easy pickings for her. Certainly I
didn't have the strength of character to resist pressure like that, so
I joined the Devonshire regiment. By November, I was in
France."

He stopped abruptly, swallowed a goodly portion of his stout,
put the glass back on the table, then shook his head. There was an
expression of bitterness upon his face.

"The following February, just three months after I got there,
I had a letter from Amy telling me the engagement was off –
she'd met somebody else. She didn't say who – and I didn't find
out until I got back home. My parents knew, of course, but they
didn't have the heart to say even though they wrote regularly. I
found out when I got back – on a stretcher, with half my right
leg blown away. As you know I've limped through life with a
stick in my hand ever since. Des Blanchard it was she'd met –
Plymouth man, and a career soldier. He was a lieutenant when
she met him – I didn't have a chance. By the time I got home –
on my back – they were married, and had a house in Tavistock.
He was in France, of course; went right through without a
scratch – ended up a major, and stayed in the army for a dozen
years or so after the war, so came away with a pension, though

not a full one. A good soldier was Des, but as we know, not much good at anything else – certainly hopeless at business. A decent man, though – good natured and basically a gentleman. Certainly too good for Amy, who gave him a dog's life in many ways with her demanding selfishness. Looking back, her breaking off the engagement was a very lucky break for me – just twelve months later I met my Dorothy at a concert in Tavistock and no man ever had a gentler, more thoughtful, loving wife. But at the time I was upset and very, very angry. And I must confess that forgiving and forgetting has never come easy to me. So even though I realised long ago that Amy breaking off our engagement was very much to my advantage, the feeling of betrayal regarding her treatment of me has never gone away – partly fuelled, I reckon, by the fact I heard of it in a hell-hole of a trench in the middle of a bitter winter in France where I'd not have been had it not been for her; and I've never forgiven her for it – and although it's not something for me to be proud of, I never will."

"I can understand that, Reg – I fancy I'd feel the same way. I never knew of this, of course – there's no reason why I should – but she certainly treated you in a shocking way, though true to character I would say. For sure, though, it's not the sort of thing you forget."

The farmer's sympathetic words and tone encouraged the council official to further expand on his involvement regarding the saving of the barbershop. "Well, I'd have done my best to help keep old Lol there for the sake of the village, and himself, of course – there's no way you can dislike old Lol, after all, is there. A lovely chap, really, despite the state he's let the premises get into. But as I say, whilst I'd have worked at getting Lol out of the mess he's in, despite the fact it's largely his own fault, I'd never have worked so hard had not Amy been involved. For, yet again, she's pursuing her own interests with no thought for anybody else, not giving a damn she could ruin somebody's life and upset half the village at the same time. So, I've been spurred on to find a way of saving Lol and scuppering Amy – and to a certain extent I've succeeded." He smiled broadly. "I'm being modest, boy –

'cause I've succeeded to a very large extent. All she's got out of it is a rise in rent from Lol of fifty percent, and whilst that sounds a big increase, in real terms because his rent is so low to start with, it isn't a great amount. Even with the increase it's probably less than he should be paying for the shop, even taking into consideration its dreadful state."

"Well, yes – I saw that on the letter yesterday when Lol showed me. He didn't seem very impressed, mind you, that he had to pay that much more, but it seemed to me that when you think of the disaster he was facing, he's got away ridiculously lightly. But how did you do it, Reg – how did you get her to change her mind?"

"I gave her no option, boy, that's the long and the short of it. I thought about the way she had approached it and sought ways to make it turn round and bite her. On the surface of it, she was on a definite winner regarding Lol. The premises are in a terrible state, and he almost certainly would be responsible for bringing them up to standard – her solicitor would have checked that the lease stated Lol had to take care of all repairs and maintenance, and that failure to do so could lead to the surrender of the lease without compensation.

"It struck me, though – as it does every time I go in there, and I reckon it hits you as well, that the outside, the entrance and yard, is in a state not much better than the inside of the shop. And not just outside Lol's, either – all of it is the same, outside the cottages, the workshop, the lock ups, all the way from the main street. Now I suspected that the ownership of that was Amy's as well, even though clearly it's a public right of way – so I checked. That's where it's helpful working for the district council. I was able to check with our records and the land registry, and, yes, she does own that public area – so its upkeep is down to her.

"Now, to be frank, I've no idea how she's got away with it as long as she has, although seeing as I've hobbled and stumbled across it for years without making any formal complaints answers that question – simply none of us have ever bothered. What has surprised me is that nobody living in the cottages has ever complained – or they haven't to my knowledge. It's not too bad in the daylight, but at night it's lethal.

"Anyway, armed with this information, I went round to see her; not a pleasant meeting, I would have to say. To be fair to Amy, ever since she jilted me, on the few occasions we have come face to face, I've made not the slightest attempt to hide my contempt for her, and hostility towards her – and she, being the type she is, has always returned it with interest. Still, I called on her one day last week and, although I was kept on the doorstep – a painful business even now with my leg if I can't sit down – I was able to make my point, and concentrate her mind. Standing up probably helped from my point of view – I quickly got to the point, and the ache from my leg, plus the memory that is was her who had got me to go off to war in the first place all those long years ago, made me even more aggressive than I intended. I pointed out to her that the yard and all around was in a deplorable state, in fact, a dangerous one and that if she proceeded to throw Lol out of his shop then I would make sure that the District Council sent a surveyor to record the state of the open spaces, then to fulfil its statutory obligation to ensure it was brought up to standard immediately; no idle threat, Harry, and she knew it. There's not a lot the Parish Council could do in such a situation, but as to the district, that's very different. If some open space or right of way is deemed in any way dangerous, then their powers to ensure things are rectified are total.

"So I told her that such was what I intended to do – and that it would cost her a fortune. Certainly, no matter what she did with Lol's shop, it would take her the best part of the rest of her life to get her own expenditure back. And so it would, all the cobbles would need either relaying or replacing, which would be devilishly expensive, 'cause it couldn't be done in any slap-happy fashion. It would have to be done by very skilled tradesmen, laying them back with a minimum of cement – the surveyor and building inspectors would demand it (and I'd make sure they made very, very regular inspections, you can be certain of that). Labour costs would be massive, boy – huge. And

d

there's plenty of other things need doing as well. As you know, a highish retaining wall has partially fallen down in places, and a couple of low ones around the cottages need repair. And there's a fair bit of general tidying up to be done as well. Whatever, I laid it on thick to Amy – told her no lies, mind you, but made the most of every problem she faced there.

"It was only a few minutes before her approach changed. She asked me what would happen if she let Lol be – left him in peace. I told her that nothing would as far as I was concerned – and as the district council have not yet become officially involved, I wouldn't imagine she'd hear anything from them. There seemed no reason things could not go on as they are at present; there would be no need for any change at all.

"She offered no great resistance after that, except on the subject of Lol's rent. She wanted to double it, saying the amount he was paying at present was a mere pittance. There, she's right – it is, and he should be paying more even with the state the place is in. So I said I'd agree to her putting it up by fifty percent. Even with that increase, it's ridiculously low as I said just now – though Lol doesn't think so. He's no cause for complaint, though – he's come out of this better than he deserves if truth be told. I've seen folk thrown out of premises, business and private, because of their failure to keep them up to standard even though they've been vastly better cared for than Lol's.

"As far as my involvement in it all is concerned, I'd never have fought his corner the way I did had it not been for the fact that Amy Blanchard was the landlord. I've waited a long time to get revenge on her but, at last, I feel I have done so – partially, at least," he added.

Clearly the way she had treated him half a lifetime before had left bitterness and anger he would carry to the grave. Assuredly, to his way of thinking, she had been responsible for the best part of forty years of pain and reliance on a stick.

Harry Martin finished his pint, then lent back in his chair. "Thank you for telling me that, boy," said he with a gentle smile. "I knew, somehow, your hand was in it somewhere, and in a

74

major way. It'll go no further, Reg, you know that. The parish, though, owes you a debt, for whilst, as most agree, Lol brought it on himself, it's hard to imagine the village without him and his dusty old shop. Now, we won't have to." He got up from the table, picked up the glasses prior to going to the bar for a refill, then looked down at the parish clerk. "There's only one small minus to it all, Reg, as far as I can see."

Perkins, instantly, gave him a quizzical look. "What's that, Harry?"

The farmer laughed. "We're going to have to pay more for the worst shave and haircut in England."

# III

# Clarence's Compromise

Marion Small (née Symons) was a very pleasant lady; such was the view of virtually all in the parish who knew her. She was courteous, helpful and kindly, involved in many activities in the village where she had been born and bred and had lived all of her life. Indeed, she performed, and had done for a great number of her fifty-two years, sterling, dedicated work for the local branches of the Townswomen's Guild, the Women's Institute and the Mothers' Union; the lady's conscientious help was much to the advantage of all of them.

Audrey Allen (née Symons) also was a most pleasant, popular member of the local community, ever industrious, dedicated to the good of others, generous of both her time and worldly goods, ever respectful of the rights and views of others. She, also, throughout her lifetime in the parish of her birth had been a stalwart of many local institutions. She had for some years been chairman of the youth club committee – a village facility which surely would have closed down years before had it not been for her hard work and organisational abilities, especially in terms of fund-raising – and was also a stalwart of the church. A devout woman, she often cleaned and tidied the ancient house of worship, and did sterling work arranging flowers – much of which she bought herself – organising bazaars, sales of work, fêtes and so forth.

Thus were Marion and Audrey ladies of exemplary character,

respected, valued and liked by virtually all who knew them. They could probably justly have claimed to have no enemies – except each other. For between the identical twin sisters there was a deep, unrelenting, irreconcilable hatred, one which had existed from the day of their birth. It was a mutual antipathy, which had, to a degree, blighted the early life of their older brother, Harold. For he would often say that he spent his boyhood, when in the family environment, trying to settle disputes between his twin sisters, sometimes standing, literally, between them to prevent them physically attacking one another. Mind you, it was only when forced into each other's company were they so troublesome, as individually their relationship with Harold and their loving mother, Emily, was excellent.

Their father had died when they were only six years old – a slow, hacking death from tuberculosis. Fortunately just before he had gone down with the insidious disease, he had inherited, totally unexpectedly from a distant uncle he scarcely new, a sum of money, which was just enough to purchase the rather cramped cottage they rented. Wisely, this is what he did, so one positive for his widow was that the roof above the heads of her children and herself, was hers absolutely. Thus the three siblings, during their journey to adulthood, had the security of their home – a major plus during those so difficult early years of the century and the Great War.

Emily herself, though, had no income beyond her widow's pension – exceeding sparse – so had to work to put food on the table and clothes on their backs. A resilient, focused lady who rarely complained over anything, she worked seven days a week to provide for her family – going out charring, taking in washing and ironing, plus often flower, potato and fruit picking in the horticultural gardens of the Peninsula during spring, summer and early autumn. Her dedication to, and sacrifice for her children was appreciated, noted and, to some extent, reciprocated when they reached adulthood.

Harold, although married with two sons of his own, always ensured that his dear mother was 'looked after', he being a decent earner due to his chimney sweeping business prospering reasonably well (it being the only one in the Peninsula) during most of the year, the slack summer months partially filled with salmon fishing on the Tamar – often a precarious, uncertain business, but one which, thanks to a natural aptitude for locating the valuable harvest which the river held, usually rewarded him very well.

The twin sisters, likewise, were good to Emily, they never forgetting all the sacrifices she had made for them. Both had married reasonably well, Marion's Laurie being an insurance agent and Audrey's Clifford a cobbler, the owner of his own small shop and workshop in the village.

Thus in her later years, Emily Symons had a comfortable life, lacking nothing in practical terms, her modest requirements and needs amply catered for. She still, though, lamented – as she had since their early childhood – the mutual hatred between her twin daughters. How two people so basically loving and gentle as were they in their treatment of virtually everybody else could harbour such antipathy towards each other was something beyond her comprehension; likewise her son, likewise all others in the Parish who were aware of their lifelong feud (as were most). Still, such was life – such were the idiosyncrasies, illogicalities and sheer cussedness which defined the human race. Certainly there was nothing anyone else could do about it. Only the twins could ever bridge the deep chasm which lay between them – and chances of such were nil.

The sisters themselves had no problem in handling their mutual antagonism – they simply had nothing to do with each other. They ensured they did not belong to the same village groups and organisations, would make certain they were never in any of the local shops at the same time, would cross the road if there was any danger of passing on the same side, and would speak no word to the husband and children of the others. Marion, when Audrey became deeply involved with the church, ceased attending and went instead – on a quite regular basis – to the congregational chapel. Not that either attempted to instil in their families their own prejudice, which was to their credit. Their children – of largely similar ages – often consorted whilst their husbands, on occasions, would have a convivial chat over a pint or two in the Tamar View Inn.

Still, whilst the twins were able to live in the same village for very many years without acknowledging the existence of each other, it was inevitable that such close biological relations would one day be forced into mutual dealings. The cause of this – to both Marion and Audrey a calamity – was brought about by their mother Emily Symons: she died.

It was something of a shock to most who knew her, as she had ever been a lady of excellent health who, even in old age, had avoided most ailments and all major illnesses. She did have though, a slight weakness of the chest with mild bronchitis having come her way on occasions in her latter years. Sadly just days before her seventy-eighth birthday, an attack came her way and Pneumonia set in – something the doctor was slow to notice. By the time he had become aware of it the damage had been done – her lungs refused to fulfil their function, and Emily Symons died. She was just four days into her seventy-ninth year.

Her three children were greatly upset. She had been a loving, devoted and very caring mother to them all, something of which they were very aware. And in more recent times, she had been a friend, someone they could always turn to for advice, encouragement, even solace when needed. Harold Symons, though, whilst probably grieving no more than his sisters, was assailed by a further problem – those very twins. Their mother was dead; legal procedures had to be gone through – and a funeral had to be arranged. He foresaw problems, and he was assuredly right to do so, for the Marion/Audrey feud was to loom large in the preparations for the funeral service and interment of their beloved mother.

Clarence Langton was the undertaker. He had been burying the folk of the Peninsula for some quarter century. Prior to that the business had been run by his father Charlie who, unlike his son (who was over six feet and built like a flagpole) was a very corpulent man. Such bulk had caught up with him relatively early in life, keeling over one day in front of his own hearse as he was about to go off to the far side of the parish to fill the empty coffin which lay in the back. It was an immense heart attack – Charlie died on the spot. His son, who had helped his father, in the business on many occasions when not pursuing his own path of jobbing carpenter and joiner, took heed of his mother's pleading and took over the undertaking business, whilst still doing carpentry work when none in the parish needed laying to rest.

When Harold contacted him regarding his mother's death, he did what he saw as being his duty, just as much as it was his living, and made arrangements immediately to pick up the body of Emily Symons and perform the manifold tasks which had to be confronted when arranging a funeral. It was, though, a task which he approached with grave forebodings. For he knew the twins very well; he was very close to their age and had been in the same class as them at the village school. Thus he knew better than most of their intense antipathy towards each other. He could well remember that teachers would always ensure in the classroom they sat as far away from each other as possible – though in reality they would rarely have to take much action in that direction as the twins tended to do so automatically. Yet, he would have to concede that individually they were charming people – friendly, respectful and exceedingly easy to get along with. Thrown together though, as they would be by the imperative of burying their mother, he knew that trouble would ensue, as did their older brother.

Harold, though, being a man of wisdom when it came to neutralising the so often mischievous vagaries of human nature, felt that the more he did regarding the organisation of the funeral – with Clarence Langton, of course – then the less his sisters would be involved. Thus, in theory, a reduction in the likelihood of major strife between them.

Initially it seemed to work quite well – whilst there were snide, often malicious comments made to their brother from each twin regarding his sister, no major dispute came to the fore. Chances of the funeral taking place in a reasonably peaceable atmosphere were quite good. This, though, was before Clarence got them all together in the cramped office of his premises on the edge of the village. That they come together to ensure their mother's funeral the following day proceeded with decorum and without mishap was, clearly, a wise thing to do, and all of Emily's progeny were in agreement with the idea.

Fortunately, from the undertaker's point of view, the twins had been happy to leave most of the decisions, and the liaison with him, to their brother. He was, after all, the eldest, the male, and they both had a good relationship with him.

So Harold chose the bearers, the hymns and had an input into the other minutiae listed by Clarence, the absolute adherence to which was essential to the smooth progression, and respectful ambience, which the undertaker saw as being central to the ceremony of farewell to the occupant of the coffin.

Clarence was beginning to feel quite optimistic. He had expected little other than a war of attrition between the sisters, with Harold and himself in the middle, trying to avoid the verbal battles and restore peace. It had not happened though, and the arrangements were almost complete.

Only one matter remained to be discussed – albeit an important one – the order of family mourners as they entered and left the church, behind the coffin. The procedure in this direction was, to Clarence Langton – as it had been to his father – almost holy writ. The rules were simple in his book but sacrosanct; relations lined up behind the bier according to seniority. Blood relatives were to the fore, those marrying into a family bringing up the rear; and those at the front would be widow or widower, children, often parents, of course, when the deceased were youngish, to be followed by aunts, uncles, nephews, nieces, cousins and so forth. Mourners would follow the coffin in pairs and would always be of mixed gender.

The undertaker, having gained confidence following a peaceful and trouble free discussion between the three siblings and himself, thanks to the smooth progress which had been made during the half hour or so they had been together, briskly addressed the issue of the procession. "It's all straightforward enough, certainly when it comes to the main relatives. There could well be some more distant ones – cousins, perhaps and suchlikes – who might turn up tomorrow unexpectedly, and, no doubt, one or two who are expected not to come, but we can sort that out at the time. It's the main mourners who are important – yourselves, your families and so on. With that in mind, I've drawn up a list of close family and their progression into the church."

He stopped briefly, cleared his throat, then launched into the reading of the names he had in his hand, his somewhat relaxed tones suggesting he in no way was expecting the avalanche of outrage which was set to engulf him.

"Well, of course, we start with you three, then your children, then other blood relations, then spouses and so on – you all know the procedure. So that means, in pairs, the first couple behind the coffin will be you Harold, and Marion of course. Then behind you two will be. . ."

Who was to be the second pairing, Clarence was not destined to state for a cry of anger rent the air:

"What do you mean, Harold and Marion? What do you mean by saying such a thing? Mother had three children, Clarence, not two – she had me as well. Why am I not mentioned?" Audrey's face was almost deep red in colour registering a mixture of emotions ranging from outrage to extreme hurt – but principally outrage. "How dare you leave me out. Clarence – I'm as important as Harold and – and – and her." She spat out the final word, finding it virtually impossible to speak the name of her twin sister.

There was from the undertaker, for a few seconds, silence, he being stunned by her sudden, vituperative outburst; he then collected himself and replied, "I wasn't going to leave you out, Audrey – you'll be in the second pair, walking with Harold's older boy, Derek. Then, following you two in the other pairing, will be. . ."

"The second pair? What am I doing in the second pair? As I said just now, mother had three of us – and we're all equally important."

" 'Course – 'course, maid. I know that – well, it's obvious you're all of equal importance. But as you know when walking behind a coffin, down the aisle and suchlike, it has to be in pairs – you know that, Audrey, surely."

"Why?" The question was abrupt and spoken in tones devoid of any comprehension or compromise.

"Well – well – well – that's the way it is, isn't it. I've been directing funerals for the best part of twenty-five years – and involved for fifteen, almost, before that when I used to help father on many occasions. Folk walk in pairs – always have done, maid. Man with woman, too – unless it's a men only funeral; and you don't get many of them, except perhaps if it's the burial of a cheel; graveside too – it's always pairs, men and women," he added as an afterthought. He paused, very briefly, then put forward – a touch lamely – a further argument for folk waking in pairs, "It's space as well – there's not room for three to walk abreast down most church or chapel aisles." After he said this, he brightened slightly – he's never used such an argument before, largely because he'd never needed to. On the spur of the moment, he considered it to be quite a sound one.

Audrey Allen was not impressed. "I don't care what the reasons are, Clarence. All I know is that I'll not walk behind her." The final word was spat rather than spoken, and said without the slightest glance in the direction of Marion Small, who sat very still, staring stonily directly ahead, maintaining a fine display of aloof disinterest in the proceedings, most aware that it would seem the undertaker's list for the funeral procession would put her detested and detestable twin firmly in her place – standing and walking behind her.

"But there's no way around it, maid," replied the undertaker, increasingly bemused over a dispute which he had not fully foreseen, and to which he could see no immediate solution. "I mean, as I've said, folk can only walk in pairs and it has to be a man and a woman; there's no other way it can be done, 'cause, 'cause, 'cause that's the way it's always been done. And it's done in seniority – first Harold, 'cause he's the eldest, then Marion, 'cause she's the older of you two twins – or that's what Harold said yesterday, when I checked with him. Although to be honest, I've always known that you, Marion, were the elder of you two."

"By ten minutes," retorted that lady, tersely, a statement confirmed by her brother.

"Yes, that's right," agreed Harold. "Marion is the older by about ten minutes. I was only six when they were born, but I remember she was the first of the two."

"Nonsense – she's not older; how can she be? We're twins – born on the same day; you can look at the birth certificate if you want – we were both born on November 13th, 1899. It says nothing about anybody being older than the other – we're the same age, so it's wrong that one is given preferential treatment over the other."

"Come on Audrey," said her brother, weariness in his voice. "It's obvious you cannot both be the same age to the minute – you can't both be born at exactly the same time. No, there is no doubt Marion is the older of the pair of you – so, in a situation such as this, she is, without a doubt, the senior. I mean, I mean..." He paused briefly, searching for an example to back up the point he was attempting to make – "well, for instance, let's imagine Princess Elizabeth and Princess Margaret are twins – instead of there being a few years between them. Now when King George dies, they cannot both be queen, obviously – so the crown would go to the one that entered the world first, even if it was only by ten seconds. On their birth certificate it would state the same date for their birth, but the elder of the two would have precedence over the other – you see what I mean, Audrey. Marion was born before you – just minutes, true, but at a time like this it makes all the difference. She was born first, and so it has to be her that walks with me behind poor old mother's coffin."

Audrey, her expression registering myriad emotions ranging from anger, to outrage, to frustration, to desperation said nothing for a few seconds, but then, her face brightening, launched a counter attack. "You've every right to be at the front, Harold, I wouldn't argue with that – you're the eldest of the family. So that's where you should walk, in front, right behind mother's coffin – on your own. Then behind you, we two should walk, side by side, without one lording it over the other. That seems to be a fair way of doing it – the senior member of the family is treated as such, then we who are exactly the same age. . ." she paused briefly, then said again slowly but in tones suggesting she would accept no argument, "exactly the same age, walk as equals. I can see nothing wrong with that, Clarence – can you?" The question was put in tones of such aggressive assertiveness that it would take a brave man indeed to see something amiss with her argument and an even braver one to dispute it!

When it came to funerals and having correct order followed, Clarence Langton was a stickler for protocol, decorum and procedure, as had been his father before him. Whilst burying the dead of the parish provided probably the bulk of his living, he had always seen it as more than just a means of paying the bills and putting food on the table – it was a service he performed for the community. Laying folk to rest in a respectful, dignified fashion, ensuring they were planted into the rich Devon soil with due ritual, solemnity and, in a sombre way, a modicum of seemly style, was in its way as important as the receiving of a cheque for his services.

Charlie Langton had done it that way, had set as high a standard as it was possible to reach, and his son had not the slightest intention of allowing such standards to dip in any way even when confronted by the ferocity of a woman consumed with irrational hatred of her twin sister (a loathing which, he was aware, was mutual). So, if blame were to be apportioned for this dire feud, then it was most probably fifty-fifty. Audrey, though, was the one fomenting the trouble in this instance – so it was she with whom he had to do battle – and win. He had no doubt that whilst he disliked dispute of this kind – indeed, of any kind – that he would win. He was the funeral director and things would be done his way. Granted the family was hiring him, but his account would be paid, no doubt, out of money which old Mrs Symons would have left for her burial. Thus, she was paying him from beyond the grave; so he owed it to this good lady to do it all 'proper'. It would be, of that he was determined. If they were to process into the church, then the order would be as laid down by him – and custom; it was not negotiable.

"I'm sorry, Audrey – truly I am. I realise this is something you feel very, very strongly about and I respect that – and in no way do I want to upset you. I mean, after all, we've known each other all of our lives – we're the same age and have always lived in this village, all of us. But I cannot agree to what you suggest. You can't have anybody walking on their own – except, just occasionally at the back of the procession if there's an odd number of family mourners; nor can you have two women walking together – man and woman, that's how it has to be."

"Why? Who says it has to be that way? What rule or law says it must be like that, eh, Clarence? Tell me." Her pause was so brief; the undertaker had not the chance to speak a solitary word. "The answer is nobody – am I not right? It's just you and your routine – you and your customary way of doing it; your father did it that way, so that's the way it has to be done. You do nearly all the funerals in this parish, and your father before you – I doubt there's been half a dozen burials here that have not been organised by you two in the past fifty years and more. You've got everybody believing that because it's the way you do it, it's the only way it can be done. I mean – I mean, I went to a funeral in Tavistock a couple of years ago and I'm sure the undertaker there didn't insist on all the nonsense you're on about. I'm sure family there could file behind the coffin in any way they saw fit."

Audrey was telling the truth in so far as she had attended the laying to rest, in the town, of an old friend, but she had no idea as to whether or not mourners followed the coffin in the style insisted upon by Clarence Langton, or in any way they chose – she could have no idea, because she did not know the family. She suspected, though, that the strict rules laid by Langton Funeral Directors were personal whims, rather than written rules laid out in some worthy tome.

Clarence was about to respond to Audrey's angry attack – avoiding acknowledging she was correct in stating there was no laid down procedure regarding how family lined up behind a coffin, the rules essentially being down to the whims and sensibilities of individual funeral directors – when Audrey launched her final salvo.

"It seems to me, Clarence, you act beyond your authority – you bully people into doing things they don't necessarily want to do, hiding behind the talk that it's the way things have to be done, it's the laid down rules. I think it's nothing of the sort. It seems to me, you should take your instructions from us, not the other way around. After all, we hired you to organise mother's funeral and it'll be us who will have to foot the bill when it's all done – and it'll not be cheap, that's for sure."

Briefly Clarence was at something of a loss as to how to respond to this broadside from a very angry woman, but he soon got himself together, and responded to Audrey in as composed and dignified manner as he was able.

"Well Mrs Allen," said he in unusually formal fashion, "it is true that it is your family who has employed me to organise your dear mother's funeral. It is also true that you will be paying me for my services – although I suspect the sum will come out of your mother's estate, as is the usual way. In fact, knowing the thoughtful, practical lady she was, she probably made provision for her funeral costs, possibly through an insurance policy that will have paid out upon her death; this though is not my business. What is, though, is to ensure your mother is laid to rest in the manner she deserves. A lady held in high regard in this parish – respected and liked, a lady who, I would say, never did knowingly harm to anybody in this world and, most important of all, a lady – and I'm sure you'll agree – who was a wonderful mother and friend to you three, working her fingers to the bone to make sure you wanted for nothing even though she was widowed at such a young age. A lady good to grandchildren and all she knew; such a lady as this deserves to have a funeral which sends her off with the honour and decorum that, by virtue of the good life she had, is her due. As long as I'm in charge of her funeral, that's what she'll get. If you as a family are unhappy with the arrangements I've made, and am making, then clearly you have the right to cancel my services and get somebody else to conduct this burial, although I would say it would be difficult for you to find somebody else to do the funeral now, it being less than twenty-four hours away. Clearly I've already done a great amount of work – there's a great deal involved in a funeral. It starts the minute I come to a house, or a hospital, and collect the body, then there's the laying out, the making of the coffin, arrangements with the vicar and organist, and so much more. So probably eighty percent of the work regarding your mother's interment has already been done – which means I'll be sending in a sizeable bill for my services. It's not the best time to talk about money, I know, but it's only right to state the situation as it stands at present."

Harold spluttered as if he were about to suffer a seizure; "Cancel your services?" He stopped, and wheezed loudly – his chest always caused him trouble when he was stressed or upset; at that moment he was both. "Cancel your services, boy? What do you mean? What are you on about, Clarence? You're the undertaker – you and your father have buried the dead of this parish for probably the past three generations. Cancel your services be damned. You've known mother all your life – and she knew you, of course. You have to bury her, boy – it's what she would expect; it's what we all expect – more important, it's what we all want. All right, we've had a bit of a disagreement this afternoon – or one of us has, to be more to the point. But the thought of you not burying mother – well, I can't think of such a thing; and poor old mum will – will – will not rest in peace if you're not there to handle the burial."

The final words were a touch dramatic, he had to acknowledge that, but felt this situation that threatened to spiral out of control, called for dramatic words, if not action. He glanced across at Marion who had taken little part in the developing saga of the proposed order of the line up behind the bier; he needed an ally. "Isn't that right Marion – Clarence has to be in charge tomorrow; mother would definitely have wanted it, and so do we. Isn't that right, maid?"

His sister nodded – which was a virtual certainty as Clarence's unbending sense of funeral protocol placed her in front of the detested twin. "Of course, Harold. Clearly Clarence is to be in charge: why, I doubt there are any undertakers in West Devon that have organised more burials – and always to my knowledge, done them efficiently and – and – and reverently. I really don't know what the fuss is all about. Your arrangements seem to be totally fair as far as I can see, Clarence – so carry on." Briskly she got to her feet. "I've just looked at the time – I must be off. I've got tea to cook. So see you tomorrow, Clarence, outside the church – and you Harold. And, as I say Clarence, your order of procession into the church is exactly as it should be – and – and exactly as mother would want it and expect it to be," she added, delighted at having suddenly thought of the final dozen words: a magnificent put down – or so it seemed to her. It was lost, though, on her twin.

Audrey got to her feet also. "Mother was always the fairest of people and would have wanted things to be done in a right and fair way," said she. "There is no way she would class this present arrangement for following the coffin as being remotely fair, though, and nor do I. What's more to the point, I refuse to accept it, so I'll give warning now, Harold – and especially to you Clarence as you're to blame for this – this – this injustice – that when I come to mother's funeral tomorrow, I will not walk behind *her*. I accept I do not have the right to walk in front of her," (she said the words in tones which suggested it was an act of excessive magnanimity on her part to allow her sister equality), "but I will not walk behind her; so if you insist I do, Clarence, then I will go home – and say my farewell to mother in my own way." With that, she turned on her heels and stormed from the cramped office.

Marion then took her leave – in courteous fashion. Harold Symons got to his feet and made for the door; turning, he gazed at the undertaker and shook his head – a movement which conveyed sadness, mystification and despair.

"Sorry Clarence," said he. "You don't deserve all this nonsense, you really don't. I don't know what gets into that pair, truly I don't. It's always been the same, of course, as you well know – and it's a certainty it'll not improve now. It's been the bane of my life to some extent – and it was far worse for mother, of course. Even when they married and left home, she still spent half her life, seemingly, trying to keep the peace between them – usually without success. Yet, on their own, they're as pleasant a pair of folk as you could wish to meet." Again, he shook his head. "Still," he continued, "for what it's worth, you've my full support for your order of procession. It's a shame, Audrey's attitude, but that's up to her. If she decides to boycott the funeral then so be it. You've always arranged these matters in the correct way – seniority, blood and so forth; that clearly is the way it should be done, so it's the way it must be done."

The undertaker nodded and smiled, wanly. "Thank you, boy, it's appreciated what you said. Yes, I am in the right – it's the way things should be done, I've no doubts about that. But I hate the fact it's causing so much upset, even though that upset is down to Audrey's ridiculous attitude. If I can think of any way of avoiding it without compromising the basic principals of doing what is right, then I'll follow that course right away – not for Audrey's sake, mind you, but for your mother's. She was a good, devoted and kind lady, liked and respected by all. The acknowledgment of her passing from this world should take place without dispute or ill will. Sadly, though, I can't see any way around it."

"Again, boy, I'm sorry for all the trouble we've caused," said Harold, apologising for a situation for which he was not to blame. With that he held out his right hand; quickly it was grasped by the undertaker.

"Not your fault. In no way is it your fault. You were a good friend to your mum when she was alive, and you're every bit a good son to her now. Anyway, we'll see what tomorrow brings."

Harold Symons smiled, raised a hand in farewell, then made his way home, to be followed a few minutes later by the undertaker, who having locked the office, proceeded around the back to his house. He went in, took off the coat he had been wearing in the unheated office, then went through to the kitchen where his wife, Ethel, was preparing tea. He poured himself a cup of strong tea from the brew which Ethel said had just been made. She anticipating his arrival – a man of routine was Clarence and a good timekeeper – and then, when asked by his wife as to what was the matter (his demeanor suggesting something was amiss), told of the events of the past hour or so in the company of the Symons family.

His wife listened as he poured it all out, then at the end stated, simply, "Well, you're right of course, Clarence. You cannot change the way things are done – the way things should be done – just because one silly, nasty woman doesn't like it. The one who counts here is you. If you think it's the right way then that's the way it should be done. After all, that's what they hire you for, to see that a man or woman's send off is done in correct fashion. Mind you, I suppose if you can think of a way it can be handled that both will accept, but which will still be in keeping with the reverence and decorum of the occasion, then that would be ideal. After all, dear old Mrs Symons does not deserve to be sent off with part of her family refusing to attend the service. But you must not be seen as giving way to Audrey; you've established a name in the parish – just like your father before you – for doing things in the correct fashion. You know what folk are. If you give way to her and let her walk with her sister – two women together – then folk will start to talk. You must stick by your principles, Clarence. Any procession into the church organised by you, must be done your way – the correct way. It takes years to gain a good reputation – minutes to lose it."

Wise words from Ethel Langton, and her husband knew it. An intelligent lady, who had been educated at Tavistock Grammar School, and had worked as a legal secretary in the town until their marriage just over twenty years previously, she had instantly taken over most aspects of the paperwork involved in running their undertaking, carpentry and joinery business, and handled such matters with impeccable efficiency and authority. Clarence listened to her in all matters where the business was concerned, and indeed, in virtually all other aspects of life also. Rarely was she wrong.

"Oh, I forgot to say, Clar, there was a phone message for you about an hour ago, I've written it down on the pad." She left the room, went into the hallway, picked up the pad and brought it to her husband sat at the kitchen table.

"How didn't it ring in the office – I've been there for the past couple of hours, perhaps more?"

"Because you'd forgotten to do the transfer button here that would make it ring there, that's why. Anyway, here it is." She ripped the top sheet from the pad and handed it to her husband.

91

The words written were straightforward: 'Mrs Mary Bray and Mr Bob Parkin will be attending the funeral, but will not take part in the procession because of their health. They will go directly into the church and sit in the second pew, leaving the front pew empty for the close family.'

The undertaker nodded, "Fair enough," said he. "I know they're pretty lame these days – arthritis and the like. I didn't know they were on the phone though."

"Apparently it's only been installed a couple of weeks. They say – or, the lady said, Mrs Bray – that they have both become so bad on their legs these past few months, that her son felt it important they have a phone so that they can ask for help if either of them falls, or is ill in any way. Very sensible, of course – very wise. But who are they Clarence? I mean, I know them, but how do they tie up with Mrs Symons?" Although she had lived in the parish for a couple of decades, Ethel had been born and bred in Princetown, and had lived there for, almost, the first three decades of her life; thus she was not well informed of the details of family relationships in the parish in which she had spent her married life.

"Well, they're sister and brother to Emily Symons – both older. Mary's in her early eighties, whilst Bob must be eighty-five; bachelor, he is – never married. When Mary's husband, Donald, died – what, perhaps twenty years ago now (I remember doing the funeral), Bob moved in with her. It made sense – company for each other, and only one lot of rent to pay. They've lived together ever since. Like dear old Emily, they're both good as gold. Just like them to think of telling me what they're going to do. They didn't say how they were going to get to the church?"

"Taxi – Sam Cartwright's going to collect them and drop them off."

The undertaker did something he'd done little of that fraught afternoon – laughed. "Well, they'll need to leave early if Sam's driving them; it's less than a mile from where they live to the church, but the speed old Sam goes it could still take some time."

The man spoken of rarely drove his ancient Austin Taxi any faster than the horse and wagon he had driven, for hire, in the younger days of his life. Twenty miles per hour, to Sam, would have been excessive speeding.

Clarence Langton's enjoyment of an excellent tea and a good play on the wireless was ruined by thoughts, ever intruding, of the funeral which was to take place the following day. Probably a burial never had caused him so much worry and anxiety, and he'd been involved in, literally, hundreds throughout his life. Well into the early hours of the morning he lay, deep in thought, trying to think of some compromise with which both Audrey Allen and himself could work; one in which neither were seen to retreat on basic principles, he changing the time honoured order of procession, she having to walk behind her detested twin sister.

Over and over and over again the seemingly intractable problem tumbled around his tired mind as he lay on his bed gazing into the darkness. He could not see a solution; there appeared to be no possibility of compromise. Either he gave way to Audrey – which would offend greatly her twin, disappoint her brother and, crucially, do considerable harm to his high reputation throughout the Peninsula as a man who abided by high standards and impeccable rectitude in the laying to rest of the dead – or he insisted on the procession as stated the previous day and thus sullied Mrs Emily Symons laying to rest by provoking the storming off of a much loved daughter.

As he lay there in the darkness, his mind wandered a little from the direct problem to Emily Symons sister and brother. He smiled to himself at the thought of them being brought to the church by Sam Cartwright. He'd hired Sam a couple of years earlier to pick up some close relatives of the deceased and to follow the coffin to the congregational chapel. The solemn decorum of such a progression demanded that the hearse travel through the village at no more than twenty miles per hour, but even then he had to slow down the hearse to walking pace to allow Sam to catch up.

Then his mind moved on to the thoughtfulness of Emily's elderly and none to fit sister and brother phoning in the way they did. Like their deceased sister, they had always been the kind of folk who had put more into life and the community than they had taken out. That they had decided to go directly into the church and not cause any major slowness in the procession following the coffin was typical of their selflessness, as was their intention of sitting in the second pew, leaving the front row for Emily's son, daughters and grandchildren. Also, he was struck by the helpfulness in their phoning to tell of their intention.

His mind stayed with that phone call for a few seconds – there was something about it which, he felt, somehow had relevance to the problems he faced later that day – problems which threatened to mar his reputation as a funeral director, and prevent Emily Symons being laid to rest with the respect and decorum that was her due. Somewhere, in the message from Mary Bray and Bob Parkin, there were seeds of an idea – one which possibly could neutralise the ghastly possibilities of the following afternoon's funeral. The seeds, suddenly, started to grow within his mind – and within seconds were bearing fruit. "Yes," he said to himself – audibly, although Ethel didn't hear him as she was sound asleep. He almost cried out, "Eureka – I have found it," as that Greek fellow was supposed to have done when making some scientific discovery; one which neither Clarence, nor most of his classmates, ever really understood. Whatever, his idea could well work, and if he handled things correctly, the chances were it would work. A smile came to his face and relaxation crept over him at last; he closed his eyes, entering a deep and satisfying sleep.

The hearse, the experienced Norrie Rapson at the wheel, drew ever so slowly to a halt outside the Parish Church. Norrie had worked for Clarence for some fifteen years – and was hugely valued. A carpenter and joiner of the highest quality, he was also a good driver and had an exemplary manner with the families of clients, being ever patient, respectful, kindly and understanding. Appreciating just how crucial he was to both the undertaking and general carpentry business the astute Ethel Langton, many years earlier, had suggested to her husband that she paid this first class craftsman so well he would not easily be enticed away to one of the Tavistock firms. Clarence had heeded her advice, thus Norrie was, and remained, possibly the best paid craftsmen in the parish, and almost certainly the most valued.

Clarence, sitting beside the driver, pushed down the handle, thrust open the door, climbed out briskly, and closed it behind him, the words of advice from his wife ringing in his ears.

Just as he was leaving the house following an early lunch, she gave her views of how he should approach this so difficult funeral – and such views were stated in direct, uncomplicated and somewhat uncompromising fashion, as was her way.

"You're in charge, Clar, remember that. You are hired to organise everything, so what you say should prevail. The suggestion you made over breakfast that came to you in the night is a good one, and it could well work – but only, I fancy, if you're firm; if you take control. I know you expect things to be done in a proper fashion – insist on it, in fact – which is right; and virtually all folk are happy and content to have it done that way – the proper way. You've done it for so many years – and your father, of course – that they're happy to follow your guidance. Fortunately the Audrey Allens of the world are very few; so you've got to stand up to her – to all of them, in fact – and do it the way you suggest." She felt it necessary to give her husband the benefit of a talk, which combined encouragement and positivity with subtle instruction, for she was aware that whilst he was a principled man who adhered to the highest professional standards, he was also essentially easy going and good natured, and loathed confrontation and dispute. It was an aspect of his character of which he was aware and as the car door shut behind him he was determined to ensure it was submerged. He would keep his wife's advice to take charge to the front of his mind – and do it immediately.

Having alighted from the hearse, his eyes took in the thirty to forty family mourners standing in small groups beside the lychgate, to the fore Harold, Marion and Audrey – all standing separately. For a few seconds he composed himself then, clearing his throat, he said, in tones as authoritative as he could muster:

"Ladies and gentlemen, if I may have your attention for the moment. After much thought I have decided, as the funeral director, to deviate a little from the usual routine of family mourners following the coffin into the church." Clarence saw a slight smile appear upon Audrey's lips – a smile of triumph, she clearly feeling her demands were to be met. Marion, on the other hand, began to frown; as to Harold, his features were dead pan – all he wanted was for the afternoon in general, and the funeral in particular, to pass on its way without disagreement or incident.

"As many of you know," continued the undertaker, "the deceased's brother, Mr Bob Parkin, and sister Mrs Mary Bray, have decided not to process behind the coffin as normally they would, but have already taken their seats in the church. They have done so because, in an act of great unselfishness, they felt the procession into the church would be easier, quicker and more seemly without their presence, they both being aware that because of arthritic conditions, their progression would be slow. As brother and sister, these good people are very close relatives of Mrs Symons and I cannot doubt it has upset them greatly to forgo walking behind their sister's coffin on its final journey; In what they see as the interest of all, they have sacrificed their right to stand well to the front of the procession.

"I have thought a good deal upon this, and I have made a decision on behalf of the deceased, Mrs Emily Symons. I feel that as her brother and sister, to whom she was very close, have sacrificed their right to follow the coffin, then all should do likewise; it's what I feel Mrs Symons would have wanted. So there will be no procession into the church. Instead, I would ask you all to file into the church in whatever order you wish and join the other mourners. The first row of pews are reserved for family, with the front rows for Harold, Marion, Audrey and their children. So if you would please proceed into the church, ladies and gentlemen, thank you."

For as few seconds all stood like statues, slightly bemused by this dramatic deviation from normal procedure, until Harold Symons, aware that Clarence had thrown caution to the winds and played the 'joker' – plus realising instantly that this bold move could well avert a 'scene' that would scandalise the village for months, perhaps years, to come (and Audrey Allen storming off home refusing to attend her own mothers' funeral would do just that) – nodded his agreement with what the undertaker had said, then briskly walked through the lychgate onto the path leading to the church door some forty yards away.

Audrey, appreciating instantly that whilst she had not enjoyed total victory, Clarence's judgment had spared her having to make a stand – which she had not relished – against walking behind her twin, followed in his wake, and was soon joined by Marion who, though angered by the undertaker's snatching from her the opportunity to exhibit her seniority over the detested Audrey, saw that she was in danger of actually entering the church door – albeit in informal fashion – behind her younger sister. Quickly she was at Audrey's side and walking down the path – though they kept as far apart as possible – through the door into the church, then to their seats in the front row where they sat either side of their brother.

Minutes later, with all the mourners in place, the bearers entered the church with the coffin and carried it to the front before the altar. The vicar began the service. Words of remembrance were said of the long and positive life of Emily Symons, as were prayers and hymns sung. The service ended, and then the old lady was laid to rest in the large cemetery adjoining the church.

The devout ritual of farewell done, many mourners made their way to Harold's house for a cup of tea and for those who wished it (and many did) something a touch stronger. They were joined as was the custom, by Clarence and Norrie; a cup of tea, a sandwich and a bun, and then they would be on their way. It was, after all, a time for family and friends, not undertakers.

Their refreshment almost taken, Clarence glanced around to try to locate Harold in order that Norrie and he could make their farewells. He had no need to, for Emily's eldest child was suddenly there beside him:

"I'd have been over sooner, Clarence," said he, "but I thought I'd let you and Norrie finish your tea in peace. You certainly deserve it – especially you, Clarence. What you did today, and the way you did it was masterly. Do you know, I lay awake all night worrying about it. There was no way I could see to prevent mother's funeral being ruined and – let's be honest about it – the family name disgraced. In a place like this, boy, it would be

97

remembered for generations; and if it had happened, it would have caused another family rift – there's no way I would have ever forgiven Audrey if she'd ruined mother's send off, no way at all."

Mild tempered man though he was, Clarence had no doubt that the eldest of the Symons family meant exactly what he said. Clarence smiled, "You talk about last night, I was having a sleepless night 'til that idea came out of the blue. I didn't know if it would work or not, but it was worth a go."

"And worked wonderfully, boy – thank you, thank you from the bottom of my heart." He said the words with much emotion, then shook, with vigour, the hands of the two undertakers. He then laughed and shook his head. "The best of it is that you used Uncle Bob and Aunt Mary's – how did you put it – 'unselfishness', in forgoing the right to walk behind the coffin, because of their respect and thought for mother and the family." He laughed again – "To be honest, boy, I'm surprised they turned up for the funeral. I think they get on all right with each other, but both fell out with mother years ago. Dispute over the sharing out of what their mother – my grandmother – left when she died, what, back in the early thirties, I think it was. Not that she had much to leave, but there was certainly a big falling out about what there was – mother felt she dipped out, and she probably did. Anyway, they've had little to do with each other since then."

Clarence grinned. "Well, at least they were in the church and couldn't hear what I was saying; and your dear old mum wasn't going to say anything – more's the pity. She'll be missed, boy – a lovely lady. Still, at least the worst is over now, Harold; mum laid to rest. That's always the worst, the funeral, especially with all the strife between the twins – but it's all over now. You'll be able to relax a bit."

Harold Symon's face suddenly lost all traces of joviality and contentment. "Relax? All over? Dear me, I wish you were right, Clar – oh, how I wish you were right. Sadly, I fear far more trouble lies ahead – we've got mother's estate to sort out. Not that there's a lot of it. She won't have left much money, and what there is will probably be largely swallowed up paying your bill for the funeral – modest though I'm sure it will be," added he, hastily, aware that Clarence was the most honest and fairest of men in terms of charges – and had established a reputation as such.

"There's the cottage, of course," he continued, "which is straightforward enough. It's been let go a bit in recent years, but will bring in a reasonable sum which will be divided between the three of us – a handy cheque it will be, I don't doubt. The thing is though that mother was a hoarder – the cottage is full of all sorts of knick-knacks, curios, little china figures and suchlike. And then there's the furniture and bits and bobs – none of it worth much, but some nice enough things among them. The problem is that nothing is especially promised to any of us; so somehow we've got to agree on a fair division of everything between the three of us. Marion and Audrey already have spoken of various items they would like – often, the same piece of china or piece of furniture! It'll be a nightmare, boy. Think of the friction and cussedness there'll be between that pair – and remember who'll be in the middle, trying to keep the peace. No, Clarence, the funeral will have been the easy part – the worst is yet to come."

# IV

# The Sheep Dipping

Constable Claude Barton declined Mabel's offer of a third cup of tea, something which surprised her considerably; it was not unknown for her husband to quaff four large ones whilst consuming breakfast. Also, he had eaten a less hearty breakfast than normal, though by no means a paltry one. His very sturdy build gave evidence that it was probable he had never partaken of a meagre repast in his life (at least, not if something more substantial was available).

"What's wrong with you this morning?" asked his wife, a modicum of concern in her tone – the last thing she wanted was him sickening for something. He was not the most stoic when 'under the weather'.

"Nothing," he replied. "It's just that I'm over at Downside Farm today for the sheep dipping – didn't I say?" He realised he had not informed his spouse of the direction in which his duties would take him that morning, although he had meant to, for not only would he not require a heavy breakfast, he would not need Mabel to prepare a midday meal, either.

"Is it that time of year already? I suppose it is," she added, answering her own question. "July – dipping's always in July, isn't it?"

"Yes, Downside today and tomorrow. Mrs Martin is as good as gold. There's always tea and biscuits morning and afternoon and there'll be a master great roast about one o'clock. I'll need it, mind you," added he, hastily. "Busy morning keeping an eye on things, making sure they cut no corners. Some farmers – more than you might think – try it on now and again."

Mrs Barton smiled – to herself. She had been married to Claude for almost 25 years and over a score of them had been spent in their present abode, The Police Station (and dwelling for the incumbent constable) on the Peninsula, and every year her husband had told her a similar tale concerning the onerous duties and grave responsibilities involved in ensuring the dipping went ahead smoothly and, most crucially, in accordance with the law of the land. She suspected, though, that in reality it was a gentle, easy, most undemanding task for her affable husband, the enforcing of the law requiring little input from the Village Constable. For she was very well aware that whilst the law did require all sheep and lambs to be immersed in a deep pit containing strong smelling, quite powerful chemicals mixed with water, the purpose of which was to kill off the myriad of pests and lice which dwelt in their thick fleeces – thereby ensuring such nasty diseases as 'sheep scab' did not get a hold – it was very much in the interests of farmers to have them dipped. For they would have their stock cleansed of insidious insect life and be in a position to sell ewes and lambs at market, there being no chance of any sensible sheepman buying any which had not been properly dipped in the strong pungent disinfectant.

However, if it pleased her spouse to look upon the next few days of keeping an eye on the dipping as being a task and duty both onerous and vital, then she was not going to argue over it. Indeed, their sound marriage was down, partly, to the fact that neither ever argued very much over anything. And, of course, the following week he faced a brace of difficult days at Ridge Farm, which lay on land running down to the Tavy and catered for the flocks on the opposite side of the Parish (the two farms had for decades done the dipping for the Peninsula, the specially constructed pits having paid for themselves many times over, both farmers receiving a small fee for each sheep and lamb dipped).

Claude would spend two reasonably easy days at Ridge, but

they would not be as enjoyable as those at Downside – Farmer Doug Jarrett's wife, Hattie, although a courteous and kindly lady, never providing hospitality and sustenance in the same quantities, or of similar excellence, as Sarah Martin.

"Well, I'd better be off, maid – they usually start early. There'll be a lot of yaws and lambs to be done. They'll probably keep going until about five this afternoon, and there'll be a full day tomorrow as well. Good earner for Harry Martin," added he, perceptively. "Mind you," he conceded, " 'tis hard, hot, dirty work and he does his full share along with his son, Graham, and the men who work for him, so good luck to him – and to Doug Jarrett over at Ridge, for that matter."

He put on his thick tunic, buttoned it almost up to the neck, stuck his helmet on his head, said his goodbyes to his wife then went out the back door into the yard, took his big, police issue bike from a shed, wheeling it round the side of the house to the road. He looked about him, saw no obvious law breaking taking place, so set off along the main street of the village towards Downside Farm some three quarters of a mile away in the direction of the river, the sunny, sultry July morning already inducing sweat.

Within five minutes he was turning off the road and into Downside's yard. Stopping briefly he heard the bleating of sheep, realised the dipping had already begun, so wheeled his bike the 100 yards or so to the far side of the yard, turned a corner and saw a flock of some 50 or 60 ewes and lambs penned beside the capacious dipping pit, and four men hard at work – including Farmer Martin, who, along with Dead Eye Dawkins was doing the dipping. The sheep were being brought from the pen, one by one, by Gordon Nolan and his son Derek – who farmed Riverside, a smallish farm which, as the name suggested, was situated upon largely sloping land leading down to the River Tamar.

"Morning Harry," called Constable Barton. "Early start, I see."

The farmer looked up from his task of thrusting a sturdy Devon Longwool ewe under the surface of the murky disinfectant laden water in the deep, narrow pit. "Hello, Claude – yes, Gordon and David have arrived a bit earlier than I expected but the pit was filled and ready so we've got on with it. Got a lot to do today and tomorrow so we can't afford to hang about. I expect you'll want to check everything is all right, boy – it is as far as we're concerned, but you'll need to have a look and be happy with it. That's what you're here for, after all."

"Yes – yes – yes, of course," agreed the policeman. He leant his cycle against a nearby barn wall, removed his cycle clips, putting them in his pocket, undid another tunic button to allow a little more air into his body, then proceeded to the pit to make his inspection. Not that there was much for him to actually look at – just a pit full of water and disinfectant. He assumed the liquid was of the correct strength to fulfil its purpose (in reality he should have been there to witness the actual filling of the pit, thus to know the mixture was correct), and he could see the level of liquid was just below the rim of the pit – thus all looked to be in order. He nodded sagely; "Looks to be all right, boy," he opined. "You've been doing this so long, Harry, it doesn't need me to tell you how much disinfectant you've got to put in the water, and how often you've got to top it up and suchlike. I doubt there's anybody in the Parish knows more about such things than yourself, you've been doing it for so long now."

He was certainly right in that direction so was justified in trusting to the farmer's judgment. However, even if he hadn't been, he'd have had no real option other than to assume Harry Martin knew what he was doing, for he himself had no knowledge of the ratio of the amounts of disinfectant and water needed to create the optimum solution – one which would free the sheep from the debilitating, often blood sucking parasites which afflicted them but would not cause the beasts any harm or major discomfort beyond the unpleasantness of being immersed in an eight foot, sheer, smooth sided pit and having their whole bodies, including their heads, pushed below the grey coloured surface (and often having some of the foul brew in their mouths).

The constable strolled around the pit glancing cursorily about him. All seemed in order, although beyond the submerged receptacle there was little else to see or note. "All looks all right to me, boy," he opined to the farmer in as an authoritative a tone of voice as he could muster (never was, or had been, much good at sounding official, Claude Barton).

"Morning, Mr Barton – morning, Mr Nolan – Derek." The words came from behind the policeman, and swinging around he found himself confronted by the large form of Graham Martin, Harry's son. Ever a courteous young fellow, it only seemed right to him to utter greetings to the trio of visitors, all of whom he knew well – especially Derek Nolan, with whom he had gone to school and who was a fairly regular drinking partner of his in the village pub. He also played football with him most Saturdays during the season; young Nolan, though not a big lad, being a tough tackling, wiry right half. Also, he was the possessor of a sizeable amount of skill – probably more than anybody else in a very good side – and it was rumoured that Argyle were 'keeping an eye' on him, though nothing yet had come of it. As for Graham, although he was probably built more for rugby than football, he had always played the round ball game at school, and had no desire to change. He had no expectation of Argyle scouts tracking him, but still considered himself to be a competent goalkeeper, as good as most in the Plymouth and District Premier Division.

"You go on now, Dead Eye," instructed the farmer. "Graham's here now so he can take over. If you'd go out to the outside field and make a start singling out the swedes. It's time we got on with it – past mid-July. Have your crib and dinner out there, I should. Save you coming in. Missus'll give you an extra flask to take out with you. See you later on."

"Right boss," the worker replied and departed the scene with alacrity. Dipping sheep rated, with Dead Eye, along with threshing corn – smelly, sweaty, uncomfortable hard graft (with threshing corn the description dusty and itchy could also be added) – and his intention was to get to the large, sloping field on the far side of the farm as soon as possible. The news that the missus was going to supply him with the old, battered but efficient flask which she kept on a shelf in the kitchen, intimated that he was not expected back in the yard – and the vicinity of the dipping pit – until knock off time at 5 o'clock. Granted he had been told by Farmer Martin that he'd only be needed at the pit until Graham had finished helping Herbie with the stock, but something unexpected might still have happened which would have prevented the farmer's son from relieving him of this most unpleasant of tasks.

Seeing Dead Eye turn the corner of a barn and depart from view, the farmer glanced towards the policeman. "If you're happy with everything here, Claude – happy that everything's in order – then you'll find a cup of tea up in the kitchen, and a piece of cake, I reckon. Missus was doing a fair bit of baking yesterday and there were definitely cakes and sponges being put in the old range. Makes a master cake and sponge, does my missus," he added with some pride.

"She does that, boy," agreed the policeman with enthusiasm. "Makes a master everything to my knowledge." He had over many years, eaten often at Sarah Martin's table and knew of nobody else on the Peninsula who could bake with the expertise of that good lady, not even his Mabel, first class cook though she was. "Yes – yes, I will stroll up to the house and say 'morning' to the missus. Everything certainly seems to be all right here – and you chaps well know what you're doing. You don't need me to tell you – in fact, all I'd do is get in your way," he added, somewhat lamely. With that, he turned on his heels, collected his bike, and started to walk in the direction of the kitchen, turning after a few yards to inform Farmer Martin, "I'll be back in a while, boy – but give me a shout right away if you need me, if you have any problems."

His host could not imagine any situation arising, which would need the presence of the officer of the law and did not anticipate seeing a great deal of him throughout the day – which would suit them both, he preferring to be able to get on with this grafting, tedious task without a spectator, whilst the constable was more than happy to embrace the comfort, tea and quality victuals of Downside kitchen, rather than the smells and boredom of watching a multitudinous succession of sheep thrust below the surface of a turgid pit of liquid. The only loser was Sarah Martin, who would end up having to suffer the company of the uniformed officer for the bulk of a long day.

The constable leant his cycle against a wall of the farmhouse then knocked on the back door – which led directly into the kitchen. It was opened almost immediately, then left open whilst he was greeted by a smiling Sarah Martin. "Hello, Mr Barton – so nice to see you again; please do come in. It must be a couple of months since you were last at Downside – it was when you were asking if anybody had any information about men poaching salmon on the Tamar. It was rumoured they'd not come away from the river by road to start with but had come up the hill through the fields and woods which might well have taken them across part of Downside."

"Yes, that's right, missus," he confirmed as he passed into the kitchen. "I don't know where the tale came from, to tell you the truth, but I had to check to see if there was any truth to it. None, though, as far as I could tell. Whatever, we've no idea who took them out of the river – whether they were from out of the parish or local. I suspect, to be honest, they were local – know the lie of the land and ways of the river. The only chance of catching them would be to know where they got rid of the salmon – or who it was that bought them, not something I'll find out now, though, that's for sure." He smiled, shook his head then sat down in the shabby but comfortable chair beside the large, black cooking range, which dominated one side of the kitchen. As he laid his helmet on the floor and unbuttoned his tunic, he reflected – as he had over the many times he had sat in this very chair – that there was none more comfortable in the Parish. Sarah Martin was well aware of this, thus was her seating of the burly policeman there part of a plan which had worked very well on dipping days of recent years.

"Cup of tea, Mr Barton?"

"Thank you, missus – that would be very nice, throat's a bit dry, so it'll slip down well; must be all that disinfectant down by the pit," said he with some seriousness, neatly ignoring the fact that his presence down at the area where the work was taking place was of very brief duration – contrary to what the rules and regulations required, he, officially, being tasked with seeing that every single ewe and lamb plus the occasional ram, of course, was immersed in the cleansing liquid.

"A nice piece of sponge, as well? Victoria, it is – I baked a few yesterday. I was going to bake a fruit cake but couldn't get enough fruit, raisins and suchlike – it's shocking isn't it that though the war's been over now for more than five years there's so many things you cannot get, so much still rationed. But it's not such a problem making sponges – and we all love them. Awful family for sweet things, we are – in fact, Harry could live on sugary sweet food. The fact you could hardly get sugar and such during the war upset him more than anything else. And he's still upset you can't get sweets and chocolate. Anyway – I expect you'll have a slice, Mr Barton, won't you?"

"Well, missus, well I shouldn't really – I've not that long had my breakfast. And my Mabel reckons I carry a bit too much weight already – always on to me to cut out cakes and buns and so on. But then, a slice of sponge won't do me any harm, will it? Small one, missus, if you would – thank you."

Sarah Martin, rapidly and skilfully wielded a large knife on a sponge lying on a platter on the kitchen table, placed a wedge sufficiently large to impede the progress of a tractor upon a plate and handed it to the policeman, who, mumbling his thanks, fell on it as if he'd not eaten in days.

The farmer's wife busied herself making preparations for the roast she was going to prepare for one o'clock whilst the constable munched steadfastly, but relentlessly, through his culinary challenge. Pushing the last few crumbs into his capacious mouth, he swallowed the delicious concoction, emptied the remains of the tea likewise, got up from his soporific chair and placed the empty receptacles upon the table. "That was lovely, missus, thank you – lovely. I'll just have a sit down for a little while to let it settle, then I'll be off down to the pit again to see how they're getting on."

The policeman returned to his seat, and settled down. "You talking about the war just now, missus – all we went through, and still go through in many ways, I often think about it, you know – they was hard times, terrible times in many ways. I was only saying to my Mabel last week about the war; I was saying I can well remember. . ."

"Would you like another cup of tea, Mr Barton," interjected his hostess, almost a tone of urgency in her voice.

The only uniform PC Barton had worn during the war had been the blue serge of the Devon County Constabulary and all his 'battles' had been fought on the Peninsula twixt the Tamar and the Tavy, yet he regularly talked of the Second World War – at great length – as if he had been present at every battlefield in Europe; thus it was, Mrs Martin knew, crucial he be silenced as soon as possible.

"Well, yes missus, thank you." There was no way he was going to turn down further liquid refreshment.

"And perhaps another piece of sponge?"

"Well – yes lovely, thank you. I shouldn't, mind you – I know that. The old waistline's getting a bit thick I have to say – but that's an 'ansome sponge, ma'am, and I'm sure a bit more'll do me no harm. Mind you, I don't want to be greedy."

"Good heavens you're not greedy, Mr Barton. It's good that you're enjoying it – and there's plenty left. In a minute I'm going to take some sponge and tea down to the men where they're working. They'll need something doing heavy work like that – it's quite a while since they had breakfast, and dinner won't be 'til one o'clock. I'm doing a roast, Mr Barton – you'll join us, of course."

"A roast – well, yes, ma'am, yes, thank you. I'm very partial to a roast – even on a warm day like today it always goes down well. It's very kind of you, Mrs Martin – very kind indeed."

"You're very welcome, Mr Barton. Anyway, I'm going to make a fresh pot of tea, slice up the rest of the sponge, and take it down. They'll be glad to see me, no doubt about that."

A lady who talked quickly and moved even faster, she proceeded with alacrity to prepare tea and victuals, place it all on a tray and, with a quick "I'll see you soon, Mr Barton," speed out the back door and across the yard in the direction of the dipping. She planned, however, not to return to the kitchen too quickly – a minimum of twenty minutes absence would probably be necessary for her scheme to work. It had certainly been successful in the past.

She was warmly welcomed at the dipping pit, all well in need of a brief break and some refreshment after more than two hours solid catching and dipping of sheep, some sturdy and quite powerfully built, on a stuffy, fly ridden July morning.

"Jobs don't come worse than dipping," as Dead Eye Dawkins had said many, many times in the past – which explained why he had been so pleased to be relieved of a long session of it by the boss's son earlier that morning.

Sarah distributed cups of tea, sponge and biscuits to her husband and son and to the latest farmer, Joe Bateman whose flock was being processed – a sizeable number that would take up the rest of the morning. His worker, Cyril Chambers, a giant of a fellow, with the strength of an ox, had an appetite and thirst to match his size and Sarah could see that even though she had prepared a substantial amount of both food and liquid, little would be left after ten minutes or so when they recommenced work.

Leaving them to get on with it – calling out to her husband as she was leaving, "The roast'll be on the table at one, Harry" – she walked back via the kitchen garden at the side of the house, stopping to pull a few longish weeds which, seemingly had sprung up overnight amongst her carrots, before strolling casually back to the kitchen. "It should be long enough by now," she mused to herself as she approached the open door. Reaching it almost silently, she glanced inside and saw exactly what she wanted to – and what she had anticipated: Constable Barton was laying in the easy chair sleeping like a babe in arms. It had worked yet again, she thought to herself – it had to be, at least, the fifth or sixth occasion in recent times that she had managed to induce sleep into the policemen. Not that she had any malevolent intent – it was simply that she needed peace, quiet and her space on such a morning when she had much to do, especially on the cooking front.

The problem with Claude Barton, an habitual one for the past decade, and possibly more, was that he would come into the kitchen for an earlyish cup of tea and snack – and stay. The fact that he was supposed to maintain virtually constant vigilance by the dipping pit had never weighed heavily on his conscience. His habit had been to absorb goodly quantities of tea and some cake, then inflict his presence upon the farmer's wife for a large portion of the morning, chatting idly and inconsequentially, surmising over possible local events and indulging in general gossip.

Amicable, indeed jovial, though he was, Sarah Martin did not enjoy such a conversation, being essentially a quietish, quite reserved lady (albeit kindly and friendly) and also, most relevant of all, invariably she was busy; thus the last thing she wanted was the kitchen occupied for two or three hours by a portly policeman with far too little to do. A few years earlier, though, she had stumbled upon a solution.

One warm morning, as Claude sat chatting away in the chair – between gulps of tea – she did something she'd never done before; she offered him another slice of sponge in the hope that his chewing and swallowing would stem his flood of words. She had always doled out such large slices that it never had occurred to her that anybody would want another with a large dinner less than three hours away – even her Graham, an enormous eater, was satisfied with just the one sturdy wedge. She had anticipated that big though was the policeman's appetite, he would refuse. She was wrong, for her offer was accepted with an alacrity directly opposite to his physical movements, and thus she cut a further large slice and handed it to her unwanted guest. At least, she surmised, it could keep him quiet for the few minutes or so it would take him to devour it. Here, though, she was wrong, and was to be very agreeably surprised. For within five minutes of Barton finishing the sponge and returning his plate to the kitchen table, with voluble and enthusiastic thanks, he was sat back in his chair sound asleep.

The warmth of the summer day and the heat of the giant range had, with the addition of the 'fuel' of the second slice, coalesced into a powerful soporific force which had brought sleep to a none too reluctant policeman. He had slept soundly all morning until the time – about half past noon – when the farmer's wife deemed it time he was up and about, with dinner being only half an hour away. She had roused him by banging a saucepan down noisily upon the iron surface of the range. He awakened instantly in some confusion, insisting that he must have "dropped off for a few minutes." Then eyeing the face of the old grandfather clock in the corner of the kitchen and seeing the morning had passed him by, he had hastened from the kitchen saying that he had "better see that everything's going to plan down at the dip."

And such had been the routine ever since, it having failed not once. As her husband had said to her after it had worked three years in a row (he being a great fan of Sherlock Holmes tales), "It's a case of the second slice, my dear."

Clearly it had worked yet again; she was free to go about her busy routine unhindered by the shackles of tedious, irrelevant chatter. A well organised, highly disciplined lady, she went about her business in a smooth, orderly and very capable way, and, with the clock approaching 12.30, decided that everything was as it should be and the roast would be ready to serve at one o'clock as she had promised.

It was time to rouse Constable Barton. Picking up a sturdy, solid iron cooking pot, she banged it down, exceedingly loudly, upon one of the ancient hot plates atop the vintage range which had kept the ground floor of the house warm for decades – and fed three generations of the Martin dynasty (in association with the culinary skills of a likewise number of generations of female members of the family).

The constable awoke with a mighty start; Blearily he gazed about him, then fixed his eyes upon the clock face. With a speed somewhat at odds with his bulk, he heaved himself up from the low slung chair. "Dear me – dear me – well I'm damned," he stuttered. "Is that really the time? I must have nodded off for – for – for a few minutes, missus. That sponge of yours – that's what did it. Anyway, I'd better get down to the pit and – and – and. . ." momentarily he was not too certain as to what he was going to do when he actually got there, and as inspiration as to what his task would be when he arrived at the centre of activity eluded him, ended lamely, "and make sure everything's in order – and – and – and going to plan. Thank 'ee, missus, for the tea and cake – lovely it was. I'll see you a bit later."

"Not much later, Mr Barton. Dinner's at one, don't forget – only 25 minutes away." She was all too well aware that this was one time which her somewhat unwanted guest would not forget, his more than adequate stomach always ready for action. "If you'd remind the men down there that the roast will be on the table at one, Mr Barton, I would be most obliged."

" 'Course, missus, 'course," he replied hastily. "I'll go right down there now and remind them of the time – and – and see that everything's in order, of course."

With that he was gone, stumbling out through the open kitchen door, pulling on his tunic top despite the warmth of the day. Claude Barton, when on official duty, always tried to look just that – official. One thing Sarah was sure of – the 'men folk' would not be late for their dinner, as PC Barton, despite his comprehensive devouring of Victoria sponge, would be ready for his dinner and, knowing he wouldn't get it unless he delivered the others on time, would ensure that all involved would be in the big farm kitchen at one o'clock.

She busied herself laying the table, then made final preparations for the meal – and at five minutes to one found her kitchen invaded by hungry men who queued at the kitchen sink to give smelly, disinfectant polluted hands a very thorough wash.

Seeing as Claude Barton had done nothing all morning, he sat down at the table without washing his hands at all. He was followed by Harry and Graham and by Joe Bateman, the dipping of whose sheep had been completed just before they were summoned to the repast, and the young giant, Cyril Chambers, whose bulk would take some filling.

Always kindly, hospitable folk, on dipping days the Martins had long invited those involved with the flock dipped immediately prior to dinner-time to join them in the hearty repast – which was prepared, invariably, by Sarah – even if the dipping of their flock had been completed.

Farming just 60 acres about half a mile from Downside, Joe Bateman was mainly a grower – daffodils in the spring, strawberries and raspberries in the summer plus a large acreage of potatoes. He did, however, keep a largish flock of sheep as some

20 acres of his rather hilly holding was roughish pasture, with a small woodland, all totally unsuitable for arable pursuits. Resilient, hard mouthed Devon long-wools were ideal when it came to keeping the grass down. In fact, they prospered, his flock always being amongst the best that came yearly to be dipped. The last 'yaw' was immersed at ten minutes to one and, the flock being penned securely until after dinner when they would be walked home, the two men were, by one o'clock, seated at Downside's capacious kitchen table awaiting, keenly, Sarah Martin's roast – which would be large.

"Thank you, maid," said Harry Martin to his wife, as a mountainous plate of food was laid before him. "I'm certainly ready for this – and I fancy we've earned it too, all of us. Hard work dipping." He was aware that his statement was not accurate regarding the gathering universally being deserving of the mighty meal, but he had no intention of leaving out the severely under employed constable – for two reasons: Firstly, he was ever a courteous man, conscious of other folk's sensibilities and would hate to hurt Claude's feelings and secondly, certainly every bit as important (possibly even more so) the last thing he wished to do was inspire in the constable a rare spurt of energy and sense of duty, one which would have him down by the dipping pit actually keeping an eye on the work in progress. As things were, the policeman did not want to spend hours watching sheep half drowned in disinfectant, and Farmer Martin – likewise the customers – did not want the authoritative figure of the local constable keeping them under constant vigilance. With the exception of just one farmer – whose flock was to be dipped that very afternoon, and who would receive his full attention, Claude Barton was content to doze in the kitchen, and the farmer was delighted for him to remain there, although he knew he was being selfish as he was only too well aware that his Sarah was none too happy to play hostess for hours on end. However, he was also aware of her shrewd, and successful system regarding inducing sleep into the fellow, such knowledge neutralising his conscience to a large extent.

All fell hungrily upon the flavoursome victuals – including

Constable Barton despite his substantial intake of Victoria sponge through the morning and his lack of activity – and there was little conversation until plates were cleared.

There followed a few minutes of somewhat desultory, inconsequential talk until, once again, food induced general silence. Sarah served a magnificent apple crumble – for which she was noted – topped with copious lashings of custard, and the portions were again exceedingly large. The devouring of such, however, did not take long, and assuredly nothing was left.

Drinking strong, sugar laden tea following the feast, Farmer Martin leant back on his hard kitchen chair and voiced the feelings, probably, of all those sitting replete around the table; "Well, I wish I could go in the front room, sit in the easy chair, and get my head down for an hour or two."

There was a general agreement from his guests, with the first to voice such – totally inappropriately in view of his indolent morning – being Claude Barton. "Yes, you're right there, farmer," said he. "Warm weather like this, then a morning with plenty on, followed by a master dinner such as us have just had – thanks to the missus here," he added speedily, "makes 'ee feel drowsy, I must say. Trouble is, though, I reckon there's a busy afternoon coming up."

"There is that boy," agreed Harry, "and me and Graham can't linger here any longer, looking at the time there. Ten to two – and we've got Arnold Fuller due here at two with his flock. Hadn't better be late for Arnold – he'll be on time for sure. I can't imagine Arnold being late for anything."

Joe Bateman reacted rapidly to the news that Farmer Fuller, owner of almost 200 acre Brook Barton – amongst the biggest farms in the Parish – was due in no more than ten minutes. "We'd better be on our way then, Harry – we'd better clear our yaws and lambs out of the pens now before he arrives. There'll be a lot of them with Fullers' mark on them, for sure. Damned sight more than I've got." An accurate statement that, as the flock due to arrive would possibly contain three times the numbers of the one about to depart.

Mention of the name Arnold Fuller certainly spurred all the

men round the table into action – including Claude Barton, this being the one flock coming to Downside, the dipping of which would command the policeman's full attention.

Barton had never enjoyed a harmonious relationship with the farmer since he had come to Brook Barton just a year before the outbreak of war, from a somewhat smaller holding just north of Dartmoor. It was widely believed by folk on the Peninsula that he had been a somewhat impoverished tenant farmer in that area, but had suddenly come into major money – or, to be more accurate, his wife had, she having been left, totally unexpectedly, a sizeable amount by a very distant uncle she had never met who had gone to Canada to live well before the First World War. Having prospered, and never married, his fortune had come in its entirety to Jill Fuller as his nearest relative (her parents being deceased and she having no siblings). Not that the Fullers had ever told anyone local such tidings – they had always been a touch aloof – but an agricultural representative who came occasionally to the parish, and had also done business where the Fullers had farmed previously, had spread widely the story, one which could well be reasonably accurate. For it was certainly true that he had suddenly ceased being the tenant of a small thin soiled holding in thrall to the cold winds blowing off the Moor, and become the owner of a large, first class farm – arable, pastoral and horticultural – of rich soil situated in the much friendlier, climate wise, Tamar Valley. Also, his son and daughter had been privately educated (the latter now a doctor), the former, who had attended Kelly College in Tavistock, being a young fellow who loved the land, now farming with his father.

Assuredly, there never appeared to be any shortage of money at Brook Barton, for over the years the tradesmen and builders of the parish had done well out of them – the work being plentiful, and payment prompt. Not that their affluence was due solely to inherited wealth, for no one could say in fairness that Arnold Fuller was anything other than a first class farmer and grower. A believer in putting his 'eggs' in varying 'baskets', he ran a smallish but high quality herd of South Devon cows, had the large flock which was about to be dipped and grew some 30 acres of corn.

The main reason for their moving to the Tamar Valley, though, was his desire to grow things. Brought up at the toe end of Cornwall, the son of market gardeners, the growing of flowers in the spring and soft fruit in the summer was dear to his heart (plus 'spuds' throughout late spring and into autumn). The tough environment, and thin soil of his tenanted land, meant that the keeping of hardy livestock was their only option.

His wife's sudden wealth, however, opened doors which he had assumed would be closed to him forever. They bought the excellent Brook Barton with its growing potential and, with wise investment and consummate skills, had during the dozen or so years of their ownership, exploited the fertile land to the full, making it probably the most profitable farm on the Peninsula. He had also mechanised in a way which no other farm in the parish could match – or, in very many cases, desired. One old shire remained, but the bulk of the work was done by the small Ferguson and larger Massey Harris tractors, with appropriate implements.

Such mechanisation had been pointed out to Harry Martin in recent times by those who felt he should 'move with the times', but influenced him not a jot. "He's got the money to invest – nobody else in the parish could buy machinery like that; they'd be bankrupt," said he, with some accuracy. When it was pointed out that he could invest in, perhaps, some modern equipment, he would argue, "Downside's got a lot of hills – if it was a bit flatter, then I might think about a little Ferguson, or suchlike," blithely ignoring the fact that a level holding in this parish was as rare as a diamond mine.

Sarah Martin was left to clear away as the well fed diners quickly exited, showering her with sincere words of thanks and gratitude. In quality and amount, few in the local farming community could match her, and probably none could surpass.

Arriving back at the dip, Joe Bateman could see a cloud of dust some two hundred yards away at the beginning of a narrow lane which led directly from the parish road to the farmyard. Clearly Arnold Fuller was on time with his flock (no surprise there, as he was on time for everything) so the departing farmer needed to move his small flock from the pens immediately.

"You'll go across the field, Joe." It was more a suggestion than a question from Martin.

"Yes, that's the best way – don't want to get mine mixed up with Fuller's. He's never the friendliest man on earth, and that would do nothing to make him friendlier." He grinned as he said the words, then with the help of Cyril Chambers, turned the sheep out of the pens and into the field which adjoined them, at the far side of which there was a gate leading directly onto the parish road. The sheep once again in grass, Bateman unleashed his elderly, but still very able collie, Nellie, who quickly rounded them up and set them off in the direction of the gate some 300 yards away, Bateman waving cheerily his farewells and imploring Harry to again "Thank Sarah for a marvellous dinner," words echoed by Chambers. Just as that flock moved towards home, Arnold Fuller's came into the yard, shepherded by the farmer and his son David.

Harry moved forward to greet his next 'customer'. He extended a hand, which was briskly accepted by the newcomer. "Good to see you, Arnold."

Fuller nodded, his face impassive. "And you, Harry. All ready for us, I see."

As always there was from Fuller a brisk basic courtesy and civility, but no warmth or affability. He had not made enemies in the parish, but he assuredly had made no friends either. He was certainly not a sociable man, not having involved himself in any village activities or joined any local groups or societies. Even during the war when so many events were organised to both help the war effort and raise local morale, he took no part. The one exception to this was the local Methodist chapel. A staunch, committed Christian – and a teetotaller – he had quickly become a pillar of the chapel, even on occasions conducting services and preaching sermons. And his wife was similar. She had not joined any village organisations, although she had been invited to on many occasions. She, like her husband, however, was a devout Christian – possibly even more than he – and a very regular worshipper at the Methodist chapel.

So they were a couple who had never really integrated into the community – and had never made any attempt to do so. They were held in high regard, though, by the four men who worked for them (three of them in excess of ten years), who by their employers were treated with respect, thoughtfulness and fairness. Also, it was said they were paid slightly more than the official hourly rate for farm workers, which would have added to their approbation of the Fullers. Nobody knew for sure, though, and the quartet were certainly not going to tell anyone.

Son David, though, was very different. An extrovert, he was involved in many village activities, at only 21 most of them sporting. A member of the football club, he got the occasional game although he was no Stanley Matthews. He was a better cricketer, being one of the best batsmen in the village team. His best sport, though, was darts, having the most accurate touch in a very good Tamar View Inn side. Being a young man of strong character and independent spirit, he eschewed his parents temperance habits, going to the pub regularly since the age of 17 – though he had never been a heavy drinker. To their credit, his parents had never put pressure on him, or tried to influence him in any way, to adopt their teetotal ways. Indeed, he was, and had ever been, very close to them – especially his father. When he stated his intention to go farming, Arnold had offered him the chance of going to agricultural college – he certainly had attained a level of education which would have given him automatic entry. David, though, wanted no more education in the formal sense; rather he wanted to learn 'hands on' and having the wisdom to be aware that there were few around more knowledgeable than his father in the practical sense – and also comfortable in his relationship with his parents – he had no hesitation in deciding to pursue a farming career on the family farm.

The brief, somewhat formal greetings between the two farmers, who had had very little contact over the years save for occasional business matters (where Harry Martin had to concede, the incomer was always fair and a man of his word) was warm in the extreme compared to those between Fuller and Constable Barton, where the only acknowledgement from both to the other's presence were curt nods. Certainly there was 'history' between the two, and it was this which had prompted the somewhat indolent policeman to forego the comforts of the kitchen for the action down at the dip. His presence was motivated on two fronts – one defensive, the other positive (a rare event, indeed). Regarding the former, he did not want to give the disagreeable, pedantic Fuller any further scope for complaint about the way he policed the parish – unlike occasions in the past. As to the latter, easy going, affable man though he was, he did not take kindly to folk, not that long in the parish, finding fault with the way he performed his duties. Always he had taken them seriously, had been conscientious, and attempted to administer the law with justice and common sense – albeit, he did on occasions do it his own way, and he made no apologies for that.

Still, if Fuller wished him always to work to the letter of the law, then that afternoon he would do so, even though it would mean he would have to miss out on Sarah Martin's easy-chair, strong, sweet tea and masterly Victoria sponge. He would stand beside that pit and ensure that every 'yaw' and lamb in Farmer Fuller's large flock was dipped thoroughly – which included being submerged – in accordance with the law, and any which weren't would have to be done again. He would ensure, also, that the paperwork was in order, every 'T' crossed and 'I' dotted. Having said this, he had little doubt that the efficient Martins would dip the sheep fully in accordance with the law, and that the exceedingly precise Fuller would make no mistake in the paperwork. Whatever, he would do his job to the letter of the law, even though it might well inconvenience himself, even more than his protagonist.

It was not, in Claude's eyes, as if the man had any cause for complaint, not any of the times they had clashed. The first time was little more than a year after the Fullers had arrived in the parish, when the farmer had phoned the Police House, late afternoon, to complain that somebody had broken some windows in an outhouse and that he, as the village constable, should come out and inspect the damage. This he did, but not until the following morning which, to him, seemed eminently sensible.

After all, he was in the middle of his tea when Mr Fuller had phoned, devouring one of Mable's magnificent rabbit pies and there was no way he would abandon that. By the time he had finished his meal and let it settle, the light was fast falling so there was no point in going to Brook Barton to inspect an outdoor building when it was dark. Thus, he went there the following morning – and had nothing from the farmer other than vituperation for his trouble.

Not that Fuller was abusive in any way, his strong religious beliefs prevented him ever swearing, but he let it be known that he felt Constable Barton had failed lamentably in his duties. As custodian of the law on the Peninsula, the farmer was adamant that the officer should have come out to Brook Barton the instant he had been called, not some 15 hours later when, as Fuller put it, "The trail is now cold as ice." Claude felt that the farmer had been reading too many detective tales as, in this case, there would never have been a trail of any temperature. He pointed out that, in reality, the perpetrators of the vandalism, if not caught there and then in the act, would be virtually impossible to find unless someone had actually seen them do it, which was unlikely.

"Could be anybody in the Parish, of any age – though it's likely to be some youngsters who need a clip around the ear. If I'd caught them, that's what they would have got. But, of course, I haven't, and there's no real way I'll be able to now. Pity, of course, but that's the way 'tis, I'm afraid. If anybody tells you anything about it – if they saw some young devil hanging around, or have any ideas as to who did it, then let me know. If no information comes to light, then there's nothing I can do. Sorry about that." With that, he had bade his farewells and returned to the Police House in good time for his lunch, leaving an irate Arnold Fuller in his wake.

A few years after this, just before the end of the war, the Master of Brook Barton had again phoned the Police House complaining that he had chased a fellow, from the village, off his land, Jimmy Jones by name, who had been poaching rabbits – and not for the first time. Then he proceeded to make it plain that he expected PC Barton to go around to the man's cottage in the village and charge him with both trespass and poaching.

The law enforcement officer, though, was unequivocal in his response. "Come on," said he, "Old Jimmy's not doing any harm. Granted he should probably have asked your permission first, but anybody who catches rabbits is doing us all a good turn. I mean, there's thousands of them about – they're nothing but a pest, eating crops and so on. And they're vital to fill people's bellies. There's still a war on, Farmer – we need all the food we can get. No, I can't see Jimmy's doing any harm. The opposite, in fact, 'cause he's providing supplies for the nation, just as you are. Anyway, except for his poaching, he's as honest as they come, is Jimmy. Leave him in peace, Farmer, leave him in peace." Seeing as the policeman would take no action, the farmer had had no other option than to do just that – leave the poacher to continue in what to Fuller were nefarious ways – but his low opinion of the local policeman became even lower.

And it was to descend even further over the years. The most recent incident being just a couple of years previously, when the farmer had caught two lads from the village – about twelve, thirteen years old – playing one early July evening on top of a freshly constructed hayrick awaiting covering with galvanised iron. The lads were having a fine time jumping about on the rick and, in the process, displacing largish amounts of loose hay onto the ground, where the warm, strong, huffy wind spread it over a wide area. Outraged, Arnold Fuller laid hold of the pair, literally, and hauled them off to the farm house. He locked them into an outhouse, then promptly sent for Constable Barton.

As, when the call arrived, he was about to leave the Police House to cycle an evening beat out and about – and one which would take him past Fuller's fine farm – he actually arrived there much quicker than the farmer had expected. Briefly, he was a touch impressed by the officer's rare alacrity. It was not to last. He had thanked Claude for his speedy attention, had told of what the boys had been up to, then, being a man with strong, uncompromising views regarding the necessity to punish wrongdoing – his somewhat rigid Methodism playing a leading role – had demanded that Barton take the two boys, somewhat scared by this time, back to the Police House, charge them with

121

trespass and criminal damage, then produce them at Tavistock Magistrate's Court at the earliest opportunity.

Claude, though, had no intention of doing any such thing, and said so right away. "Well, sir, I don't know that there's any point – and need either – in doing that. No, I've found over the years that a good telling off, and threatening to tell their fathers as well, usually does the trick – unless they're real ne'er-do-wells, and there's not many like that. I've always done it that way – in fact, with all folk who step out of line, I find that it generally works to have a word, sometimes a very serious one, with them rather than hauling them off to court. Not often they cause trouble again, I find." This, essentially, was true, he having kept law and order in the parish for a generation without wasting too much court time.

The farmer, though, was having none of it. He was fed up with this, to him, ludicrously easy going policeman ignoring constantly the law breakers of the parish – and he informed the officer so in direct terms. When Claude remained unmoved by his remonstrations, letting the boys off with a mild telling off, Fuller also told the Inspector at Tavistock of his increasing anger and frustration over the local policeman's, to the farmer, indolent, laissez fair attitude. The complaint, though, produced no harvest, the Inspector telling the master of Brook Barton, initially verbally, then in a formal letter, that whilst his complaints and views had been noted, there was no evidence that PC Barton had acted in any way incorrectly or inefficiently, and that the levels of law breaking on the Peninsula had over very many years been amongst the lowest in the county, and remained so. A sound, efficient, conscientious officer was Claude Barton – or so the Inspector stated.

The farmer was hugely at odds with such an assessment but knew there was nothing he could do about it, except to view the local policeman with hostile contempt, and have as little to do with him as possible.

Thus the dipping of the fine flock from Brook Barton was to take place with Farmer Fuller ignoring the Police Officer and that official responding in totally opposite fashion – he would be as vigilant as it was possible for him ever to be; not one 'yaw' or lamb would fail to be dipped in accordance with the letter of the law.

Sarah Martin was very grateful to Arnold Fuller. She, like Harry, was well aware of the antipathy between the master of Brook and the local policeman, and equally aware that it was the one flock which in recent times had always received, from Barton, total vigilance regarding the dip. Thus, for the bulk of the afternoon, he would be standing by the pit rather than squatting in the easy chair in her kitchen. She would be able to get on in peace – which is what she did. After clearing away the dishes and plates, then washing and drying them, she made some preparations for dinner the following day – another full day of farmers bringing flocks for cleansing, so another large lunchtime meal to create.

This done as far as she was able, she made herself a cup of tea and decided it would do no harm to have a brief rest in the exceedingly comfortable, albeit well used chair which had hosted Constable Barton for most of the morning. Her sojourn, however, was somewhat more protracted than she had intended. For soon she had succumbed to the malady which had afflicted the policeman, sleep creeping over her gently and pleasantly.

How long she would have remained in such a state had she not been woken, she knew not – probably her husband and son would have been in for their tea and would have found her comatose. That was an embarrassment from which she was saved, though. For the raucous bellowing of a powerful male voice cut through the waves of deep doziness which engulfed her, and she sat up with a start. Firstly she stared at the grandfather clock – a quarter past four. She'd been asleep, and for well over an hour – it was so rare for her to drop off during the day. And it was something which almost made her feel ashamed – work and duty at all times throughout the day was a principle which had ever been central to her life.

Hastily, she pulled herself to her feet, shook her head to try to neutralise the drowsiness which still dominated it, then realised the noise was coming from Claude Barton who was stood at the open kitchen door looking somewhat hot and exceedingly bothered. "Missus – missus – I'm sorry to wake you up – sorry to bother you," he added, hastily, aware that the mistress of Downside might not take too kindly to having it suggested she had slept in the afternoon of a busy day. "I need to phone the doctor, missus – right away. It's young David Fuller – he's had an accident. Knocked himself out – and I fancy he's swallowed a fair drop of the dip."

"That's awful, Mr Barton. The phone's there, over on the window ledge by the table. Is there anything I can do? I'm sure there will be. They must bring him in here and lay him on the old settee by the wall there." She indicated a battered, but large Victorian piece, which in her husband's view was the most comfortable seat in the house. Also it was prized because, being in a decrepit state, all were welcome to sit or lay on it no matter how work weary their clothes.

The constable moved unusually quickly across the kitchen to the phone, explaining as he went that under Harry's instructions, they were already conveying the unconscious young fellow to the house. "Last yaw of the day, too, just dipped it and pulled 'un out, when young Fuller slipped and fell against the wooden safety rail along one side of the pit. Somehow it snapped at the base, and he fell in and, it seemed to me, bashed his head against the side before going under. Nasty blow, missus – done him no good at all," he added unnecessarily. Just as he lifted the phone, there was further noise at the door, and the lad was brought in, borne by Harry and Graham Martin, his father bringing up the rear, his ashen, taut face telling of the anguish which engulfed him.

Under instructions from Sarah who took immediate control of the situation, he was lain on the old settee. Immediately she bent over him to see if there was anything she could do before the doctor arrived, which according to PC Barton, replacing, noisily, the receiver, would be reasonably soon. "I managed to get hold of him just as he was about to leave the surgery. He won't be long."

Sarah Martin gazed, anxiously, down at the young man prostrate on the settee; his colour was pallid, almost grey. Certainly, he was unconscious – and she feared he was quite ill. Some years earlier she had, for just 12 months, joined St John

Ambulance. She had found it fulfilling, but with her busy life on the farm and her involvement in other societies and community events in the parish, realised she could not give the effort and commitment such a vital organisation had a right to expect. Thus, with regrets, she had left. She had, though, accrued some useful medical knowledge during that time, and she was about to make it count.

David Fuller needed attention, she was well aware of that, and she felt he could need it before Doctor Luxton arrived, even though that was expected quite soon. For the lad was breathing with great difficulty – indeed, gurgling and even choking at times – whilst his complexion became, by the second, ever more drawn and ashen. Suddenly it hit her – he had gone under the surface of the deep water and disinfectant at the pit, and would have swallowed far too much of it. How much, she had no idea, of course, but the swallowing of pure water would have done him no good, so when it was mixed with the thick, acrid chemicals which brought death to the multitudinous pests which afflicted sheep, it had, to her logical mind, the potential to bring death to an unconscious young man. Clearly, his lungs had to be emptied of such a dangerous mixture.

"Turn him over – right away. We've got to try to get the fluid out of his lungs – it could poison him."

"The doctor'll be here any minute, Ma'am," said the constable. "Best to leave it to him, isn't it?"

"No, it's not, Mr Barton – who knows, it could be too late. Just look at him – look at his colour, the way he's breathing, or rather trying to breathe. We've got to do something now."

Arnold Fuller waited to hear no more. He thrust himself forward, grabbed his son by the shoulders, and began to turn him onto his stomach, assisted instantly by Harry and Graham. The lad face down, Sarah began to pummel the top part of his back, opposite his lungs. Within just a few seconds, her actions were producing results, with a trickle of brownish, foul smelling liquid coming from his mouth. The trickle soon became a steady flow down onto the kitchen floor linoleum. Within seconds more, David began to cough, firstly in a somewhat strangulated way, then far more freely. Certainly the moribund figure of just a few minutes earlier now became one of life, thrashing around as the coughing became almost convulsive. Within seconds, though, this had stopped and David Fuller had turned himself up the correct way and was sitting, gasping upon the settee, holding his head in his hands.

"What's going on – what's going on?" he muttered, his natural desire for information answered by a series of platitudes from those around him, especially his father:

"You'll be all right, son, you just had a bit of a knock that's all – nothing much – nothing much to worry about," words that were, of course, a downright lie, which weighed heavily on that devout man's conscience but which, in the circumstances, were, he knew, justified. There was no reason for his son to know just how serious – even lethal – could have been the consequences of him falling through the guard rail into the pit.

"Patient recovering, I see." The words spoken from behind them caused the throng gazing down upon the invalid to turn in unison and stare towards the kitchen door. Standing there was the tall figure of Doctor Denzil Luxton, sole general practitioner on the Peninsula. Having announced his presence he advanced into the kitchen, an erect man with a brisk pace (both giving evidence of his 20 years as an army doctor before taking his present position). He was soon across the kitchen and examining David Fuller, whilst his Father gave a full, but concise summary of the accident, its apparent seriousness and of Sarah Martin's prompt and exemplary actions in restoring, it would seem, the young man back to reasonable health.

After a brief, quick examination (Doctor Luxton never took long over any medical matter) he expressed his agreement with Fuller senior. "Well, you've done my job for me, Mrs Martin. This young man is feeling the worse for wear, which isn't surprising bashing his head the way he has, and, by the look of the floor, swallowing half a gallon of that vile, poisonous muck – but if he goes home now and gets his head down, he should feel no adverse affects by the morning. I come past your place on the way to the surgery, so I'll look in first thing – about 8.15."

"Excellent, Doctor, thank you – it's such a relief to know he'll be all right. I feared the worst, I have to say, but my prayers have been answered." Arnold Fuller was as none outside of his family, probably, had seen him before – overflowing with emotion. Indeed, near to tears. He saw this, though, as a sign of weakness, and quickly regained self-control, doing so by addressing practical considerations. "I've got my two dogs with me, so it'll not take me long to get the flock back to Brook Barton. Then I'll return right away with the car, collect David and get him home to bed. Will that be all right with you, Mrs Martin? Will it be all right if he rests here on the settee until I get back?"

Sarah was about to say he could remain there as long as he wished, but had no chance as the doctor spoke before she could utter a syllable.

"No need to do that. I'm on my way home myself, so I can give David a lift. You get your flock home and I'll see to my patient." He looked towards Sarah Martin. "After your heroics of the afternoon, Mrs Martin, you could probably do with some peace and the opportunity to relax. Perhaps you could turn out a couple of old blankets – after the trauma his system would have experienced, it'll do him no harm to be wrapped up despite the warmth of the day, and it'll protect my upholstery."

The farmer's wife moved quickly towards the stairs to seek the blankets requested – she would be relieved to have her kitchen to herself, and the opportunity to sit with a hot, sweet drink before turning her attentions to the preparation of tea. It had been a fraught, emotional afternoon. Knowing exactly where to lay her hands on the blankets, she was back in the kitchen in little over a minute. David having been swathed in them, was guided from the kitchen by the doctor, followed by Harry and Graham and Claude Barton. Bringing up the rear, deliberately, was Arnold Fuller. He saw the others depart the kitchen, then turned to face Sarah. As was his way, he spoke quickly and to the point.

"Mrs Martin, we are deeply in your debt, David, my wife and myself. Without your prompt, and clearly, knowledgeable actions our son could have died. Thank you from the bottom of my heart. I will not forget what you have done today."

The farmer's wife was a touch taken aback by the sincerity and integrity of the words from this rather austere man. "Well – well, Mr Fuller, I'm just pleased I was able to help. There have been a couple of occasions in the past when I was able to use the knowledge I gained when in St John Ambulance, but none quite as dramatic and vital as today. It's said that no knowledge is ever wasted – and what happened this afternoon proves it."

"Indeed it does. But again, thank you." The farmer dipped his head slightly, then turned on his heels and headed out into the sunshine, seeking Claude Barton just a few yards away watching Doctor Luxton drive off with his passenger. He instantly called out to the constable. "PC Barton, I'd like a word if I may."

Claude turned around and saw Farmer Fuller approaching him. "Of course, Sir," he replied, politely. "What can I do for you?"

"Several things, Constable," came the brisk reply. "Firstly you can make out a report regarding this afternoon's events – the breaking of the guard rail around the dipping pit, the subsequent falling in of my son, and his consequent life threatening injuries. Then you can file charges against Mr Martin – criminal neglect of his equipment being foremost amongst them and certainly dangerous and defective safety procedures."

Barton stood several seconds as if turned to stone. Then spoke in a disjointed, yet outraged tone. "You – you – you want to bring criminal charges against Harry Martin? Against Harry? Why man, his wife has just saved your son's life. Just behaved wonderfully as the good, able, fine woman that she is. Just done the most brilliant medical tricks I've seen in my life. Yet, you want to bring her husband to court – what sort of man are you?"

"A man who believes in what is right – in justice, and in people shouldering their responsibilities, Constable. I will never forget what Mrs Martin did for my son. I've told her that, and I've thanked her for it. But this is nothing to do with her. She played no part in the sheep dipping. That's her husband's job – his job to do it, and to make sure it's done correctly regarding both dipping the sheep and all aspects of safety. Clearly that handrail was defective, something which he should have been aware of."

"How – how could he know there was anything wrong with the

rail – that's if there was anything. I mean to say, I saw your son slip and fall against it – bad luck, true, but he hit it brave and hard and, and, well these things happen."

"But they shouldn't happen; No matter how hard he hit the rail, it should not have snapped at the base. That is what the rail is for, for heaven's sake, to stop people falling into the pit. It is not as if my son is a particularly big or heavy chap crashing against it. No, this is incompetence Constable. I pay Harry Martin a sizable sum for him to dip my sheep; I've no complaint over that – that's my side of the bargain. His side is to ensure that everything is in order, that the sheep are dipped correctly and that all men and animals alike are safe from harm. This he has clearly failed to do. So I want statements taken from all of us involved and charges brought."

The policeman could still not fathom the man and his argument. "How was he to know there was anything wrong with the rail as I said just now – that's if there was. I mean how could anybody know if there was rot in it or suchlike – you can't look into the middle of a bit of wood."

"No, you can't – but you can replace them. Wooden rails such as this should be replaced, say, every ten years at least. When were these last replaced, Constable? Have they ever been replaced? I'm told that sheep have been dipped here since before the First World War; I reckon those rails have been here the same length of time. Lethal – or they could have been. And to be fair to Farmer Martin, it's not only his responsibility to make sure things are safe – it's yours as well. In fact, in law it's probably more your responsibility than his. You're in charge – you, officially, give permission for the dip to go ahead.

"The fact those rails clearly should have been replaced years, possibly decades ago, is primarily your fault. You should have ensured they were. You've clearly not done your duty – and it's not the first time, unfortunately, I have cause to say this."

Claude Barton said nothing for a few seconds. Rather, his face began to redden and his breathing came in ever shorter, sharper gasps. Anger and this basically genial man were unlikely bed fellows, but they did come together on exceedingly rare occasions – and this was one such.

"Not done my duty, Sir – not done my duty. How dare you, Sir – how dare you say such a thing to me. I've been doing my duty in this parish for, for the best part of 20 years, without fear or favour. I treat people right, with fairness – I make sure the law is followed and obeyed. Not done my duty, indeed – damn it, I've done nothing else throughout my police career. And my duty now is to tell you that you are talking a load of nonsense – malevolent nonsense too, in my view. So I'll tell you what I'm going to do about this business – nothing. There'll be no statements taken and no criminal charges brought. And shame on you for trying to blacken the name of one of the most respected men in this parish; A fine man, Harry Martin, and his family's lived in this parish for generations."

"Not going to do anything? You've got to, the law's been broken. Your duty is to enforce it, and I demand that you do."

"Demand, Sir – demand. Nobody demands of an Officer of the Devon Constabulary. We make our own judgements on what should be done, and here no action needs to be taken because no law has been broken. It's clear to me, considering everything, that no human being can be blamed for what happened here today; Rather, Sir, this was – was – was . . ." for a few seconds he struggled to articulate exactly what it had been. Suddenly it became, to him, vividly clear. "This," he stated authoritatively "was obviously, an act of God." With that, Constable Barton turned on his heels, then stalked, with an unusually rapid pace, towards his bike leaning against a wall of the house, leaving a nonplussed Fuller gazing after him in stunned fashion.

The policeman mounted the bike and headed in the direction of the village, and the Police Station. He needed one of Mabel's excellent teas, and a good night's sleep if he was to recover from the non-stop work, strain and stresses of this long day. And, of course, he had to revive himself to face another demanding day of dipping at Downside on the morrow – with all the pressures and worries it could bring.

# V

# The Birth

Sam Cartwright was a law abiding man; it was difficult to imagine him ever coming to the attention of the Devon County Constabulary. If, though, by some misfortune he ever did, then it would not be for breaking the speed limit. Part of the reason for this was the fact that he was into middle age before he had started to drive in the mid-1930s. He had timed his acquisition of a car, and his learning to drive it, impeccably, as he obtained a driving licence just months before the government of the day, alarmed by the exceedingly high number of accidents in relation to the numbers actually driving on the highways of the kingdom, brought in a law making the obtaining of a licence dependent on the passing of a driving test. Up until that time, Sam had driven horses – in the pursuit of his, like his father before him, dual methods of making a living.

Firstly there was farming. Sam's grandfather had obtained, during the mid-Victorian era, tenancy of a small farm – no more than 30 acres – from the Earl, who owned virtually the entire parish at the time. High up, in the middle of the Peninsula it was windswept and of relatively poor, stone strewn soil, and the Cartwright Family had struggled to make a living from it.

Sam's father John took over the place upon the death of his father and, with a large family of five children to provide for, realised very rapidly that there was no way he would ever make sufficient from farming to support them in appropriate fashion, the place only large and productive enough to support a few milking cows, some store cattle, a dozen sheep, half a dozen pigs and a motley collection of laying hens; also beyond a few acres of potatoes, the soil had insufficient body to grow cash crops to a quality and quantity which would swell the family coffers to any adequate degree.

Thus did John Cartwright, Sam's father, seek a sideline – which he soon found. Owning two prime shire horses, it occurred to him that they were being underused, spending more time eating grass and fodder than working; so he started up a service which within just five years was far more rewarding than working the land – he did haulage work throughout the parish and beyond to Tavistock, even occasionally, the dozen or so miles to Plymouth.

If it fitted on the wagon, he would carry it. Produce from the fruit, flower and vegetable gardens were collected from those market gardeners who did not have their own transport and taken mostly to the quays on the Tamar where it was loaded onto steamers and hauled off to Plymouth. On the occasions when boats where not available, the longish journey to the big city to the south would be undertaken, whilst the shorter one to Tavistock was done with regularity. With the coming of the railway to the parish, again regular pick-ups were made at the market gardens, and the produce hauled to the station to be transported across the kingdom. Also the Cartwrights would do furniture removals, move heavy goods about the parish – indeed transport virtually anything locally which needed moving.

Upon John's untimely death in the same week as that of King Edward VII, Sam, being the oldest of the children and the only male, took over the haulage business, largely leaving his mother and siblings to run the farm (though he still did quite a bit on the land, farming remaining very much a way of life he loved). The haulage and carrier business continued to prosper reasonably despite the austere times in which they lived.

Within a year of his father's demise, Sam had extended the business by buying a good quality, though quite elderly, trap plus a horse of like description to pull it. Thus the haulage side of the operation was augmented with a Hansom cab service – a canny move on his part. For the old hunter type mare – quick and fit despite her advancing years – was kept in almost constant employment, especially in the taxi work; the picking up of folk from the more distant parts of the parish and transporting them to the railway station being her main task. She was often called upon to make longer trips, the six mile hike to Tavistock being the most common, and did service upon occasions at weddings – sometimes carrying bride and groom – but more often at largish funerals, when the local undertaker would need his own transport augmented, numerous mourners having to be moved to and from church and so forth.

Sam never pursued his carrier and taxi business in a major way, not taking on more work or commitments than he could usually handle himself, although there were a couple of fellows in the village usually willing to help him, for suitable remuneration, if needed and convenient to themselves. He always baulked at the high expenditure which would be involved in buying the extra wagons, traps, horses and general equipment essential to making it a larger enterprise, including the wages involved in taking on, at least, a couple of full time workers. Also, he was a farmer at heart and had no intention of getting rid of his land (which would have been inevitable if he had greatly increased the haulage side of things).

Even though no great profit was ever made from the farm Sam had, however, been able to raise sufficient to buy the holding when the Earl sold off most of the farms in the parish in 1921. The 30 acres plus the house and farm buildings represented both security for himself and Clemmie, and ownership of that where they would be happy during their latter years. Assuredly he had been most fortunate with his choice of wife. A farmer's daughter, Clemmie shared her husband's affection for that way of life, and had superior skills and judgment when it came to working a farm and making a living from it.

Through the dark years of the First World War, then the uncertain times of the 1920s, Sam and Clemmie continued to make a fair living. By the later twenties, though, the non farming side of their business was slowing down perceptibly – the age of the horse was passing. Increasingly on the Peninsula cars, vans even the occasional small lorry were to be seen – a faster, more cost effective form of transport for goods and passengers alike. In the early thirties Sam and Clemmie were well aware that a decision of some magnitude would have to be made and in 1933 they made it.

They were, neither of them, in the first flush of youth, their two children had grown up, left home and were making, successfully, their own lives. In consequence they decided to cut their losses – so, the farm being the first love for both of them, they closed down the haulage side of matters. Sam though, was aware that seeing as nobody in the parish ran a taxi service, there was, in that direction, a quite sound future; thus, he bought his first car, was taught by the undertaker how to drive it (though not well) and proceeded to augment the farm income by becoming the Peninsula's first motorised Hansom cab.

It was not often the large Austin saloon, built, heavily, in the mid-1920s left the parish (though Tavistock was not an unusual destination), most of Sam's work being the collecting of folk from slightly more remote houses and farms dotted around the parish, and dropping them at the railway station which lay just outside the village.

Sam had two characteristics as a taxi driver, one admirable, the other most irksome to most of his clients. On the plus side, his time keeping on arrival was impeccable (if ever late for a pick-up it would be due to some unforeseen and serious hazard on the road); the minus side was simple – he drove ridiculously slowly.

A man who loved horses, and had spent almost the first fifty years of his life driving and handling them, usually on a daily basis, he saw no reason why a car should be driven any faster. Certainly, he would never feel at ease moving the tank-like black car at a greater speed than he would have manoeuvred a horse and trap, thus he did not.

People using his service, most of whom were local, knowing his habits well, would generally make sure they ordered his service sufficiently early to guarantee getting to the station in good time to catch their train. There had, though, been occasions when he had taken so long that trains had been missed. Despite all this, he had retained the confidence and custom of most people.

One of the reasons was that he was local, and they generally likewise, and he was a character, so as they trundled along he would impart to his passengers local news, gossip, opinion, even the odd bit of scandal. Mind you, not only did he speak to them, he would talk to the old car as well – just as he used to address his beloved horses; and used similar words. When applying the brakes, a loudish "Whoa maid!" would emanate from his lips; on the rare occasions he decided to go a little faster, "Get on, there – get on, there," would be spoken loud and clear; and any obstruction in the road successfully avoided, would be greeted by a "Well done, maid." This had been his habit during the nearly twenty years he had been driving, haphazardly it had to be said, on the narrow roads of the Peninsula; and not driving very well if truth were told.

Indeed, many of his passengers were quite pleased he drove slowly as they would possibly have feared for their lives if he'd gone a normal speed. Whatever, the people of the parish knew that if you were in a hurry to get anywhere, then Sam Cartwright was not the man to take you.

Still, he had provided a valuable service to the community through most of the thirties, the war, then the difficult years which followed and now into the fifties. He himself was facing old age, along with Clemmie, but both were in good health and had no intention of changing their ways of life or the way they made a living. They still kept ample stock on the farm and he was kept reasonably busy with the taxi work – though less than it had been before the war (at the end of it, too, for that matter) more folk owning their own cars, or having access to lifts through family and friends.

Stanley Johnson was the Cartwright's nearest neighbour, living with his wife Sadie in a cottage about a quarter mile from their farm. They had moved in following their marriage about four years previously, he having lived in the village all his life, his wife born and bred in Tavistock. A decent, pleasant young couple, she had worked in a shop in Tavistock until her marriage, whilst he was a shipwright in Plymouth Dockyard, travelling to and fro daily by train.

Sam Cartwright had informed his passengers some months previous to what was to prove a traumatic November night, that Sadie Johnson was "In calf," and the 'nipper' was due October/ November time, news given him by Clemmie who was usually up on village happenings, and always seemed to know when fresh life was due to come into the local world. The fact that their daughter Jill was a part-time secretary to Doctor Clarkson in his cramped surgery next to the Police Station, was the key to this (the maintenance of patient confidentiality not being amongst her greatest attributes).

Sadie Johnson's pregnancy, however, was due to dominate Sam Cartwright's attention during the early hours of a foul November morning. A southwesterly gale had been building throughout the day and it struck in full fury mid evening. So stormy was it, the wind howling about and down the chimney, rain beating against windows, that the taxi driving farmer found it impossible to sleep, which for him was rare. For the Johnsons, this was just as well, for when Cartwright slept he did so deeply; for sure he would not have heard a 2am knocking on the front door, especially with the background noise being provided by the storm.

As it was, laying feeling tired and bad tempered in his bed, cursing the weather and his insomnia, Sam heard a noise above that of the weather. For a couple of minutes he thought it might have been connected to the storm – something blowing around outside in the yard perhaps. He realised quite soon, though, that somebody was knocking upon the front door – though battering would have been a more apt description.

Clearly something serious – and urgent – was afoot, so he climbed as quickly from his bed as ageing, aching legs would allow, told Clemmie (who had been asleep) that somebody was trying to knock down the door, then, clad in his thick, stripy pyjamas went downstairs, put on the lights, drew back the bolts and opened the front door.

Standing before him, hatless and ill clad for such a terrible night, was the stocky figure of Stanley Johnson, the colour of his face ashen, the tone of his voice one of panic.

"Oh, Mr Cartwright. Thank heavens I made you hear. I'm sorry to wake you in the middle of the night. I really am sorry, but I need your help – we both do, and right away. It's Sadie, her waters have burst – the baby's on the way, could be born anytime. It's urgent Mr Cartwright, really, really urgent."

"Step inside, boy, or you'll catch your death. It'll do you no good standing outside in weather like this."

The young man did as he was bid, the farmer closing the door behind him.

"Right boy," said Sam, "you're telling me the baby's coming and you need my help. I'd have thought it's the doctor whose help you need – and right away."

"But he can't come, Mr Cartwright – that's the problem." The expectant father wiped the rainwater from his eyes and face with a somewhat grubby handkerchief, then explained himself. "As soon as Sadie said her time had come, I nipped along to the phone box – and it's only just over a hundred yards from our cottage. I phoned Doctor Clarkson and spoke to his wife. He can't come – or not at the moment, that is. His wife says he's had to go out to a house down by the Tamar where some chap's had a heart attack. He could be some time, she said, so she gave me the number of a doctor in Tavistock who's covering for him, but he can't come either; again he's out on call somewhere out in the country – somebody with severe stomach pains. Both will come, apparently, when they've finished what they're doing now, but that could be hours and Sadie needs help now. I tried to get an ambulance – dialled 999. The trouble is they've only got one in Tavistock and they're out dealing with somebody trapped in a car crushed by a tree that's come down in the wind, along with the fire brigade. They can probably get one out from Plymouth but they say, on a night like this, with the roads either awash or covered in branches – even trees – it could take well over an hour, perhaps two. By that time, Mr Cartwright, it'll be too late – Sadie could give birth virtually any minute. The lady at the ambulance station said I should try to get her to the nearest hospital or maternity home as soon as I can – well, that's Tavistock, and not very far; the trouble is I've got no car, and although my father has, it's in the garage having rear axle bearings replaced. In the middle of the day, there'd be several who would help us out, but in the middle of the night – and one like this – there's just nobody I can get hold of; well nobody I can get hold of right away who can take us to Tavistock and the maternity home. So suddenly I thought of you, Mr Cartwright. I mean, that's what you do, isn't it, take people to places for whatever reason. I'll pay whatever you say, Mr Cartwright, but if you could get your car and take us both to the maternity home in Tavistock, we'd be so grateful we'd never forget it. Sadie needs help and she needs it now. Will you do it, Mr Cartwright – will you help us?"

The older man instantly nodded his head. "Of course I will, boy and I'll not need paying for it either – we're neighbours aren't we? I'll go up and get dressed, tell the missus what's happening, then we'll go round, pick up Sadie and get her to Tavistock – though on a night like this it'll not be an easy trip, even though it's only six miles."

With that he turned on his heels and climbed the stairs as fast as his aged legs would carry him. Rapidly he dressed, telling his wife of his errand of mercy to Tavistock as he did so.

In less than ten minutes he and Stanley were at the Jackson's cottage helping a clearly distressed Sadie into the back seat of the car. Her husband made her as comfortable as possible, then climbed in beside her. Immediately they set off in the direction of Tavistock and were soon clear of the village. It truly was a dire night; gale force wind (possibly even stronger), the rain sheeting down, the roads strewn with nature's debris – leaves, small branches, even a few trees down, though none of sufficient size to block the road. Sam Cartwright was to say for the rest of his life that he had never before driven on such a night, and never would again.

Clearly distressed when she got into the car, Sadie rapidly got more so as they wended their way – so slowly – towards Tavistock. There was just cause for this, as her contractions were becoming ever more closer together – the baby's birth was near, possibly imminent.

Her husband was not of major help either. Always a man who panicked quite easily, he rapidly disintegrated to a state little short of terror, confronted with a situation unknown to him – the birth of a child, and more relevantly, his child – with them in the back of an old taxi driving along treacherous country roads on the roughest night of the year, in the hands of one of the slowest drivers in England.

Sam Cartwright, though, was not a man to panic; he had probably never done so in his life, even though he would have been confronted with situations – potential calamities, in fact – which would have induced such in most people, especially during his lifelong dealings with horses, some of whom, being the large powerful creatures they are, could, when frightened or antagonised, be dangerous to both limb and life. The old haulier just kept his ageing – and by no means sharp – eyes upon the road ahead, giving constant instructions to the taxi – "Get on, maid, get on." – "Don't like the look of it ahead." – "Whoa, maid, whoa." – then, "Get on, maid," again.

And all the while the volume of noise from the back seat of the car rose, with Sadie understandably crying out in both pain and fear as the birth of her first child moved rapidly towards immediacy, and her husband exhorting the driver to go faster, saying, "Can you put your foot down, Mr Cartwright – please, please. The baby could come any minute – and we're not half way to Tavi yet. I know it's terrible weather, but please go faster – I fancy we've only a few minutes before the birth. We've got to get to the maternity home before then – with it being Sadie's first she doesn't know the ropes when it comes to birth, and I definitely don't. So please, Mr Cartwright – if you could go a bit faster, please, please."

"Going as fast as I can, boy – dangerous night to be on the roads. I've had to stop twice already and clear away branches and other stuff. It would be daft to go too fast on a night like this; there's three of you on the back seat, remember; mustn't do anything that might affect the cheel," replied the driver, urbanely.

"Don't want us hitting fallen trees or anything like that. Better to be a bit late getting to the maternity home."

It was much to the fore of Sadie and Stanley Johnson's minds that if they did not get to the refuge of the home with its complement of midwives (well, there was sure to be one, at least, on duty) very, very soon there would be little point in getting there at all. Potential calamity could well have struck, with the baby coming in the back seat of Sam Cartwright's old Hansom cab car on a tempestuous night, miles from warmth, light, succour and, most crucially, professional help. Such a situation was too dreadful to contemplate for either the expectant father or mother, whilst the steadfast driver was so intent on staring at the treacherous road ahead exposed by the twin beams of somewhat ill-aligned headlamps – and giving instructions to the old car – to have any time for such thoughts.

Suddenly from the rear seat came a piercing scream. "It's coming, Stan – the baby, it's coming; I can feel it coming. Oh god, oh god, what are we going to do?" Sadie screamed loudly and long, a piercing call induced by high levels of pain and fear (though terror was possibly a more apt description).

Her husband reacted instantly. "You've got to stop the car, Mr Cartwright – it's coming, the baby's coming. There's no way we're going to get to Tavistock in time. There's two or three miles to go yet. The speed we're going it'll take us another quarter hour – it'll be too late. Good god, what are we going to do?"

"Don't fret yourself, boy – 'tis a bit of a shame, true, that we can't get to the maternity home in time, but that's the way of it, isn't it – that's nature. The cheel's ready to come so we've got to do our best to make sure he or she comes safely into the world." Sam spoke the words with all the dearth of emotion characteristic of somebody giving a weather forecast on the wireless. "There's no reason why we shouldn't be able to do it between us; but first I've got to pull the old maid in off the road – there's a wide gateway only a couple hundred yards along so I'll pull in there."

Probably nobody on the Peninsula knew that road as well as the haulier, having driven horses and wagons, and in more recent times, the car, along it for half a century.

"But I've no idea what to do, Mr Cartwright." Stanley's voice was little other than a wail – though one loud enough to make itself heard above the cries and screaming of his distressed spouse.

"Well, I've been around for one or two births in my time, boy, so we'll see when I've pulled up."

"You mean you know what to do?" Hope was to be heard in Stanley's voice now, though it was still secondary to immense fear. "You know how to deliver a baby? That would be wonderful if you could do that – oh, good god, that would be wonderful."

By this time the car had been pulled into the gateway, and Sam was clambering slowly, and a touch painfully, from the driver's seat. He stumbled to the back, opened the door, got in, and closed it on the storm which still terrorised the night.

"Right boy," he instructed, "let's see if we can help Sadie here bring the next generation into the world."

The husband, his thought processes immobilised by worry and total ignorance of any way in which he could give assistance, moved out of the way, allowing Sam to push past him to minister to his wife.

This he did for several minutes, a period of time which both Sadie and Stanley were to say seemed hours – hours in the grip of pain, fear and no small measure of drama. A cry rent the air, and suddenly the trauma was ended – for it wasn't the cry of a mother, but that of a child.

Sam Cartwright turned away from the exhausted mother Sadie, and presented to the almost traumatised father, a small baby, crying and spluttering as he attempted to clear his lungs. "Your son, Stanley – a bit small at present, but he'll certainly grow. You hold him a minute, until his mother feels up to it – which won't be long I reckon. After all she's gone through to give birth to him, she'll be wanting to hold him, and very soon." He reached up to beyond the top of the back seat, pulled down a rather threadbare rug, then handed it to the baby's father. "Not the best, boy, I'm afraid, but it's a cold, rough night and he needs to be kept warm – so it's better than nothing."

"Thank you, Mr Cartwright – for the blanket, but mainly, of course, for the baby. You were great, brilliant – without you, well

141

I daren't think what would have happened without you, thank you – thank you."

The baby's mother spoke for the first time – softly and slowly, her drawn face speaking volumes as to the exhaustion she felt following probably the most alarming, stressful hour of her life: "Yes, Mr Cartwright – thank you: we'll never forget it, ever. As Stan says, it doesn't bear thinking about as to what would have happened had you not been here to help us."

"I don't think I made much difference, maid – the baby was coming all right as far as I could see. He'd have come along even without my help. It could be I speeded it up a bit, that's all – though that's no bad thing I suppose."

Stan shook his head. "No – it was more difficult than you make it sound, I'm sure of that; it really was. It wasn't straightforward like that – and it wasn't just the cheel, it was Sadie. Her health's never been the strongest – she had scarlet fever when she was very young and she's been a bit delicate ever since. She was getting weaker by the minute and more distressed – something terrible could well have happened to both her and the babe if you'd not done what you did.

"What's your first name, Mr Cartwright?" The question came from Sadie. "I've always known you as just that – Mr Cartwright – though having lived in the village for the past three years I probably should know. I don't though."

"Sam," the answer came not from its holder, but from her husband.

His wife nodded. "Stan, we've mentioned a few names during the past week or so as to what we'd call the baby, but as obviously we didn't know if it was going to be a boy or a girl, we've not fixed on any. Why don't we call him Samuel after Mr Cartwright; every time we speak his name we'll remember this night and how he'd possibly not be in this world if it wasn't for this good man. It would please my mum as well, she being regular at the Congregational chapel, and Samuel being a good biblical name." The last sentence was added as an afterthought, she suddenly thinking that the old haulier might be a touch embarrassed that he was the sole cause of the baby's name.

142

Before her husband could make comment on his wife's suggestion, Mr Cartwright made a reply. "Well, that's most kind of you my dear – most kind indeed. Yes, yes it's a lovely idea; much more than I deserve, mind you – as I said, my contribution was small – but a lovely idea; I'm honoured you should suggest it; my Clemmie will be delighted."

Stanley Johnson was nonplussed for a few seconds, but if he'd had any other ideas regarding a name, he knew that the die, now, was cast – Samuel it was to be. "Good idea," said he, in positive tones. Then, a fresh turn of thought flashing through his head, added, "A godfather – you must be a godfather to Samuel as well. What do you think, Sadie?"

"Oh yes, yes, yes, Stan – wonderful idea. Please say you will, Mr Cartwright."

The driver for a few seconds looked bemused; he then smiled and nodded. "Well, yes, thank you – again, I'd be honoured. Clemmie will too – likes anything like that, does Clemmie," he added vaguely. Then, before this so thankful couple could think up any further ways to express their gratitude, he took command of the situation; "Anyway, it's time we got moving," he said in as authoritative a tone as he could muster (he'd always been far more masterful with horses than with people). "Mother and cheel need the maternity home now, not the back of an old car on the roughest night for years. You and young Sam here need tending to by those who know what they're doing – you both need food and a warm bed, so I reckon we should get right on into Tavistock. Ten minutes – quarter of an hour, should do it."

He moved across to the door and was about to open it when Stanley Johnson posed the question which had dominated the young man's thoughts for the past couple of minutes. "How did you know what to do, Mr Cartwright? Where would you have delivered babies? You've never worked in the medical profession, have you?"

Sam laughed, quite heartily. "Medical profession? Me? No, boy, I've never been able to make my living as easy as that. No, I just learnt over the years. Our two were both born at home and I helped a bit with that, though the doctor was there both times so he did most of it, naturally. Mainly though, it's through the farm; I've pulled off hundreds of calves in my time – some a lot easier than others; and years ago, we used to keep some yaws, so many's a lamb I've helped into the world. No great difference between that and a baby being born, really – it's the same basic process, the same way. It's all nature, boy, isn't it? The only real difference, I suppose, is that calves are a lot bigger."

With that he was out of the back door and into the driving seat, leaving a stunned pair of new parents in his wake. Starting up the engine, then uttering an encouraging, "Get on, maid," he steered the burly taxi back on to the road and proceeded at a pedestrian pace through the stormy night towards the haven of Tavistock. Despite all the drama, it had been for him a very good night indeed – he was to have a young baby named after himself, and become, for the first time, a godfather.

# VI

# Sunday Cricket

Thoughts of playing cricket on a Sunday had never once entered the head of Ginger Hocking, even though he had dwelt thirty-one years on this earth. Granted, his service in the Devonshire Regiment during the war had broadened his outlook, having learnt of different pursuits, beliefs and ways of life, but folk playing the game he loved – passionately – on the Sabbath, was not amongst them. He had never heard of such a remarkable happening as Sunday Cricket and knew of nobody else who had. Assuredly the idea of his village team, of which he was the main fast bowler, and had been captain for some five years – playing on the Sabbath day was one which had never come near him remotely, and probably might not have for years to come had he not, with his wife Maude, made the long train journey to Yorkshire for a brief holiday.

His Sister, Nora had met a fellow from Harrogate, named Roland, during the war – a marine stationed in Plymouth – had married him directly afterwards, and had moved up to the man's native county to live (more than five years now). For some years, the Hockings had promised to spend a bit of time up there on holiday, and at last they got round to doing it, Ginger, in his capacity of jobbing builder, having just finished one job and with a few empty days on his hands before he could consider the next – late in May.

It was a week during which seeds were sown in Ginger's

fertile, quick mind that were to grow with remarkable rapidity. His brother-in-law was almost as keen a cricketer as was he – although not as skilled.

Having arrived on the Saturday evening following the long rail journey north, at lunchtime the next day the Devonshire builder was somewhat taken aback to see Roland attired in cricket whites – although 'creams' would have been a slightly more accurate description of the ancient, well worn trousers.

"Hope you'll come along and watch us this afternoon, Ginger – you'll be very, very welcome, you and Maude." Roland's invitation was delivered with enthusiasm. "Nora'll be there as well, 'cause she's helping to do the teas. It should be a good afternoon, with good cricket. We're playing a decent side today."

"Cricket? Today? But it's Sunday." Ginger's shocked tone of voice suggested that if his brother-in-law had said that Martians had landed and were about to overwhelm the nation, his surprise could not have been greater.

"Yes, we often play Sunday matches. Half a dozen a summer – probably more. We've done so for years now. A lot of chaps prefer it. Let's face it, if you work on a Saturday, as many do, then it's a godsend. I mean, Ginger, you're a self-employed man. There must be times on a Saturday afternoon when there's urgent work you need to be doing – perhaps a rush job of some sort, even an urgent one, an emergency; the chance to earn good money. Now if you played some games on a Sunday, then you could pocket the cash for that job on a Saturday but still have your sport the following day. We find we get more folk watching us as well – far more; which is understandable. After all, for six days a week, folk have got work and family commitments, plus other things to fill their lives; Sunday is the one day they've often got on their hands. Mind you, we still play the bulk of our games on Saturdays and some mid-week evenings throughout June and early July when the light's at its best, but I can see the number of Sunday matches increasing in the future. In fact, I reckon the day will come when games are played most Sundays. There'll probably be Sunday Leagues, even Sunday teams – I mean clubs will have room for more players, some performing mainly on a

Saturday, others on the Sunday. Yes, I can see all this happening, Ginger, and not that far in the future either."

However, Ginger's initial surprise at the playing of cricket on a Sunday soon turned to a moderate scepticism, despite his brother-in-law's enthusiasm (Roland, lovely fellow that he was, tended to be enthusiastic about most things). Possessing the Devonian's innate distrust of change, he could see little point in playing sport on the Sabbath, even though he was not a church or chapel going man. Cricket, football, all outdoor sports were played on Saturday afternoons mainly, just occasionally perhaps of an evening in mid week.

That Sunday afternoon in Harrogate, though, was to see him converted, radically and irreversibly, to the belief that much of the future good health of England's traditional national summer sport lay in its being played on the Sabbath.

He had taken himself off to the cricket ground that afternoon, he and Maude along with his sister and brother-in-law, and had thoroughly enjoyed himself. Roland's side had, according to the man himself, been strengthened by the inclusion of three players not usually available on a Saturday (the opposition likewise, it was said) and so the overall quality of play was raised; and the number of spectators for a friendly contest between two modest local teams was remarkable – possibly 500 or more; and most of those playing did so without the distractions of upcoming Saturday night leisure commitments – dances to go to, films to see, social gatherings in general to attend. What better way to spend the 'day of rest' than in gentle, relaxing, convivial sport.

When he got back to his West Devon home, he determined to pursue through the cricket club – providing he had some support – the possibilities of Sunday cricket taking place in the Parish of his birth; and if Ginger Hocking decided on a course of action, then it would take mighty adversity and opposition (of unsurmountable proportions) to deflect him from it. Not though, that he anticipated much opposition; he was a democrat at heart, a believer in folks living their own lives – pleasing themselves – as long as they did so under the law. If some wished to belt a cricket ball on a Sunday afternoon or evening, then they should be able to – likewise watch it, of course – just as others clearly were free to go to church, do a bit of gardening or read the papers.

Some pursuits, of course, would be unacceptable. You couldn't have folk shopping in the village or going off to the bigger stores in Plymouth to do likewise. Not the day for that at all, the Sabbath – the day of rest. Indeed, that was the major objection to such a habit; those working virtually six days a week in shops (five and a half at least) needed some respite.

Cricket, however, that most English of pursuits – that seemed a perfectly sensible, acceptable and pleasurable way to spend a Sunday. Nobody could object to that – surely not, surely not, surmised Ginger Hocking.

They could though, and they were about to, with a vengeance – or so reality dictated.

The very day following the return home of Maude and himself, found Ginger, early evening, calling upon Cedric Sleeman at his bungalow on the edge of the village on the Tavistock Road.

A man nearing sixty – a Plymothian by birth – Cedric had been a teacher at the village school for some thirty years, head for the past dozen or more, and would no doubt see out the few years which remained to him before retirement in that capacity. Assuredly he was very good at his job, year in, year out coaching and encouraging a larger percentage of his pupils into passing the Eleven Plus exam for the Tavistock Grammar School than virtually any other local school in the area, whilst for those unable to vault that hurdle, ensuring they had a good, basic education plus guidance and advice as to the 'road ahead' in life which would enable them to obtain good jobs, apprenticeships and often careers where they could rise and prosper.

Cedric was also Chairman of the Cricket Club Committee, a position he had held since showing the white flag to age in his late forties, and making the decision (so painful to him) that he was no longer quite fit and agile enough to meet the demands, modest though often they were, of village cricket. He could possibly have carried on ability-wise for a few more years – an excellent eye for a ball and sturdy arms meant that decent run getting would not have eluded him right away, whilst being an adept spinner of the ball, he could probably have 'turned his arm over' for a while longer. The time involved, though, became ever more irksome, finding increasingly that he and his wife, Helen, had other things they wanted to do some summer Saturday afternoons and evenings – plus his energy levels were in rapid decline. Also, the post-war years appeared to have produced a far sharper competitive edge amongst local sides. Men seemed to want to win far more, in friendlies as well as league encounters; thus sportsmanship and that very English sense of 'fair play', of which cricket was the supreme sporting epitome, was not what it once was.

This in no way had lessened Cedric's basic love for the game, nor much of his commitment to it, and to its continued good health in the county of his birth, and this parish where he had resided for decades. Indeed, he had proved an excellent chairman of the club, guiding it with vision and financial prudence, setting realistic targets for its progression. And progressed it had. Since the War, the village side had become, possibly, the best side in West Devon and throughout a goodly part of the Tamar Valley, having established themselves in the best of local leagues, the Premier Division of the Plymouth and District – all achieved with a team comprising, solely, local men living on the Peninsula.

Thus, when Ginger called on him in order to voice his enthusiastic views regarding Sunday cricket, he knew that Cedric would be receptive to his radical ideas and give advice as to the way forward. He would, too, point out any drawbacks or obstacles – not that the fast bowling captain could foresee any, though he was worldly-wise enough to know that few things in life were ever straightforward – and suggest ways to overcome them. And he would not prevaricate – not in any aspect of his life did Cedric Sleeman ever indulge in indecision or time wasting. Almost assuredly – to Ginger's mind – the chairman would see the playing of cricket on the Sabbath as yet another step forward in the upward progression of the cricket club, and, indeed, the growing parish community as a whole.

Thus, no sooner had he entered the bungalow and accepted Helen's offer of a cup of tea, than he had launched into his reasons for calling on this early June evening – his declaration of his conversion on 'the road to Harrogate'. Sitting himself in the comfortable chair the opposite side of the fireplace to his host, the obligatory comments regarding weather rapidly spoken, he dived into answering Cedric's question, "What can I do for you, Ginger? Whatever it is, you look excited about it."

"Too right, Cedric, too right – I am – well, yes, I am excited about it. Maude and me have been up to Harrogate on holiday, visiting my sister and brother-in-law. Like us, he's a big cricket man. And we went to see him play one afternoon and evening – on a Sunday. Yes, a Sunday – and according to him it's the way of the future, or largely anyway. And I think it could and should be something we go for here in this parish too, and go for it now. There's so many advantages to it. Players have got more time, with fewer commitments and pressures than on a Saturday. I mean, hardly anybody works on a Sunday, do they? And folk have got far more time on their hands to come and watch and perhaps get involved in other ways – helping to run the club and suchlike. It's certainly the way forward. It'll always be played on Saturdays as well, of course, and mid-week as well in mid-summer, but Sunday could soon be a major day – and it should be. I reckon we should go for it and start arranging fixtures. We can do so right away – it's only June, so there's no reason why we can't play half a dozen matches before the end of the season, weather permitting."

The chairman nodded, albeit slowly – and with an expression of doubt upon his face. "Well, yes, Ginger, there's much in what you say. The world we're living in is ever changing and I fancy there could be a demand for Sunday cricket being played in the parish. There's a lot of young fellows often at a bit of a loose end of a Sunday who would be glad of a game, some who don't play much at all at present. And there are those who work on a Saturday; shop workers, some shift workers and on farms and so forth, who again would welcome a match on the Sabbath. And there's probably some decent players amongst them too. I remember one or two of them at school – very good prospects, who never had the chance to play because of work duties."

"Yes, exactly," agreed Hocking enthusiastically. "And I know that some of the lads in the side now, though they're happy to play league games, don't always fancy playing friendlies. So no doubt they'd be delighted to have the odd Saturday off and play on a Sunday. So, Cedric," he looked intently at the chairman as he spoke the words, "will you phone around one or two clubs locally and see if you can arrange a Sunday fixture or two – within the next month if that was possible? They'll probably not have heard of Sunday cricket, of course, but I bet there'll be a fair bit of enthusiasm amongst them when they give it some thought."

Cedric smiled. "I fancy several will know about it, boy. I'm surprised you've not heard of cricket on a Sunday before. A few teams in Plymouth play the odd fixture now on the Sabbath. An old friend of mine is secretary of one that does. And I've a feeling there's some village clubs up in the northern part of West Devon that do as well – up in the Okehampton area. They probably look in the Exeter direction for matches. Closer to home, it could be they play on odd occasions across the Tamar on Sundays; I fancy they do – Callington, St Dominick, possibly Calstock. That could be the direction for us to look in if we do start playing. Still, that's to the future, Ginger – and it could be a bit more to the future than you imagine."

The captain looked a touch shocked. "Why? Why can't it be soon – very soon. I mean we'll easily be able to raise a side – and a good one – and you say you think there are several clubs'll be happy to play the odd game, so what's the problem?"

"Well, there probably won't be much of one if all the games are played away. Most of the places I've mentioned probably own their own pitches, so can please themselves when they play. We don't have that same freedom on our own pitch though, do we Ginger? If we want to play cricket on a Sunday, then we'll have to get permission from our landlords – the Parish Council. We, like the football club, play in the Recreation Fields that they own – as the pavilion and changing rooms are theirs also. We clearly will not be able to play on a Sunday unless they say we can. There'll be nothing in our rental agreement with them to say we can at present, you can be assured of that. And if they do agree to

it," added he, with a sudden thought, "we'll probably have to pay
a bit more yearly rental – though we are in reasonable funds, so
that would be no great problem."

"Well, yes, I suppose so," conceded Ginger Hocking. "I'd not
thought about that." His momentary frown quickly evaporated,
though. "Fair enough, Cedric," said he. "And as you say, we'll
probably have to pay a touch more every year, but we'd get that
back two or threefold by the amount we'd collect from the extra
numbers of those watching on Sundays. And I don't see why it
should delay us more than a week or two. I mean, if we get a letter
into the Parish Council right away, they'll consider it at their next
meeting which'll be soon – they meet every month. So we could
get permission by the end of the month."

"If we get permission at all," stated the chairman, in somewhat
sombre tones.

"Well, well – of course we'll get permission. Why shouldn't
we? It's a cricket pitch, and we want to play cricket on it – not
race 'osses. Nothing could be simpler; why should there be any
trouble about us getting permission, Cedric? Surely they'll have
no cause to refuse it. I mean, it's not as if we're ever late in paying
the rents or any such thing."

Cedric Sleeman smiled – a touch wanly, almost grimly – then
shrugged his shoulders. "I know virtually all the folk on the
Parish Council, boy. Generally a decent, fair-minded bunch of
men and women. If they could make up their own minds on the
matter, without any interference, then I've not the slightest doubt
the majority of the 13 members would give Sunday cricket the
nod. Probably do it within seconds, without any debate even. But
they don't have that luxury, do they? Oh, they've got their own
views, of course, and opinions – some of them strongly held,
because generally they are people of firm, independent minds.
They are, though, first and foremost, elected representatives of
the people – the rate payers – of this parish. So whilst in the final
analysis they should, and some possibly will to some extent, vote
according to their own belief and conviction, many – in fact, most
probably – will take note, rightly, of the prevailing views of the
people of the Peninsula and could well vote in accordance with

that. To be fair, they should do – and even more importantly from their point of view – they'd be daft if they didn't. It's elections next May for the Parish and District Councils. I know you're not one to worry too much about council matters, Ginger, but you'll be aware just how political – and probably not just with a small 'p' either – this Peninsula is. Some parishes struggle to fill numbers when it comes to local councils – it's the opposite here; the last election, 23 put up for 13 seats. I remember once, back in the thirties, when 28 put up. Unbelievable, in a way – but good nonetheless. The way it should be – democracy at grass roots; it's what we fought the World Wars for – what the great sacrifice was all about."

The cricket captain nodded his agreement – "Yes, you're right Cedric, everything you say, I know all about a World War – I was in one. Four years, 1941 to 45 as you know; North Africa, Italy, then D-Day. Years that'll be with me always – saw so much sacrifice, suffering, mates and comrades who didn't come back, or who came home shattered. Yes, the Parish Council, in its way, represents all this – the local democracy we fought for. I can see all that as clearly as you; but it simply beggars the question, why should there be any doubt they'll vote to allow us to use the cricket pitch. I mean, the great majority of people in this parish will be in favour for sure – why shouldn't they be? The council will just have to reflect that mood and vote, democratically, to allow us to start playing cricket in the Recreation Fields on a Sunday."

"But that's the point, Ginger," retorted the chairman, with the slightest touch of exasperation about his tone. "There is no guarantee that a majority is, or will be, in favour of Sunday cricket. The one thing that struck me about this parish when I came up here from Plymouth to teach all those years ago, is the strong influence of the chapels, Methodists mainly, although the Congregational also has a major say; and little has changed really. The war has had some effect on attitudes, but not as much as you might expect. This is still a strong non-conformist parish. Two thirds would be chapel going as opposed to church going. Granted, a lot will rarely, if ever, go to either, but this sanctity of

a Sunday will remain with many who are not remotely devout –
the feeling that it is somehow wrong for anybody to enjoy
themselves on a Sunday. That's where the Roman Catholics score
– they go to church in the morning, confess their sins, then start
accruing the next lot at a party in the afternoon. It doesn't work
that way here, though; Sunday is the Sabbath, the day of rest, and
even if you do not go to a house of worship, you will spend the
day in seemly pursuits – which would not include playing cricket.
Non-conformist in religion, and traditionally Liberal in politics –
that sums up the Peninsula, boy. So what I'm saying is that many
people, when they hear of the proposal to play Sunday cricket –
and as soon as we make application to use the cricket pitch on a
Sunday, everybody'll know about it, as, of course, they'll have a
right to – will object immediately. Some mildly but many
vehemently; they will oppose it with all the passion and fire
they'd use to fight the Devil himself. It's not to say we'll not get
support, mind you – we will, and quite a bit. Many folk would
welcome it – sport on a Sunday, and, to them, the chance to break
some of the shackles the chapel folk try to use on the rest of us in
what is now the second half of the twentieth century. What counts
though, Ginger, is who is able to influence the Parish Council
more. If there's a clear majority in favour of Sunday cricket, then
there'll be no problem. If though, which could be the case, it is
closer to fifty/fifty then they could well play safe, go for the status
quo, and turn our request down."

"But surely folks will support us, Cedric – surely the majority
will, and a big one as well, surely?" Ginger Hocking's voice was
pregnant with shock, even incredulity. He could scarce believe
what the chairman was telling him – believe that such narrow
minded refusal on the part of some folk to allow other good
citizens to live and enjoy their lives in their own peaceful way
could exist in this age. Were it not for the fact he held the
headmaster and chairman of the cricket team in such high regard,
he would have doubted all that the older man had said.

In reality, he knew that Sleeman was rarely wrong about
anything, so what he was saying about the opposition they would
face from many 'chapel folk' was probably true. He mounted one

154

final plea to fairness and sanity. "I mean, if we were some business or suchlike just out to make money, then perhaps they'd have a case. But we're just a cricket club who want to bowl a few overs of a Sunday – just want to give the opportunity of playing to young fellows, many who cannot play on a Saturday because of work and so on, and to put on a bit of pleasant, harmless entertainment for people with a bit more leisure time on their hands than would be the case any other day of the week, including Saturday."

Again the chairman smiled. "It all sounds perfectly fair to me, Ginger, and will do to several others, including, no doubt, some members of the council. But there will be, as I've said, many in the parish who will be deaf to any arguments in favour – that's the way they are or, perhaps to be a touch fairer, such are their beliefs. In many cases deeply and sincerely held. And they are strongly adhered to – my word they are. You probably will not know – you were away fighting – but back in the latter stages of the war, two or three local farmers on a couple of occasions, wanted to put on events in various reasonably flat fields they own – sports, a few stalls, some food and drink (or what could be got together), plus in one instance a sheep dog trial – to raise money for the welcome home funds, to bring a bit of cheer, and express our gratitude to you lads when eventually the war was done and you did return to these shores and this parish. A very popular cause, of course, far more popular it must be said than anything to do with cricket – and virtually all in the parish were supportive, initially; then they heard that it was proposed the events should take place on a Sunday and largely for the reasons you articulate regarding cricket on the Sabbath – far more people would have time and opportunity to be involved and, most important of all, much more money would have been raised. Sadly, it didn't happen – not on a Sunday, that is. On both occasions, such events were mooted, they were moved to the Saturday – and, as I recall, on both occasions it rained. And why were they moved? Because the chapels – especially the Methodist under the leadership of Reverend Godfrey Jennings, who is still there in charge of course – raised Cain, called it ungodly, and put every pressure they could on all organising it to change it to the Saturday. Aware the world was in danger of being destroyed by strife, the farmers and organisers, although they felt angry and aggrieved, realised that the only way forward amicably was to move events to a Saturday, which is what they did with, it has to be said, nowhere near the success they would have had if it had been a Sunday; thus, nowhere near the money raised had it been on the Sabbath. There, Ginger, was displayed the power of local chapel folk. Granted, it has weakened, probably, since the war – though that's not long ago – but it remains powerful nonetheless. I mean, there are still farmers in this parish – Doug Jarrett at Ridge Farm, Walter Matthews at Oakhill and, and, yes, Arnold Fuller at Brook Barton, although he's not really a local man only having come here just before the war – who will do no work on a Sunday, except the essentials like milking cows and, wintertime, feeding the livestock and suchlike. Even now, if they had a field of hay down and it was ready to save on a Sunday, and they knew it was going to rain and ruin it on the Monday, they would still leave it; I've known them do it. Do you believe, Ginger, that men such as that will do anything other than fight like demons to stop you playing cricket on a Sunday?"

The captain of the cricket team said nothing for several seconds. Then, being essentially a positive fellow of action, he got to the heart of the matter. "I hear what you say, Cedric, and as it's you saying it, I do not doubt there is a great deal in it. I never thought in terms of there being any opposition at all to something which is harmless, but clearly there will be. Despite this, though, it's got to be the right thing to do – the way forward. We've come so far as a cricket club since the war because we've never been afraid to make changes, to plan for the future and to improve in all directions. That's why we've been successful and moved up three divisions in the league. And most of it's down to your leadership, Cedric," he stated in all honesty, "although I hope I've played my part as well. The question now, though, is how we carry this idea forward – and you're the man to see to that."

"I go to see Dick Conway over at the newsagents, that's how. He's Chairman of the Parish Council, and as good a councillor as

this parish has had in a generation. I'll have to write formally to the council, of course – send it to Reg Perkins, the Parish Clerk, then he'll bring it officially to the council for their decision. But a chat first of all with Dick could help a good deal. He's no chapel man, Dick, and always a man who believes in folk living their lives in their own way as long as they keep to the law, so I doubt he'll personally have any objection to cricket being played on a Sunday. But, like me, he'll assuredly know of a goodly number who will oppose it – and with a vengeance. He could well have an idea as to the best way to take it all forward; I hope so, anyway, 'cause I'm not sure I have. Still, this is no time for prevarication. The thing is that yours is a good idea, Ginger – the best I've heard in a while. I'm not really sure why I've not thought of it myself, because as I said just now, I've been aware of Sunday cricket being played on occasions in the area for a few years now. For some reason, I never thought of us doing likewise here – I'm getting old, boy, that's the trouble," he laughed. "But as you said just now, so rightly, over recent years we've never been afraid as a club to make changes, to keep moving forward – and it's worked so very well. And this clearly is a way forward, for the club and the village as a whole. You've got my total support, Ginger, and I'll do all I can to make it happen. Starting tomorrow when I go to see Dick Conway."

A man of his word, the following lunchtime saw Cedric Sleeman head out to confer with Councillor Dick Conway. He did not make for his newsagents and stores, however, but went instead to the Tamar View Inn, as he – like most of the village – was aware of the shopkeeper's habit through many years, of spending most weekday lunchtimes in the bar of the pub, over a few relaxing drinks, especially whisky. His newsagent duties requiring him to be out of bed at just after 5am on most days of the year, he felt – and his wife Cindy readily concurred – that he earned a relaxing respite in the hostelry which daily usually lasted from about one o'clock until just before two.

Entering the bar at about ten past one, the schoolmaster espied the council chairman sitting alone at the bar, sipping his Scotch – or, at least, what remained of it, which was little more than a tablespoonful.

"Afternoon, Dick," said he affably, "another Scotch?"

The newsagent looked a touch surprised to see Sleeman (he was not that frequent a visitor to the pub, and certainly not at lunchtimes) but moved on rapidly to accept the man's generous offer. "Yes – yes – thank you, Cedric; that'll settle my nerves beautifully," he replied with a smile.

The fresh whisky bought, plus one for himself, the cricket club chairman asked courteously if it would be convenient for him to have a chat with Dick on a council matter and was told, instantly (as he knew he would be, the man always being accessible to the people of the parish), "Of course it is. Let's go and sit back here at the back of the bar" – which is what they did.

No sooner had they sat together in relative privacy in the sparsely populated bar than Cedric Sleeman had launched into the subject of Sunday cricket. He spoke of the opposition he felt that the proposals would bring – and sought the vastly experienced councillor's views as to the best way forward, a way which would give the cricket club the best chance of getting permission, by causing the council the least amount of aggravation.

Conway listened far more than he spoke. He was most certainly sympathetic to the idea of the Recreation Field being alive with people on a Sunday either playing or watching cricket; to him it was a splendid idea, and he concurred with the chairman of the cricket club that it was surprising nobody had thought of it before. He also agreed with Sleeman, that many 'chapel folk' would not take kindly to the idea – a great many, in fact – and that there would be intense opposition. Whether or not it would be insurmountable he would not – indeed, could not – comment, for he did not know.

He had been born, bred and had lived in the parish all his life, but whilst he had seen many changes, in attitude as well as in other directions, he was not at all sure that a majority of folk were ready to move into the new age of playing and watching sport on the Sabbath day; and more to the point, members of the Parish Council would not be sure either, and thus most would be vulnerable to pressure to support or, possibly more likely, oppose the granting of permission for Sunday cricket. That though, of

course, could be described as the democratic process – the observation of, and respect for, all points of view, and a democratic vote from elected members after much deliberation, as to whether the answer be 'yeah' or 'nay'. There was, though, in instances such as this, where a situation was arising which could divide a community, another way forward – an even more democratic way, with which few malcontents, no matter what their views, could fairly argue.

As Cedric Sleeman stated the cricket club's case, Conway's agile mind was already moving towards such a possible way forward which would lift much of the pressure that inevitably would fall upon the Parish Council, and get them collectively 'off the hook'. After all, how could anybody possibly object to an elected body giving the community the chance to make an important decision themselves – the chance for everybody to have a say. At the same time, he would be surprised if most parish councillors would not be relieved and delighted to delegate. This though would be something for him to discuss with fellow parish councillors, but first of all with Reg Perkins, the parish's long-serving, exceedingly knowledgeable and wily clerk.

For Conway had a very personal reason for wishing to try to 'draw the teeth' of a matter which had the potential to savage the entire council – and none more than himself as chairman. Generally, this would not have bothered him too much – "No good doing this job if you've a thin skin," as he'd said on numerous occasions. "All you can do is what you think is right, then shrug your shoulders and walk away. You're always going to upset somebody. That's the nature of it." Regarding this matter, though, where he suspected the parish could be reasonably evenly – and strongly – divided, there was the potential to upset a goodly number of people no matter what decision was made. And there could be no worse time, probably throughout his long council career, for his potential alienation of fifty percent of the electorate than now. For the following May would see elections to the Parish and District Councils and, for the first time, encouraged enthusiastically by his Cindy, he intended to stand for election to the Tavistock Rural District Council.

The Peninsula returned three members to the district authority which, as it's name suggested, was centred, and met, in nearby Tavistock, and he felt that, as long as nothing unforeseen took place, he had a good chance of election. At the previous Parish Council vote he came top of the poll and he felt that in the past three years he had done nothing to lessen his sound standing in the opinions of local folk.

Being the experienced and somewhat cynical man that he was, however, he was fully conscious of the fact that issues and situations not of his making and certainly beyond his control, could put dynamite in the path of his ambitions and blow them into oblivion. Such mercurial, dangerous volatility lay with the question of Sunday cricket, as its potential to upset so very many men and women who would within the next twelve months make a cross on a ballot paper, was enormous and, from his point of view, quite possibly catastrophic.

Thus, following his discussion with the cricket club chairman and his suggestion that the club's request be put into writing as soon as possible and forwarded, likewise, to the Clerk of the Council, Conway downed his Scotch, made excuses to the headmaster that "Thing's are a bit hectic at the shop," (totally untrue) and left the pub some half an hour earlier than he would normally have done; so early, in fact, that Landlord Billy Gladwin was mildly concerned for his health.

Finishing his own drink, Cedric Sleeman left about thirty seconds later and was surprised to see the newsagent moving rapidly in the distance, not towards his shop but in the other direction, towards the northern edge of the village. "Oh well, mine's not to reason why," he mused to himself, and proceeded to walk home to his bungalow, there to put pen to paper and create the letter concerning the possibilities of the cricket club playing on a Sunday which, when it became official, was expected to bring civil war to the parish.

Within two minutes of having left the Tamar View Inn, the Chairman of the Council was deep in conversation with the Parish Clerk, explaining the bombshell which was about to explode, and seeking ways to avoid the internecine parish war

which could so likely ensue – and which could so dramatically derail his personal ambitions for higher office, an ambition, though, which nobody other than his wife knew about – a secret which he aimed to maintain for the present.

Reg Perkins, who walked with a pronounced limp (and with the aid of a stick) due to the losing of a larger part of his right leg at Vimy Ridge in the Great War, knew more about local government than any other half dozen people put together in Conway's view. For not only had he been Parish Council Clerk for decades, he had worked as a middle ranking official for Tavistock Rural District Council for over thirty years, and was due to retire just a couple of years hence. Reg knew most things, he knew 'where the bodies are buried' as the saying goes (in terms of local council matters), tended to know those who counted, trusted very few and could, in council matters, usually espy the way forward which would cause least hassle and upset fewest people.

After listening to the Parish Council Chairman's resumé of his conversation with the Chairman of the Cricket Club, and agreeing that the letter about to be sent officially requesting the club be given permission to play cricket on a Sunday had the potential to cause havoc in the parish, he agreed entirely with Conway's perceptive proposal as to a solution which might well leave the council tolerably unscathed.

"Totally right, Dick – which doesn't surprise me," stated the clerk. "You're right about most things when it comes to council work. I sometimes feel this parish would be far better off if you and me were left to run it," said he somewhat immodestly – but with a sharp laugh. "Not that it'll happen, of course. There's far too many want their say to allow that. Not that many will want to have too much say in public about this Sunday cricket business, you can be sure of that – councillors I mean. Too much scope there to upset far too many. No, your idea is the one, boy – Parish Meeting in the Parish Hall, followed by a Parish Poll. All of it laid down in electoral law – and I should know, 'cause I've been dealing with local election matters through most of my working life. Not that I've had that many Parish Polls in my time, but I must have had three or four. Some biggish local issue that's controversial in some major way, it's an ideal way to sort it out – and democratic, of course; there can be no fairer way of sorting anything, can there? Everybody on the electoral roll of the parish has the right to vote on it. If we go along that route, I'll need to get several hundred voting slips run off, of course, so we've enough for everybody who turns up to the meeting. Then we have a simple question on the slip – probably 'Are you in favour of the Recreation Fields being used for official cricket matches on a Sunday?' – 'Yes' or 'No'. Nothing could be more straightforward. Folks'll vote one way or the other, the vote will be counted there and then – it'll not take long – and the result will be given. And, of course, the beauty of it is, it will be binding; just a simple majority – one vote either way – will decide. People, even if they've lost, will generally feel they've been fairly treated – one or two won't, of course, that's always the way – and the Parish Council will not be held in any way responsible by either side, for they won't have made the decision."

"The only thing is, though, Reg, the Parish Council will have to agree to this as a course of action." Conway spoke the words with a modicum of doubt shading his tone.

Reg Perkins rapidly assured him that in his view such an eventuality was certain. "They'll agree to it, Dick, 'course they will. Whether for Sunday cricket or against it – and there's three or four, I fancy could well be against it – they'll be perfectly happy to have the Parish Poll. Nobody, boy, take my word for it, will be keen to get involved in this one – as you're clearly well aware, this is potentially electoral suicide for all of you. If you give the decision to the people of the parish, you slide out of that danger right away and, of course, you earn praise for giving folk the opportunity to decide for themselves an issue of importance and potential conflict throughout the parish."

The newsagent smiled in satisfied fashion. "Good – good – good. I'm feeling a lot better now, Reg, I can tell you that. Still, what happens now? You'll have the official letter from Cedric Sleeman within twenty-four hours for sure, so what will happen then?"

"Once I've received it, I'll call an extraordinary meeting of the council. By law, seven days notice have got to be given, so probably it'll be the week after next. I'll just put the one item on the agenda and moot the possibilities of a Public Meeting and Parish Poll seeing as this is a matter of relevance and concern to the entire community. That way the possible solution will be put before members in plenty of time for them to decide the way forward. As I said just now, I'll be astounded if that solution is not adopted very promptly – it's the ideal one. Mind you, it is obviously a matter for all you elected members – nothing to do with me," he added hastily, aware that there were times when he, as a mere official, did tend possibly to be just a touch too forceful in his personal 'advice', something which had on occasions caused resentment – indeed, stern criticism – amongst some councillors.

" 'Course it is, Reg, we all know that. Hopefully, though, it is the action everybody will go for, without too much discussion or debate about it, either. The more low key we can play this, the better for all."

Cedric Sleeman's letter duly arrived, and the Parish Clerk fulfilled his duties by calling the extraordinary meeting of the council necessary to put in place a Public Meeting and poll. To Dick Conway's huge relief, the council gathering went exactly as he'd hoped. There were mutterings from a few councillors that there should be a debate on the matter of the cricket club's request, whilst a couple of others felt the council should make a decision themselves on it. Eight of the thirteen, however, were, within minutes of the opening of the meeting, of a mind that the people themselves should decide, very conscious of the emotive and divisive nature of the debate which would rage in the parish – indeed, was raging already. They wished to distance themselves from it as soon as possible.

Thus, soon after, did nine Councillors vote in favour of the Parish Poll, with four abstaining. It was left to the Parish Clerk to organise matters, which he did with his usual diligence, common sense and astute judgment of human nature.

The Public Meeting and Parish Poll was to be held in the

Village Hall a fortnight later, on the first Tuesday evening of July
– and during that fortnight, the issue dominated virtually all
discussion and talk on the Peninsula. Major arguments and
disputes erupted. Though none became physical, some led to
lasting feuds and estrangements, even the severing of long term
friendships. The letters pages of both the *Tavistock Times* and
*Tavistock Gazette* overflowed with correspondence on the matter
– much of it from outside the parish, the issue having become
quite high profile throughout the Tamar Valley and West Devon.
Rarely was to be seen any correspondence of a neutral or
conciliatory nature; rather these were letters of very decided
opinion, few of which made even the slightest attempt to see any
aspect of the other's view. Indeed, some were so vituperative and
vicious, it took all the editor's skills to make them acceptable to
family newspapers – a few were so offensive they could not be
used at all. Thus, by the time the day dawned for the big meeting
in the Parish Hall, a state of civil war, in ideological terms,
existed throughout the large parish.

The hall was packed, with a goodly number standing at the
back – all ages, backgrounds, outlooks and beliefs were there. As
Reg Perkins commented, "No matter what happens, nobody can
say it fails on the democratic front. Everybody's got a chance to
speak and vote." And it seemed to Dick Conway, who by virtue
of his office of Chairman of the Council had to chair the meeting,
that virtually everyone did speak, or certainly wished to. (And the
word 'chairman' had little relevance literally as he spent most of
the evening on his feet attempting – with reasonable success – to
keep order.) He managed, with great difficulty, to restrict the
number of speakers to about a score, endeavouring, quite well, to
ensure that equal numbers of 'pros' and 'cons' regarding the
burning issue being debated, were able to speak – and that none
spoke for more than a couple of minutes, which was exceedingly
difficult to enforce. Finally he wound matters up by permitting
one member of each group five minutes to sum up matters and
arguments for their side. Both were most articulate men, as might
be expected – the Reverend Godfrey Jennings for the antis and
Cedric Sleeman for the advocates of Sunday cricket. Both put

forward their cases with erudition, conviction and considerable passion.

The final speaker was Dick Conway himself, who thanked the multitude for turning up, made platitudinous comments about the laudably healthy state of local democracy – complimented the orators, commented on how evenly divided the gathered throng appeared to be (when he said it, he had, obviously, no way of knowing just how evenly) and finally urged one and all to use their vote, for or against – which certainly was unnecessary as most were desperate to do just that.

With the chairman's speech done, several councillors, there to help on the night, began to distribute the voting slips to the impatient electors. This having taken several minutes, they then immediately retraced their steps and collected the completed slips, the writing of an X or a tick on each taking but a second. Several minutes again elapsed before this operation was completed, but soon a large mound of papers lay before Reg Perkins and three other councillors who had agreed to do the count, on a largish table on the hall stage, certainly very much in the view of the audience.

Dick Conway got up onto the stage again and made an announcement that was a touch unnecessary. "Ladies and Gentlemen, three councillors and the Parish Clerk, Mr Perkins, will now proceed to count the vote. I will, of course, announce the result as soon as they have finished." In this, though, he was to be wrong.

Some ten to fifteen minutes elapsed, but whereas a decision was expected to emanate from the stage, there appeared only to be confusion. The Town Clerk motioned for Conway to come over to the table. He lowered his head and said, in a whisper which was mightily conspiratorial – "I know it takes some believing, Dick, but we've got a tied vote."

The chairman looked stunned. "What – on numbers like this. I mean there must be 400 here at least. How can we have a tie, on numbers like this. It's not possible – surely?"

"It seems all too possible, boy. By our count, there are 207 for Sunday Cricket and 207 against. We'll have to have a recount – there's no other way."

The chairman shook his head, registering a combination of shock and disbelief. "Ridiculous – ridiculous. How can it be? On numbers like that, how can it be?"

"Well, it's an amazing coincidence, I'll give you that, Dick, but that's the way it seems to be as far as the four of us here can tell. Anyway, as I said, we'll have to have a recount and I fancy, so that everything can be seen to be above board, that it should be done by four others – say four of the councillors that helped distribute the voting slips. What do you think?"

Conway, still bemused, nodded his agreement, and the clerk, despite his lameness, hastened off into the body of the hall, rapidly collected together a quartet of councillors, explained the somewhat bizarre situation to them, then led them up onto the stage, where they took their seats around the table and commenced a recount of the votes.

Another quarter hour passed, with the counters, their heads bowed to their task, deeply engrossed in their work, leaving the gathered voters to sit and await events. It was clear to all that a recount was taking place, and people were remarkably patient. Indeed, a degree of excitement began to grip them, as it was obvious the result was going to be exceedingly close – and nobody in the hall could have any real idea as to who the victor would be.

At last, the four councillors arose from their task. One of them, Sam Pullen, the plumber, called Reg Perkins over and passed him a slip of paper. The Parish Clerk glanced down at it briefly, shook his head in involuntary fashion, then motioned to the chairman to come up onto the stage, which he did – without enthusiasm. Something told him that things were not ideal. Confronting Perkins, he awaited the verdict.

"No change, Dick, I'm afraid – they got it right the first time; 207 votes each. It's a tie. No good having another recount. Two lots of people counting aren't going to come to the same totals unless they're the right ones. No, it's a tie, all right – so no decision."

"But we've got to have a decision," insisted the chairman. "Things can't carry on like this – there'll be bloodshed in the parish. It's a miracle there hasn't been already."

"You're right, boy," agreed the clerk. "There has to be a decision made – and you as Chairman of the Parish Council are the only one who can make it: You'll have to give a casting vote, one way or the other. I'm sorry, Dick, but I can see no other way. This has got to be sorted out, as you say. There is a precedent, a Chairman of a Parish Council giving a casting vote in a Parish Poll." He said the words with such masterly authority, Conway believed him. In reality, he knew of no such precedent, but surmised there had to be one, sometime, somewhere – the law of averages demanded as much. He felt, though, that he needed to back up his exhortations regarding the chairman making the supreme decision. "It's no difference to a council meeting, Dick, when you look at it. There you'll give a casting vote on occasions, by virtue of your office. Here you're doing exactly the same – albeit, it's a bit bigger vote," he concluded, weakly.

"I'll say it's a bigger vote, Reg – it's a vast vote. But I suppose there's no way around it. Talk about the 'best laid plans of mice and men'. Well, I'm about to upset half the parish and, more importantly, from my point of view, destroy any hopes I – I – I. –" He checked himself, aware that neither Reg Perkins or any parish councillor were remotely aware of his ambitions to become a district councillor. He had no intention, at the moment, of letting anybody know of such aspirations – it would be better to just shelve them without anybody else knowing and thus avoid humiliation: "I might ever have to go any further in later years – possibly – possibly when I retire," he concluded. He shook his head, then looked out over the packed, serried ranks throughout the village hall. He shrugged his shoulders then said, largely to himself – "Oh well, it's got to be done – so I might just as well get on and do it."

He moved slowly towards the front of the stage, stood gazing briefly towards the back of the hall, and became aware that despite the great numbers present, virtual silence reigned – an expectant, excited one as the four hundred, plus, there gathered awaited the verdict from the Chairman of the Council.

As he filled his lungs to speak as loudly and authoritatively as possible, his eyes scanned the back of the hall, with numerous parishioners standing there, then swept over – and quickly returned – to the solid, uniformed figure of Constable Claude Barton standing just inside the back door; there, no doubt, to maintain law and order. Assuredly a very British sight – a public meeting, a public vote and the local policeman there to ensure fair play.

Again, he was about to speak; but suddenly he was seized with inspiration. Now, having gone to Tavistock Grammar School back in the twenties by virtue of passing the Scholarship, he would class himself, without conceit, as being a reasonably well educated man as well as being of tolerable intelligence. Also, he had proved a good, hardworking businessman in the parish of his birth – though such sound enterprise was down, in considerable measure, to the sharp brain and energy of his dear Cindy. Inspiration, though, blinding light showing minutely the way forward had never before visited him – until this glorious moment. He would soon discover how divine it was, but it had the potential to avoid personal calamity, restoring the possibility of his local authority ambitions being realised, despite all.

At last sound came forth from his throat and spread over the patient parishioners who had watched, with some alarm, the facial contortions which had seemingly been afflicting the Chairman of the Council for the past thirty seconds or so. "Ladies and gentlemen," he cried, in his clear, quite powerful voice. "It will be apparent to you all by now, that it has proved very difficult to arrive at a decision concerning this so important and emotive matter which has, I'm sorry to say, ripped the parish apart. It was clear from the debate just how evenly divided you are on the issue – and the vote has proved it, in the most dramatic and remarkable way. For the vote has been tied, 207 for Sunday Cricket at the Recreation Fields, 207 against. Naturally, we had a recount, one done by four different councillors; again, quite surprisingly as there are often discrepancies between votes in recounts, we find that the vote is still tied, 207 each being the correct numbers. Obviously this matter cannot be allowed to drag on; a decision has to be made right away – it is only fair to do so in the interests of all parties concerned. The problem is, how to do it fairly. I have given this long thought," – nothing could be further from the truth, he mused to himself, but this was no time to worry too much about such trivialities – "and come to the conclusion that as this issue has produced much real strife between the people of this parish and as we seem, even by our vote, unable to resolve it in the traditional democratic way, it should be taken out of our hands – and put into those of fate or, possibly, even higher authority. I would not presume to comment on such matters, of course, although we have amongst us this evening two gentlemen of the cloth who possibly do have the knowledge and understanding to do so. However, I am not going to call on them to decide – rather, I propose to invoke the element of chance, and the influence of the powers of that, or those, which decree such matters, to decide for us." He stopped briefly, and gazed towards the back of the hall. "I see Constable Barton at the back, and would ask him if he would do me the honour of coming forward and coming up here onto the stage; Constable Barton, please."

The officer was, momentarily, nonplussed, but a man rarely to be deflected for long from 'doing his duty' and certainly not a diffident one, he walked in his slowish, but upright, fashion down through the centre aisle of the hall, then up the four steps to the stage.

The chairman shook his hand firmly, then turned to face a puzzled but highly expectant audience. He raised his hand for silence – which was somewhat unnecessary as there was not a whisper to be heard; from four hundred plus. "Ladies and gentlemen, as I said just now. I feel that the powers which possibly decide our actions and our lives are those which could make this decision for us – thus, I propose this matter be decided on a straight drawing of lots."

Those words galvanised the audience even further, most feeling it was the most exciting thing that had happened in the village for many a long day, though a number of chapel going folk were not impressed, seeing such a move as being gambling. As for the Reverend Jennings and, to a slightly lesser extent, the Reverend Cuthbert Kenny, the Congregational Minister, they saw it as the ways of the Devil, but both realised there was nothing

h

they could do about it. The issue of whether or not cricket would be played, officially, in the parish on a Sunday, was no longer, in their eyes, down to matters of moral principle, but to the vagaries of chance, where the ways of blasphemy were as empowered as the ways of the Lord and of right. And, they were all too well aware, the great majority of the gathered electors would accept the result without demur. Even the antis would accept defeat without major grumble as they would deem that the decision had been reached fairly and openly.

"I will ask the Parish Clerk, Mr Perkins, to hand me two blank sheets of paper of exactly the same size." Taking the sheets from the official, the chairman picked up a black pencil and began to write upon one of them. Within seconds he was handing it to Claude Barton. "I have asked Constable Barton on to the stage, ladies and gentlemen, because by virtue of his position in this parish, as having been – which he remains – our village policeman for more than two decades, he is above local disputes and jealousies. In fact, he is, as we all know, a man of integrity with a high sense of duty. Thus nobody is more suited here this evening to, in effect, make the decision as to whether or not cricket is played on a Sunday." Lapsing into silence, momentarily, he scribbled on the second piece of paper, then straightened up. Looking at the policeman, he said, "Would you kindly take your helmet off, Constable, and pass it to me – if that's all right with you." The officer did so, instantly, then awaited further instructions. "Would you please read out loud the words I've written on the paper I've given you, then fold it and put it into your helmet."

Barton nodded, then read – "The playing of cricket on a Sunday in the Recreation Field – NO." The policeman, like the Council Chairman, needed no amplification to make himself heard, his voice carrying clearly to the far corners of the hall. The words read, he folded the sheet into quarters and deposited it into the helmet held by the Town Clerk.

Dick Conway proceeded to hand the second sheet of paper to Barton; he exhorted him once again, to read out loud its message, which he did. "The playing of cricket on a Sunday in the

Recreation Field – YES." Again, he folded it into quarters, and deposited it into his helmet.

"Ladies and gentlemen, the Parish Clerk, Mr Perkins, will give the helmet a good shake so that the two pieces are moved around, then he will hold the helmet aloft, and I will invite Constable Barton to put his hand in and draw out the first piece of paper his fingers touch. I will then ask him to read out the words written upon it. Whatever those words say, will bring to an end this very destructive dispute which, I believe, has done damage to the morale of this Peninsula. Whatever is said on the paper, will be final – and must be accepted by all sides." The Chairman of the Council had said the words with a brisk authority which he, in reality, neither felt nor, possibly, possessed; but it was a time for discipline to be brought to matters which were on the brink of getting out of hand – and he was determined to bring it.

Claude Barton raised his right arm high, then dipped it down into his helmet. He did not rush, for he had become aware that this, almost certainly, was one of the high points of his police career – possibly, the supreme one. He would savour every second of it. Slowly, from the helmet, he produced a quartered sheet, lowered his arm, and proffered the paper in Conway's direction.

"No, Constable, thank you. It is you who are in charge here. You who hold the people's trust. May I ask you to open up that piece of paper and read out loud the words written upon it."

Constable Claude Barton of the Devon County Constabulary nodded, straightened his back and filled his capacious lungs. Assuredly he was the centre of attention – and was not averse to it.

"Ladies and gentlemen, the words written upon this paper – 'The playing of cricket on a Sunday in the Recreation Field – ' " The Constable, with an admirable sense of theatre, and determination to mine this moment to its richest seam, paused for just a few seconds, then uttered the solitary word, " 'Yes.' "

Pandemonium broke loose in the hall. The pro-Sunday Cricket faction absolutely jubilant; and likewise, Billy Gladwin, Landlord of the Tamar View Inn – his was going to be a very buoyant trade

171

for the next couple of hours until closing time, so he wasted no time in hurtling home to help his wife and their sole part-time barmaid cope with the rush. The anti-Sunday sport contingent took their defeat, generally, in good grace, most merely shrugging their shoulders and accepting 'chance's' spurning of their case. Certainly a night of winners and losers – principal amongst the latter, possibly the Reverend Godfrey Jennings who really did view the playing of any sport on a Sabbath as being the work of Satan.

As to the winners, Ginger Hocking, whose idea it had been originally to play Sunday Cricket, was clearly a major one, along with all connected with the Cricket Club. Claude Barton, too, had enjoyed possibly his finest moment as the Parish Policeman – never before had he received such praise and prominence. The Parish Council, also, had come out of it all reasonably well – certainly unscathed which would not have been the case if they had had to make the decision regarding Sunday Cricket. This they owed in large measure to their chairman. Deftness of touch it was which had brought about the Public Meeting and Parish Poll and, even more adroitly – indeed, inspirationally – whose instant decision to allow the so fractious issue to be decided by the drawing of lots, at the hand of a man whose even handedness was beyond question. This was something none of the elected members would forget.

Dick Conway deserved reward – and received it. Just under a year later, in the election of the trio from the Peninsula who were to represent the parish on the Tavistock Rural District Council, in a field of no fewer than seven candidates, he was to triumph – top of the poll.

# VII

# Terminal Enthusiasm

Dick Conway had many things in life which gave him enjoyment and right up there with the leaders was the consumption of whisky. Mind you, he was not averse to the occasional pint of black and tan, and on a warm summer's day a glass of good, locally brewed Devon farm 'scrumpy' took a bit of beating. Whisky, though, was to him the King of Drinks, and (although he would not have admitted it in public) one of the major bonuses to him brought about by the ending of the war was the restoration of supplies of Scotch to most pubs – so often unobtainable during the conflict. Still, even though the guns had been silent for some five years now, the amber, fiery liquid was not always available in the quantities which Billy Gladwin – landlord of the Tamar View Inn – would have liked. For a goodly number of the regulars at the pub (arguably amongst the worst named in the land as it was almost two miles from the Tamar and being in a hollow had no views save that of hillsides) often could still not consume the spirit in the quantities which they desired – and this included Conway, although he was ever quick to declare that whilst he enjoyed a 'few nips and a few jars' he could certainly live without it; however, he had no ambition to do so.

He relaxed over a drink, especially at lunchtimes. His working day began at 5.30 every morning, including most Sundays, when he was up, first collecting newspapers from the railway station then sorting them for delivery and sale in the newsagents and

173

general village store he and his wife Cindy ran a mere 200 yards from the pub. Some three quarters of an hour spent in the pub most lunchtimes consuming a comforting beverage or two, in relative peace, was important to him – and was done with the full agreement of his supportive wife.

Having drained his glass of a smooth pint of beer, he took delivery of a double Scotch and sipped it appreciatively, an expression of contentment upon his weathered features. That expression was destined to be fleeting. For the door to the bar was opened in a fashion, and with a force, which in a Western movie would produce a gunfighter seeking to wreak havoc. The fellow who stood in the doorway, however, sought not to bring mayhem but rather to impart dramatic and, to him, most mind concentrating news, to the gathered throng in general (somewhat small) and to one of them in particular.

"Dick – I thought you'd be here; you usually are at this time of day."

The words were spoken – hurriedly, almost breathlessly – by Sam Pullen, the local plumber and a fellow parish councillor.

"Have you heard the news?" Having uttered the question, he moved rapidly, stumbling slightly towards the bar. Seeing the landlord reach for a tankard in which, clearly, he was about to deposit, from the huge weathered barrel behind him, a pint of scrumpy, the plumber's regular beverage, he shook his head in almost violent fashion – "No, no thanks, Billy – not this time. I need something stronger than even scrumpy. I'll have the same as Dick, here – whisky; and a double as well. And after you hear what I got to tell you boy," he continued, talking to the newsagent, "you'll need another double in that glass."

Conway looked somewhat surprised – then just a touch alarmed.

"Whatever is it, Sam? What's so important; well, more than that, so terrible? You've got me a bit worried. Somebody died?"

Pullen shook his head, took a fair portion of the whisky which the landlord had thrust into his hands in a single gulp then shook his head again – somewhat violently.

"No, no, no, nothing like that. But it's grim news never-the-less boy. It certainly will do nothing to brighten your day when you hear what's happened."

"I don't doubt Sam," he retorted, slightly annoyed at the fellow's perpetual proclivity for prevarication. So many times over the years he had, when his patience had worn thin (it did not take long), implored, on occasions, demanded, an immediate imparting of information from the plumber when that good man had some to give – which was not infrequent, he seemingly most adroit at gaining news, gossip and the like before most other folk in the parish. It was possibly the fact he was often in possession of intelligence not known to most others which encouraged him to impart it in his own good time.

"What's happened – what is it that's got you drinking Scotch of a lunchtime?"

Such a departure from the plumber's usual drinking habits was more than ample evidence as far as Conway was concerned, that something serious, dramatic or grave – or all three – had happened. He was to be informed, though not with alacrity, the news bringer still finding it exceedingly difficult to get to the point. Still, he did make a valiant attempt to do so.

"It's the council, boy – the vacancy following poor old Gordon Dixon's dropping off the perch a couple of months back."

Momentarily, an image of the twenty stone Dixon upon a perch – five years of war and almost double regarding rationing not having reduced his bulk by as much as an ounce – flashed across Conway's mind. Aware that falling from a great height had not contributed to that good councillor's death whereas a massive coronary (exacerbated no doubt by his weight) had, he returned his attention and concentration to the matter in hand – the desperately important, and almost certainly grave news which the plumber was frantic to impart.

"Well I thought you should know as you're chairman – and know right away. I remembered that nominations would close at noon, so as I was passing the phone box just now, I thought I'll phone up the rural district offices in Tavistock to see if there were any nominations – even though it's a vacancy on the Parish Council here, all nominations go to the returning officer, Frank

175

Fellows at the district offices, of course. Luckily I caught him just as he was about to go to dinner – a bit later than usual, so he told me."

"The time he goes for his dinner, Sam, isn't of any great importance as far as I can tell," retorted the chairman of the council in exasperated tones. "We're here, all of us," he indicated those present with a theatrical wave of the hand, "hanging on every word you're saying 'cause clearly you've got some vital, and I fear, worrying tidings to give us, boy – so please, please tell us what's happened, who's put up?"

"Well believe it or not – and it takes a lot of believing, 'cause we said here in the pub not more than a week back that there didn't seem much interest in the vacancy, and we could see it ending up in us having to co-opt somebody. . ."

"Well clearly that's not going to happen Sam, is it – somebody's put up, that's for certain. You'd not be in here in such a state if nobody had – so tell us, who is it? And what's so bad about them. Something must be – you'd not be drinking Scotch at dinner-time if it wasn't somebody who's going to be a damned nuisance, or is a fool – or even worse. So no more prevarication, Sam, who is it?" The final three words, whilst not exactly shouted, were spoken in loud, direct tones, and would brook no avoidance or further delay (or at least, no major further delay).

"Well, to start with there's bound to be an election as two have put up. There we were thinking that it could be that nobody will have a go, and there's two – I never expected that."

The news bringer ceased speaking and indulged in a session of shaking his head, his astonishment that such a 'horde' were seeking public office clearly having had a profound effect upon him.

"Well," rasped Conway, making no effort to disguise his exasperation at this convoluted, exhausting conversation with a fellow who seemed incapable of giving information even though he gave the impression he was bursting to do so.

"Well, what boy?" came the reply.

"For God's sake, Sam, who are the two putting up for the council?"

The outburst came not from the chairman but from the long serving – and suffering – landlord of The Tamar View, who took an interest in the parish of his birth well beyond that of a man merely seeking to sell his range of liquor.

The outburst from the usually easy going Billy Gladwin hit the mark – the plumber prevaricated no longer.

"Well, first, there's Sally Marsh – that's the good news."

"Well, yes it is," agreed Dick Conway with some warmth. "Excellent woman, Sally. I mean she was on for several years – started a couple of years before the war and resigned a year or two after it. She gave up, as I recall, to nurse poor old Phil during his final three months – he died slow and painful, sadly. It must be, well, three years at least since he died. She was marvellous through the war, helping with events for the war effort and suchlike – also always doing things for the evacuees as well. Not a talker Sally, a doer. Always willing to roll her sleeves up and get stuck in; not many like her about – it would be first class if she was elected back on. Still," he continued, "looking at messenger Pullen here it's clearly not that simple; somebody else has put up that won't be quite as welcome, that's clear from all your huffing and puffing, Sam. You give the impression 'tis old Nick himself, but surely it's not as bad as you make out. Who is it for heaven's sake?"

The plumber downed his Scotch in a gulp, dropped the glass dramatically onto the bar and said two words which seemingly drained the ruddy, rural Devon colour from the chairman's cheeks.

"Murray Jarvis."

Conway stood stock still for several seconds, whisky glass in hand, apparently stunned by the news. Returning at last to something approaching consciousness, he, like Sam Pullen, downed the remainder of his Scotch in a solitary gulp (a rare form of consumption on his part, he habitually preferring to sip the spirit); returning the glass to the bar, he looked at the convenor of the tidings.

"Are you sure, Sam?" he rasped, somewhat superfluously.

"Of course I am," came the reply, with a measure of asperity.

"As I said, I've just phoned the returning officer in Tavistock – he's not going to get it wrong, is he?"

"No, no of course not. Sorry, boy – it was a daft thing for me to say; it's just that, that – well, it's knocked me sideways to be honest. Murray Jarvis. . .' He stopped talking and shook his head in bemusement – "I never thought of him putting up for the council; but perhaps I should have – after all, he's got a finger in so many pies, so why not the council as well. It's a shock though, no doubt whatsoever about that."

"Frank Fellows told me that he submitted his nomination papers within just a few minutes of the earliest time that he could do so – which, of course, is Murray all over; with him, to think is to act. He's always been the same when you look at it. Like you, though, I never thought of him trying for the Parish Council, but when you think of everything else he's involved in, perhaps it's surprising he's never put up before."

The chairman nodded his agreement.

"Yes, you're right – it is strange we've never had to put up with him in the past. But I fancy we'll have to in the future. He's very well known, and, to be fair, popular with many folks – he'll be favourite for sure."

His companion nodded in agreement.

"Oh yes, he'll be favourite without doubt. Mind you, Sally's popular too – many will remember she was a first class councillor when she was on before, very hard working, treated folk right, very sensible and listened to what the voters said. Despite this, though, as you say, Murray'll be the one that will get the votes – a fair majority, anyway."

"You're right about the Scotch, Sam." The chairman of the council shook his head in weary, possibly bemused, assuredly highly despondent fashion. "I certainly need another following news like that. You'll have one as well?"

He did not wait for an answer, so certain was the reply.

"Two whiskies Billy, please."

Rapidly the landlord replenished the brace of glasses and placed them before the seemingly distraught regulars. He received the proffered ten shilling note from the newsagent, gave the change, then set out to solve a riddle which was puzzling him.

"Sorry gents," said he, "but I could hardly help but hear your conversation about there being a by-election for the Parish Council – and I'm a bit puzzled to be honest; what's wrong with Murray Jarvis putting up? He always strikes me as. . ." His view of the potential councillor was not forthcoming, his voice trailing off at the insistent ringing of the phone behind him. Reaching round and picking up the receiver he listened and said: briskly: "Yes, he's here, I'll put him on."

He looked directly at the chairman of the council.

"It's Arthur Mason, Dick; wants a word – its urgent he says."

Conway promptly got up from his stool, went around to the business side of the bar, and was soon giving brief replies to the torrent of words being hurled his way by another parish councillor.

"So I've heard." – "No I can't believe it either." "Yes, I'm afraid he'll win." – "Granted, Sally is quite popular, but like you say, she's nowhere as well known as Murray." – "True, if she canvasses really hard, she could do it, but it's unlikely I fear." – "Oh yes, I reckon most of us on the council will do all we can to get her returned, but there's a limit to what we can do. Well, what I mean by that is that we've got to appear to be impartial; we must certainly not say anything against old Murray." – "True there's not much you can say against him in terms of character; I mean he's a decent chap, is Murray, honest and straight as they come. But no, like you said, we do not want him on the Parish Council; my God, we do not. Yes, we'll talk again Arthur."

The phone returned to its home on the shelf just below the whisky, Dick Conway went back to his stool.

"Arthur's just heard the news. I don't know how mind you. He's been tail lopping all morning and has just come in for his dinner – so who's told him, I wonder? Apparently they only had the phone put in last week and this is the very first call he's made. Said he hated the thought of using it as he felt he'd be all over the place talking to somebody he can't see – but he thought it was urgent as he felt I might not have heard about it and, being chairman, he thought I should know right away. Not that there's anything I can do about it."

"I bet Ida's used the phone more than once," opined Sam Pullen, somewhat irreverently. "Never knew a woman who talked more than her. Very different from Arthur – he just speaks when he's got something to say. Good councillor though, 'cause it's nearly always sensible."

"Well he had a fair bit to say just now about Murray. And knowing the sort of man Arthur is, it's clear just how shocked he is, that he took the trouble and time to use what he calls a queer, new fangled contraption. There's not a lot we can do about it, though, as I tried to say to him."

"But how did he know about it, Dick? That's what I don't fathom," puzzled the plumber. "After all, the nominations only closed just over an hour ago and, by his own words, this is the first call he's made – and he lives on the far side of the parish so wouldn't see anyone much. Course, somebody might have phoned him – although I imagine he would have said so if they had."

"Alfie Spurr – that's how he knows, I bet," interjected the landlord. "Murray will have told him this morning when he was delivering the post; just think about it. Murray lives about a half a mile from the end of Alfie's round in that old bungalow of his, and Arthur Mason lives virtually at the very end. Murray will have told Alfie and he in turn will have told Arthur, he being on the council."

"And everybody else in between," stated Conway shaking his head. "Neither the wireless or the *Tavistock Times* can ever spread news – or rumour, or gossip the way Alfie can. And Murray knows that as well as anyone else – good way to spread the word and do a bit of canvassing. He's no fool and that's for sure."

"No – that's true," agreed the plumber. "Which begs the question, why hasn't he been putting the word around before now? I mean, it's been the best part of a fortnight since his nomination went in. How is it that he hasn't told all and sundry that he's standing? Not like Murray that – I'd have thought he'd have been telling folk, and out and about, right from the minute the papers went in. As we know, he's never lacking in energy."

"He's been on holiday." The words were spoken by Roy

Hillman, a burly fellow possessing the best bass voice in the area, who was sat at the far end of the bar soothing his larynx with Guinness.

"He's been away ten days or more. I know 'cause he's missed a couple of choir practises. He was there last night, though – he said that he and his missus, who has not been well lately, had been up to Sidmouth so she could recuperate. Their train had got in not more than an hour before. They'd gone straight home, then he left her to unpack and he'd come straight on to the church."

"That explains it; he missed a meeting of the parish hall committee last Friday. He sent apologies but didn't say he was on holiday." Sam Pullen shook his head in slight annoyance. "I should have realised he was away – you know Murray, he never misses meetings."

"I suppose I should have as well," opined the landlord. "He wasn't at the carnival committee meeting on Thursday. Again, he very, very rarely misses – I thought he might be poorly or something. Didn't think to ask."

"Well, if he's got Alfie Spurr spreading the news, the best part of the parish will soon know that he's standing for election – which will put poor old Sally at a disadvantage right from the start," said Pullen, with another shake of the head.

"She's quite well known, mind you, and well liked and respected – but everybody knows Murray – and most folk like him; he'll win for certain."

The landlord seized the moment of silence which ensued, and returned to the question he had attempted to ask earlier.

"As I said before, I really cannot see why you all seem so upset at him putting up for council. I mean, it seems to me that. . ." again how it appeared to the landlord was destined to remain a mystery for the time being, as the door of the bar burst open and the lofty, exceedingly skinny figure of Councillor Harvey Collins stumbled in.

"Dick, Dick – I thought I'd find you here," he spluttered a touch breathlessly, before even closing the door behind him. "Have you heard the news? You'll never believe it but Murray Jarvis has put up for the council. I just heard from Alfie Spurr. He was just coming back into the village from his round. Murray Jarvis – I can scarcely believe it!"

"Half and half, Harvey?" enquired Billy Gladwin, reaching for a pint tankard in anticipation.

"No, boy, no – I'll have a rum; double, Billy if you will. I need something stronger than beer after hearing news like this."

Rum was always Harvey's choice on those relatively rare occasions when he eschewed ale, he having got the taste for it during his fifteen years of service in the Royal Navy which had ended in the mid-1930s when he had returned to the parish to take over his father's market garden – rich but steep land which ran down to the Tamar – upon that good man's somewhat early death from a heart attack. Having been brought up on the land, he was soon able to work it to the high standards of his father and even during the hard times of the late 30s he was able to make a decent living. During the war and the years since, he had made a very good one – "Folk have to eat," as he put it. He had been spared a recall to serve His Majesty by virtue of both age and being in a reserved occupation – something which suited him very well.

He drank most of the rum, placed his glass heavily on to the bar, then indulged in the epidemic of head shaking all around him.

"It really is grim news, isn't it? – Murray Jarvis; and he'll win, that's the trouble. He's so damned popular. Poor old Sally won't stand a chance; a lovely woman too and a good councillor when she was on last time."

He lapsed into silence, again shaking his head. Billy Gladwin filled the void, in determined style – returning to the question he had been trying to ask for the past half hour.

"What is the problem – what is wrong with Murray putting up for the council?" asked he with asperity. "I know him reasonably well, and he always seems to me a good bloke – in fact, to be blunt, you would be hard pressed to find anyone better, kinder or more helpful in the parish. He'll do anything for anybody, and at any time."

He paused slightly, but seeing the chairman of the council open his mouth to make possibly what might be a counter argument, returned instantly to the offensive.

"When you think what he does for this parish and for all the folk in it. As we've said, he's on the parish hall committee, is chairman of the carnival committee; he's the Scout master, and a Special Constable – and think of all the money he raises for local things, charities and suchlike."

He paused again, but before other views could be put, continued with the case for the defence.

"He's in the church choir – as Roy was saying just now – is a church warden; and there's the allotments – he's secretary of the committee that runs them, or I'm pretty sure he is anyway; and there's the football club – he regularly gives a hand when marking out the pitch and does a bit towards sorting out the fixtures and suchlike even though I've heard him say he doesn't much like football."

Again he paused, but once more returned to his diatribe before there could be intervention – essentially an easy going man, he was nonetheless always relentless in pursuit of what he thought was right and fair.

"And in the war, think of the work he did raising money for the 'Welcome Home' funds and organising events for the lads when they did return; and the 'Spitfire Fund' and other things to help the war effort. Then there were all the dances and concerts and shows he organised and worked on in the parish hall to keep up the people's spirits, and to raise funds, of course. I could go on and on about the things he does and he's done – but won't. In my view, gents, he's a thoroughly kind, friendly man – probably the most helpful, energetic chap I've ever met, always involved in things, always ready to lead from the front, always full of ideas, plans, new projects – a dynamic sort of bloke. So what's wrong with that? As far as I can see he's an asset to this parish and would be a first class addition to the Parish Council."

Billy Gladwin's impassioned defence of Murray Jarvis, provoked by his increasing disbelief and disgust over the display of head shaking and 'hand wringing' from the assembled councillors that had turned a normally quiet lunchtime session into a drama of King Lear like proportions, came to an end. A response from at least one of Jarvis's critics was called for.

"You're right, boy," said the chairman after a brief silence. "Every single word you've said is true. Murray Jarvis is a lovely man – you'd not find a better chap in a month's march. And he's an asset to the village and most folk in it – a major one as well. The trouble with dear old Murray, though, is that he is so unceasingly, so eternally, well – enthusiastic."

"I've never met his equal," cried Pullen, desperate to have his say. "Whatever he's involved in – and as you pointed out, Billy, that's virtually everything locally these days and, again as you said, was the case during the war, and before come to that – whatever he's involved in he's always awash with ideas, brain waves, ventures, and usually expects others to go along with him. He gets so immersed – even overwhelmed by everything, I sometimes fear for his health. Like most of us he's not that young. One day I can see his heart just giving out, and on the certificate of his cause of death, the doctor, in honesty, should write just the words. . ." – he paused briefly for dramatic effect – "Terminal enthusiasm."

Dick Conway smiled – "You could well be right there, boy."

Harvey Collins said nothing – he just sipped his rum and nodded in agreement.

Billy Gladwin was not finished.

"But I still do not see what would be wrong with him coming on to the council. Surely he would be an asset!"

"No boy, he wouldn't," Collins suddenly entered the discussion. "Councillors are elected men and women representing the ratepayers. We don't have the luxury, or the right, to play around with off-the-cuff ideas or schemes often driven more by the heart than the head. These things nearly always cost money, and if councils spend cash it's not theirs, but yours and mine – public money. Everything we do has to be thought through, approached with caution – we'll certainly be in trouble from the district auditor if it isn't. Dear old Murray would have enthusiastic ideas that, inevitably, would cost a fair bit to put into effect. The majority could stop it, clearly, but I can see the council being in a constant state of turmoil, and meetings lasting for days."

"The parish clerk might well resign, or demand a doubling of salary because of this extra work, and there'll be by-elections every other month, members resigning because of the length of meetings and the general state of chaos that will dominate council proceedings – and I could well be one of them." The chairman was speaking in support of the market gardener. "You might think all this is alarmist, Billy – but I doubt it. I've been on for over twenty years now, and I've seen what can happen when keen folk get elected to the council – and none of them were in the same league as Murray in terms of unbridled enthusiasm. No, sadly his election, if it happens, will be a bad day both for the council and the ratepayers."

Fate, though, was in mischievous mood. For a few days later, Sally Marsh was summoned to hospital – almost three months before expected – to undergo a hip replacement operation. Realising this would prevent her from campaigning for the by-election she decided to withdraw, planning, if all went well in terms of her health, to submit nomination papers for the normal elections some two years hence.

Thus Murray Jarvis was elected, automatically, to the Parish Council; the whirlwind was about to be reaped.

# VIII

# The Usual Drill

'Darkie' Dalton did not in any way owe his nickname – used universally, and to such an extent that few outside of his family knew his real name, Francis – to any non-white pigmentation of the skin. The contrary was the case, for ever since his childhood, he had possessed as pale a skin as it was possible to have; indeed, his pallor often was of such whiteness that both in childhood and as an adult, folk often feared illness was either upon him or certainly about to strike. As a boy – and hater of school – he used it to great effect, often convincing his mother (a very caring, and it had to be said, somewhat gullible lady who herself had a ruddy, healthy complexion) that he was on the brink of needing the services of an undertaker, and that he assuredly was not fit to go to school. His father Stuart, was not so easily fooled, but was always happy to leave such decisions to his spouse, he generally being away from the house and working in their market garden before his son was due to depart to pursue his education.

This, though, clearly was not the reason he was known as 'Darkie', that simply, being down to his shock of thick, usually longish, jet black hair, which, because of his paleness, looked all the darker; thus with the penchant of country folk to assign nicknames in accordance with the way people looked (especially men), he became known, from a small boy, as such – and that remained his name, even though now he was in his early thirties.

Now, although his basic health had always been good, he did have a medical problem – he was arthritic; not chronic, mind you, but enough to have caused him major problems and disappointment in terms of a career.

Darkie's father Stuart had, like so many others, been swamped with patriotic instincts in 1914 and had joined up. His, though, was an unusually positive tale, for whilst he had fought across most Flanders Fields, had experienced and witnessed so much which would remain in his mind forever, he reached Armistice Day in 1918 without a scratch; and, despite all the horrors around him, essentially he had enjoyed army life. So whilst one day he intended to return to the parish and work with his father (Darkie's grandfather), on their sizeable horticultural holding which sat on the edge of the village, running part way down towards the river, he decided that his immediate future lay with the army, so signed on as a regular.

Stuart served a dozen years, in this capacity, and would have served longer had not his father died of a heart attack in 1930. As he had always intended to come back to the Tamar Valley and be a grower, as the previous three generations of his family had been, he realised that circumstances dictated it had to be some five years earlier than he had intended. Still, on his leaving the army he became the recipient of a pension which, whilst it was by no means large (well below what he would have received with longer service) was a most useful addition to what he could earn during the hungry thirties from the land; indeed, what would have been a meagre living became, at least, an adequate one.

Having had a reasonable time in the army Stuart had imbued in his son, Darkie, the desire to emulate him and join the regiment – albeit inadvertently as he had said never a word of encouragement to him as a boy, he hoping more that his son would join him in the market garden which he felt could probably support them all adequately even if Darkie married and had a family of his own. Stuart was to get his way, though being a good father he regretted the way it happened.

When war broke out, Darkie was just nineteen. He had left school at fifteen and had been happy to follow his father's suggestion that he come to work with him on the land – certainly no hardship to the lad as he enjoyed the way of life and had a 'feel' for growing. Also, although young he had sound ideas as to how they could grow slightly different crops – one or two rarer types of vegetables mainly – which had prospered in the rich Devon earth, and had been relatively lucrative in financial terms. Nevertheless, he did not lose sight of his desire to be a soldier, and told his father so – something Stuart accepted without any argument or any attempt to dissuade him.

Thus, with the outbreak of war, came the time for Darkie Dalton to don the King's uniform, and he went off to the recruiting office in Plymouth with his father's encouragement (though not his mother's). Dalton senior, though, retained much affection for the army and, even more relevantly, was a patriot. He had done his bit in the Great War, now it was only right and proper his son should do likewise in this one, and Darkie was destined to do so – but not in army uniform and not in any way he could have foreseen. As to his strong desire to wear khaki in the service of King and country, such hopes were dashed by an army doctor in the Plymouth recruiting centre.

His enthusiasm, clear intelligence and sharpness of thought, plus his father's exemplary record made him an ideal recruit, a certainty for 'the King's shilling'; all he had to do was to pass the medical, and with the forces so desperately needing men, few failed.

Sadly for Darkie, he was to be like the Battle of Britain pilots the following summer – 'one of the few'. It was his arthritis; it was not such that it restricted his life in any meaningful way – he had never been able to play sport, running had always been a problem, and there were occasions when his joints swelled, especially the knee – but this made no difference to his life generally. Certainly it never really impeded him in terms of making a living from the land, a way of life which often called for hard physical labour. The army doctor, though, felt his condition was sufficiently serious to put a question mark on his overall fitness to face the rigours of battles which assuredly he would have to fight. Thus was he rejected – the bitterest and most disappointing moment of his life. It could be, of course, he mused, that at a later time the call could still come for him – but he was all too well aware that, in a sense, whilst such might be a positive development for him, it would not be so for the country; for if rejected men like himself were called up, it would mean the fit had been decimated – thus the war was being lost.

Still, Darkie was destined to wear a uniform – the heavy, dark blue serge of the fire brigade. The village engine had been horse drawn until the early thirties and had been manned mainly by a body of mature men all living in the village, engaged in a wide variety of occupations. During the early years of the century they had been summoned to action by the ringing of the church bells but in more recent times a siren, attached to the fire station – a rather flimsy looking building on the edge of the village which backed on to the Dalton's market gardens – wailed loudly when calamity threatened anyone dwelling on the Peninsula, and no matter where any of the retained firemen were at the time, as long as they were within a three mile radius of the alarm, they were sure to hear it (which had not always been the case with the bells).

The older firemen had no problems with the new summoning system, but they did have problems with the new motorised fire appliance which replaced the horse drawn machine. Being men of an age when retirement from the, on occasions, physically demanding part time service would soon be required, some of them decided (they being 'old dogs' and the coming of the 'internal combustion engine' to their local fire brigade requiring the learning of 'new tricks') they would retire early and gracefully, just a few years before their time, their places being taken by a quartet of local lads all in their twenties.

These four would probably have remained in the service for very many years had it not been for the coming of the war. The world changed radically and dramatically in the autumn of 1939 – dangers and emergencies locally and nationally had moved well beyond house fires, which was understood by three of the four who had joined the village brigade just a few years earlier. Thus it was that with the ever escalating Nazi menace that dominated the summer of 1940 – with the coming of the Battle of Britain –

this trio felt it was time to take up arms against the German threat, so enlisted.

In consequence, the local fire brigade had three vacancies, and Darkie, encouraged by his father, applied to join – with not the slightest expectation of being accepted. After all, if he had not been medically fit for the army, why should he be so for another uniformed service, albeit a civilian one. The reason he was accepted was twofold. Simply, as a retained fireman who would receive no pension from council or state if ill health were to force him out of the service, the authorities took little risk in a financial sense by employing him – thus barriers to him being accepted were infinitely lower than for His Majesty's forces. Nevertheless, in normal times it was probable he would have been rejected – these though were not normal times. Thus the second caveat kicked in – personnel were needed to fill numerous vacancies in the retained fire service, county wide and throughout the country, created largely by men joining the armed forces. Seeing as the King's uniforms were filled by the bodily fit, those of the retained fire service had to be worn by those not quite fit enough, or too old, to wage war.

So in August 1940 Darkie Dalton became a fireman on the village appliance and was destined to advance at a remarkable rate. For within six months, he was officer-in-charge of the Peninsula fire station (acting). This was due to a combination of circumstances, partly down to his personal qualities, but in equal measure, due to the 'slings and arrows of outrageous fortune'. His own abilities were considerable; he had always been extremely able with his hands, a man of a strong practical bent who displayed, almost immediately, a natural aptitude for devising innovative but logical solutions to the problems which regularly came the way of a fire and emergency crew in a rural area. Also he was an intelligent young man at ease with the paperwork which came to those in charge, plus the possessor of that most elusive of gifts – leadership qualities. Just as importantly, though – he was lucky, opportunity coming his way very quickly, and most unexpectedly.

He had been in the part-time job for only a couple of months, when one of the two leading firemen at the station, Errol Wallace, was promoted to a management position in Devonport Dockyard where he had worked since leaving school. Determined to make the most of such an opportunity and astutely foreseeing that with the war escalating daily, the nearer he was to his vital job the better, he decided to move to Plymouth to live. Thus did he leave the village, creating a vacancy for a fireman and one for the rank he had occupied. Being one of the 'new boys', Darkie was well down the list in terms of promotion, but due, almost entirely, to the fact that virtually nobody else wanted to step up (for reasons as various as not wanting the extra responsibility, or the paperwork, or the slightly greater time commitment, or simply lacking in ambition) the position was offered to him. Thus within two months of having joined he became leading fireman, joint second in command of the station – at the age of twenty.

Then, remarkably, early the following New Year, he became officer in charge of the station when he was promoted to the rank of sub-officer (acting), still a month short of his twenty-first birthday and officially being old enough to vote. George Anderson had been sub-officer, for the best part of a dozen years; a jobbing builder about the parish, he was a popular man and most able at both his full-time work and his emergency service duties. Just turned fifty, he had planned to continue in the brigade for a further four or five years before hanging up his axe, and leaving "Getting out of bed at all daft times of the night to douse a chimney fire; or worse, trying to put out a blazing hay rick," to somebody else. Fate – or to be more exact, ill health – intervened much sooner, sadly. For having suffered for months a hacking cough and in more recent years a substantial loss of weight, he finally did what his wife had been begging him to do for so very long – went to the doctor. The medical man spared him the brutal truth but did tell him his condition was bad and that there was no guarantee he would survive it (the Doctor knowing, in truth, there was no real chance of him surviving – and George strongly suspecting such was the truth).

The news had gone around the village the speed of a forest fire – George Anderson had consumption, and whilst the doctor had not officially classed it as being terminal, virtually everybody else had, that not being hard to do, as the fellow in appearance, gave increasingly the impression of someone in the ever tightening malevolent grip of advanced tuberculosis. The immediate upshot was that George went sick, officially, from the fire brigade, for an 'indefinite period'.

The station, though, had to be commanded by somebody and with immediate effect. The man in line to do so, clearly, was the senior leading fireman, Phil Craddock, and it was to him the job was offered. Surprisingly, as far as the authorities were concerned, he turned it down, but it was logical from his point of view. For along with his wife, Sybil, he ran the bakers in the village, beginning work at 5am on six days of the week. There had been the odd occasion he'd been out on a major 'shout' at that ungodly hour, but because rarely would he have been in charge of the personnel at the incident, he'd been able to 'slip away' and attend to his ovens. If, however, in command – and he would always be so by virtue of his rank if he took charge of the station – then the option of a rapid return to the 'day job' would not present itself, he would have to see proceedings through to the end, and the bread would be late going into the ovens – thus the loaves would be long overdue going into their shop, and his customers already much reduced options regarding food for their families would be reduced even more. Crucially, his business would suffer – thus his answer to promotion was a firm 'no'.

So, if the senior leading fireman did not want the job, then clearly, highly inexperienced and young though he was, it had to be offered to the junior one. He firmly – and instantly – said "Yes," much to the delight of his father who had been so upset by the army's refusal to enlist him.

"In charge, boy – and not twenty-one. Wonderful, Darkie – wonderful achievement. And you'll have no problems, boy – at least, not ones you can't overcome. Proud of you, we are, your mother and me – and you'll make us even prouder, I don't doubt that."

Over the years which followed, Darkie was to do just that – certainly there was an 'old head' on his youthful shoulders, one with intelligence, sound judgment and a sense of what was right and wrong. Also he was a young man of courage and strong character; indeed his physical weakness impinged in no way upon the high standard of his overall performance as a fire brigade officer. However, his long term mastery of handling the myriad problems, emergencies, calamities, trivialities, absurdities which came the way of a rural fire brigade – something for which five years after the war he had established a sound and most high reputation – was down in no small measure to his short term experiences.

The term 'baptism of fire' proved to be apt to a degree which, had he foreseen it, would quite possibly have dissuaded him from ever going remotely near a fire engine. Darkie Dalton had attempted to enlist for King and country because he wanted to go to war; within weeks of taking command of the village fire brigade, war was to come to him and his valiant crew – war of a savage, frightening, mind-scarring nature. Not that it came directly to the village (though all felt the effects to a greater or lesser degree); rather those malevolent forces of destruction which were to blight, terrorise, and, indeed, end the lives of so many, passed overhead, carrying their loads of death and devastation, then deposited their deadly cargo some ten miles to the south. As most came at night, they were not to be seen; they were, though, easily heard, the drone of engines from hundreds of Luftwaffe bombers ensuring that few folk on the Peninsula would sleep – and assuredly none in Plymouth.

It was early March when it began, and in reality, it did not last long – though it seemed forever to the hardy citizens of that fine old port. The mighty Royal Naval dockyard was the main target, but the bombs did not discriminate – virtually all the city felt the vicious fury of the Nazis, with large parts totally destroyed.

Up until that time, the war had bothered the village fire brigade, directly, very little, though they had experienced a busy autumn and winter, the colder than normal weather causing a surfeit of chimney fires and one or two more serious – entire houses suffering considerable damage from substantial blazes, though fortunately nobody suffering from more than minor

j

injuries from the conflagrations. Thus did Darkie Dalton have a fairly hectic introduction into the responsibilities – and, on occasions, stresses – involved in being, firstly, in charge of the appliance, then after the doubling up of duties, being in charge of both the appliance and the station. This though did little to prepare him for what was to come – the blitz of Plymouth.

Within hours of the first raids, it became apparent to those in charge of public safety in the city that in no way could their own emergency services cope with destruction on such a scale; thus from all over the south west did emergency vehicles, appliances and crews descend on the city – ambulances, police reserves, home guard and, especially, fire brigades. Being close by, the village appliance was summoned and dispatched early on – "Which meant," as Darkie was to say for decades afterwards, and with some bitterness, "we spent longer watching Plymouth burn than most other crews." And how it burned; with incendiaries falling like hailstones, great areas of the city rapidly became infernos, cauldrons of fire which the gathered firemen (and there were many) could so often do little about. For the chilling realisation came rapidly to many of the crews from outside the city that they could not connect to the hydrants in order to attempt to douse the flames as their equipment was of a different gauge and, simply, would not fit; and so often when it did fit, there was no water to relay as the mains had become fractured under the intensity of the bombing.

First World War veteran Jan Jordan put it succinctly as they stood one terrible night beside their scorched appliance, impotently unable to make any significant contribution towards tackling the holocaust which was all around: "This is a bit like the Somme without the bullets."

The reality of the nights and days they spent in the shattered city – often without any real break except when exhaustion demanded sleep – was that they spent most of their time doing battle with rubble, searching for those buried in its midst. There were the occasional triumphs – joyous moments – when a man, woman or child were pulled from the dusty, brutal tombs, life still within them; but too often they were hauling forth corpses. Thus a grim task which instilled in them little other than despondency – except for hate.

Those desperate days and nights would stay in Darkie Dalton's memory for the rest of his life – not in the dark recesses either, but always close to the front, ever there not just because of the fearful, wanton destruction and the wicked loss of life, but because of their inability – through no fault of their own – to be able to do anything of significance to either prevent or mitigate it. This young man came of age standing, literally, with half a dozen stouthearted comrades, surveying a firestorm raging around them; his entire birthday, and the night and day following that, was spent in roughly the same place, they all doing their best, futile though generally it was, to alleviate the suffering and tragedy all around.

When he looked back to it, he was very much aware that those days saw him reach manhood in both the legal sense and in his mind set. Assuredly he grew up during those days, and he most certainly would never be quite the same again; and that included those who served with him. They had, in just a few days, seen more death, suffering, terror and destruction than most would see in a lifetime. They were to make many more forays into the city during the war years, but, fortunately their services were never needed in the way they had been during March 1941. This was basically a positive, of course, but to Darkie it did have a 'sod's law' element about it; for had their fire fighting expertise been required later, they would have been able to play a full part because the equipment would have fitted; government regulations ensuring that all such fire fighting paraphernalia throughout the land was of the same size and gauge.

The years since the war had seen Darkie lead a busy life, though one slightly impeded by his arthritic condition – which was getting worse, albeit slowly. However, generally the increasing physical problem affected him more when tilling the land than it did when directing operations in his sub-officer's uniform. It concerned him somewhat, as he was still only in his early thirties; thus many years, decades, in fact, of earning his daily bread lay ahead before he would draw his old age pension

– and he knew nothing other than horticulture (at which he was both efficient and reasonably successful). Assuredly, whilst his fire brigade activities brought him a modest stipend, it was, of course, the land that kept him, his wife Joy, and their two sons fed, clothed and housed. So he hoped and prayed his health would not deteriorate too much – sufficient to force him off the land, which would have been calamitous financially, or out of the fire brigade which would have greatly lessened his self esteem, plus, he felt, his standing in the parish.

Certainly a decade of being officer in charge at the station had given him a position of some influence and authority in the village, partly because it was, in the tight knit rural community, a role of some importance but mainly because he was able – indeed, excellent – at it. Whilst clearly never confronted by anything remotely like that faced during the blitz on Plymouth he did nonetheless, over the years, find himself in charge at some tricky, sometimes fraught, situations – and never once was he found wanting. House and chimney fires, barns and hay ricks ablaze, cornfields alight, cows and horses trapped in gulleys and confined spaces, the odd flooded cellar to be pumped out, increasingly road traffic accidents with, on a couple of occasions, passengers to be cut out (including two who were dead) – a miscellany of calamities and misfortunes which inevitably must come the way of a busy community of some 3000, many involved in hard physical work, especially on the land.

Darkie Dalton and his team had handled all these situations in a manner which had long since earned both the confidence and respect of the parish, and encouraged some to summon the brigade when it was not always easy to spot either danger or emergency in the incident they were called out to attend.

Such was the situation one breezy October morning the day following Tavistock Goose Fair. Darkie was working in his greenhouse situated at the bottom of his gently sloping land when the siren went. Although his speed was impaired slightly by his mild disability he would, if at work, usually be the first to arrive at the station – which was to be expected seeing as his workplace, even at its far extremity, was little more than a quarter mile from the station.

This day was no exception, he entering the rather shabby looking building at least a minute before anybody else would arrive. He went immediately to the office to check the nature of the incident they were to attend and its location. He ripped the sheet of paper from the printer, then groaned and shook his head; "Not again," said he to the empty office; then he brightened somewhat – there were positives. There was no rush, so they would not have to risk life and limb to get there, with bells clanging and sirens wailing, scattering all in their path, and when there, a nice pot of tea would be produced – and possibly some glorious saffron buns: there had been the last time, anyway. The rest of the crew arrived – or, at least, those who were available; four of the station's complement working, daily, away from the village, thus only available during evenings, at night and on weekends. Andy Paynter, who usually drove the appliance, stumbled into the office, somewhat breathless, as he had run the half mile from the local butchers where he worked, and promptly enquired:

"What is it?"

The sub-officer looked at him, then read out loud the message he held in his hand: "Proceed to Chapel Bungalow; Ernest Chapman stuck in tree and cannot get down,"

Paynter groaned – loudly. "No – no – not again. That must be the third – perhaps even the fourth time this year."

"Fourth, I fancy," replied the sub-officer with a smile – part disbelief, part resignation. "Still, there you go – we've been instructed to proceed, so that's what we'll do." He strode from the office, followed by the butcher, and was confronted by five other firemen who had just arrived – one on a cycle, one on a motorbike, Tadpole Drake in a battered old van whose tyres were as smooth as glass, and two more running. All asked, almost in unison, what the 'shout' was.

On hearing Darkie's terse response, they responded once more almost in unison – "No – not again."

"Well, look on the bright side, lads – it's a damned sight better than a barn fire; should be a cup of tea in it as well."

"Yes, that's true, and last time dear old Mrs Chapman brought out some home made saffron buns as well – lovely they were, too," commented Tadpole – very much a 'sweet tooth' – with some enthusiasm.

"Well, let's get going." Darkie looked at young Johnny Lomax; "You the last to arrive, boy?" He did not know he was, but Johnny who always ran to the station, and carried a little too much weight, usually brought up the rear. "Sorry then, boy, but we've got a full crew – daren't carry more than six. We'll leave you to lock up the station – then you can go back to whatever you were doing."

Lomax nodded. He was not too disappointed to be returning home because, as he had a day off work, he had had a long lie-in, and had been in the middle of devouring a mighty fry-up when the siren had sounded. Knowing his doting mother would have put it in the oven to keep warm in anticipation of a quite speedy return, it would await him.

The others clambered aboard the appliance, and started to dress in their heavy gear – all, that is, except Andy Paynter, who put on his helmet, started the engine, steered it out onto the road and proceeded at a quite leisurely pace in the direction of Chapel Bungalow and the unfortunate Ernest Chapman.

"How is it, Darkie, we get called out like this? I mean, it's not an emergency, is it? No way is it an emergency. How does Mrs Chapman convince them it is? Not that there's anything necessarily wrong with us doing it, but they often charge for non-emergencies – quite a bit, as well. I remember a few months back, that fellow down by the river – he's not lived there long. Anyway, he locked himself out and lost his keys; there was no emergency about it – and he was the first to admit it. We got him in all right, but it was a fair caper. Whatever, the brigade billed him for it, I'm told, so why doesn't it happen with Ernest?" The driver was mystified.

" 'Cause I fancy brigade headquarters, and control, think he's a young lad – so, perhaps, in danger."

The driver laughed. "Yes, I see what you mean; it's funny the way, when she phones through, she always refers to him as Ernest

Chapman. I don't know if she does it with the intention of fooling anybody."

"No – no, not Mrs Chapman," retorted Darkie, vehemently; "no, it's just her way – she's very formal; very polite and courteous, a true lady; one of the old school. I mean, she will use the word 'mister' when she speaks to us – no Christian names with her, even if she knows them. It would seem only natural and right to give the full name of someone she sees as a member of her family – so, Ernest Chapman."

The driver nodded. "Yes, I see what you mean, and you're right – she is a lady; not many about like her, sadly. She was a schoolmistress back before the First World War – taught my father. She's well into her eighties now."

"And mine – he thought the world of her did dad; very kind and a good teacher. Gave up teaching when she married old Archie; a man of many parts he was – a piano tuner and will writer amongst them; and in his spare time he conducted the village brass band and did a bit of wort charming too. Good he was – he certainly got rid of mine; been dead a few years now."

Without too much ado, they pulled up outside the Chapel Bungalow. A rotund, though very tiny figure (she was fractionally under five feet tall) was standing in the narrow front garden awaiting them. Alighting from the appliance – just the driver remaining with the vehicle – they entered through the small front gate and were confronted by a concerned Mrs Chapman.

"Oh, Mr Dalton, thank you so much for coming – and you other gentlemen as well, of course. It is so very kind of you. I'm afraid Ernest has been very naughty again; the same branch on the old elm. I don't know how many times it's been in recent years he's got stuck there."

She turned away and walked as fast as her short, slightly rheumatic legs would take her, around the side of the smallish bungalow towards the sizeable back garden, five assorted firemen following her.

"It has been a regular occurrence in the last couple of years, Mrs Chapman, I must say that," stated the sub-officer in a slightly disapproving tone. "It could be that brigade control might query our attendance here in an emergency capacity, and class it as performing a non-emergency service and, well – charge for it."

It was the first time he had ever brought forward the possibility of a charge being made, but he felt it only right and fair to do so, as an authority always looking at ways to limit expenditure – and raise income – would surely realise that the village fire crew could not continue, at ever decreasing intervals – and considerable expense – to be dispatched to Chapel Bungalow to rescue Ernest Chapman from a tree. Mr Chapman would either have to stop climbing trees or learn how to climb down from them – or pay the fees involved in being rescued by the fire brigade.

"I quite understand, Mr Dalton – it is very naughty of me to keep phoning for your assistance, it's also very naughty of Ernest to keep climbing up there. He's getting old, that's the problem. Even, say, three years ago he would have been able to get down from there – jump down, in fact – with relative ease, but not now. It's not as if it's very high up, is it?"

As she spoke the last words, they turned the corner of the bungalow, and gazed across the back garden, an area of somewhat neglected lawn dominated by a fine old elm tree. Clinging to one of the lower branches – his branch – no more than twelve feet from the ground was Ernest Chapman.

"There he is, the naughty boy." She stared up into the tree. "You are very, very naughty, Ernest – again I've had to ask Mr Dalton and these other kind gentlemen to come and rescue you. One day they might say no – what will you do then?"

There was no reply from a quite elderly ginger tom cat clinging on grimly atop a narrowish branch of the elm. There was, though, upon his face an expression of pure malevolence – not one to forget old foes, was Ernest. He and the fire brigade had established an increasingly poor relationship over the years; increasingly stiff his limbs might well be, but his memory was as sharp as ever. Eventually Ernest did deign to reply, however – with a loud and long hiss.

"All this palaver over a cat," opined Tadpole Drake bringing up the rear of the gathered throng – a comment he made invariably, and with which no one ever argued.

"Well, Mrs Chapman, we'd better get to work and rescue poor old Ernest from his perch; he looks none too happy up there. Tell you what ma'am, it being mid-morning and a fair time since we had our breakfast and a brave while to go yet to dinner, a nice cup of tea would be appreciated."

This good lady who had been standing as if transfixed by the, not rare, sight of her cat clinging grimly, and crossly to the bough, suddenly snapped out of her stressed reverie, and looked at the sub-officer. "Oh, Mr Dalton, what must you think of me – I'll go right in and put the kettle on. I should have done so already, but I've been so concerned about poor Ernest. As one gets older, I'm afraid one's constant companion is worry. I do so worry and fret over things which just a few years ago I would have taken in my stride. I'm off to the kitchen now to make some tea."

"That's very kind, Mrs Chapman – much appreciated. By the time you've made it we should have Ernest down out of the tree and ready to tackle the local rats and mice" – though more likely birds, Darkie mused to himself.

The elderly homeowner tottered off towards the back door, then inside to the kitchen to make a brew, leaving the crew to bring her cat to earth. No sooner had she disappeared from view than a question came the way of the sub-officer:

"Usual drill, Darkie?"

He nodded. "Yes – usual drill, but, as always, we need to be quick – get old Ernest down before Mrs Chapman comes back."

With that, a couple of the men, without being instructed, ran back towards the appliance in the road whilst Darkie gave specific instructions to Tadpole, who had been the cause of the 'usual drill'. A couple of years earlier, he had been part of the complement than manned an appliance sent to stand-by in Plymouth when the city brigade had a major shout on. Just the day before, his face had been scratched quite badly – and most noticeably – by Ernest whilst attempting to rescue the ill-tempered beast from his lofty eyrie; he was not the first member of the brigade who had been assaulted by Ernest – nor, indeed, by other cats as well. Enquiring as to the cause of Tadpole's injuries, and being relieved to learn it was not the result of a domestic dispute, a leading fireman within the city brigade had informed the visiting village crew of the drill to be followed to fetch cats from trees, avoid personal injury and complete the operation swiftly.

"Always works if they're no more than say twenty feet off the ground," the junior officer had stated with confidence.

Darkie had taken note of the suggestion, and his crew had, on the seven times since then they had been summoned to rescue felines better at climbing than descending, used the 'special drill' method on four occasions (successfully each time), including the past three rescues of Ernest. It was of some importance, however, to keep the method of rescue from the eyes of loving owners as not all would have been totally content with the new process of rescue, even though they would be fully satisfied with the results.

Thus was Tadpole instructed, by the officer in charge, to loiter, as inconspicuously as possible, near the back door of the bungalow and to raise the alarm if Mrs Chapman was showing signs of reappearing before Ernest's rescue had been completed.

The two fellows who had gone out to the appliance appeared around the corner of the bungalow, one of them, Roy Travis, unfurling a length of hose; he continued to do so until it had run its length, ending close to the elm. Then from under his arm he took a large, brass nozzle and clipped it firmly into the end of the hose; he was joined by his partner, Bart Boston (eternally known as such by all, including his parents, who after giving him such a grandiose Christian name as Bartholomew realised they were not too sure as to how it should be spelt), who also placed his hands on the business end of the hose. They glanced in the direction of Darkie, who gave a brief, almost, imperceptible nod of the head.

"Water on," they chorused at the top of their voices – certainly loud enough to reach the ears of Andy Paynter who was stood by the hydrant no more than twenty-five yards from Mrs Chapman's front gate. (It was a small bonus that in a parish desperately short of fire hydrants – an issue the sub-officer was always raising with the highest authority, with singular lack of success – that there was one so close to this property where in recent times it had been often needed.) The driver turned on the hydrant, then awaited further instructions. Spluttering – seemingly gasping – the water rapidly filled the hose, then surged through the nozzle held in the firm grip of the two firemen. Leaning back, they raised the nozzle and the powerful jet arched upwards towards the lower branches of the elm; then, eyeing Ernest Chapman – still gazing out malevolently at the world, and hissing – they directed the jet in his direction. Their aim was good, striking the old creature on his left hand side; Ernest wobbled on his narrowish refuge, then toppled over and hurtled towards the tufty, moss-strewn lawn below. As cats usually do, he landed on all fours – then kept very still.

"Water off," cried Darkie Dalton, and as soon as his command had been obeyed, rushed towards the prostrate feline pulling an old towel from inside his tunic – the one always kept in the cab of the appliance and which fulfilled manifold purposes. He quickly picked up the still prostrate Ernest and began to rub him quite vigorously – even the trusting Mrs Chapman might well ask questions as to why her dear pet was sopping wet on a cool but dry morning, following a similar night.

He had been rubbing the fur on the ginger tom for some thirty seconds when it occurred to him that Ernest, usually the most boisterous – even savage – of beasts, in such a situation, was offering no resistance at all. He stopped rubbing, held the cat away from him and, for the first time since the operation had begun, looked intently at the creature. There was no sign of life.

Darkie Dalton was a man with nerves of iron, but he felt a cold, numbing panic begin to creep over him. He laid Ernest on the ground, then knelt down beside him – still there was no movement from the cat – indeed, not the slightest intimation of life.

Tadpole, who had been watching proceedings, sensed there was something wrong so promptly abandoned his vigil at the back door, striding rapidly across the lawn towards the prostrate Ernest.

The two who had manned the hose were about to join them when Tadpole, far more in control of matters than was the officer in charge, turned to them in urgent, though by no means loud tones: "Get rid of that hose before Mrs Chapman comes out – she mustn't see it; we're all in trouble if she does."

Seeing the wisdom in his words, the pair rapidly hauled the length of hose around the side of the bungalow and out of sight of the elderly owner before proceeding to roll it up. Tadpole, meanwhile, joined a somewhat traumatised Darkie.

The sub-officer glanced at his companion then down at Ernest laid long and still on the grass. "I think he's dead, Tadpole – good God, I think we've done for him."

Tadpole knelt down briefly before the prostrate cat, then got to his feet. "Yes – yes, sorry Darkie – I think you're right. No sign of life in him; he's gone I'm afraid. Old cat, of course – probably had a heart attack."

The sub-officer shook his head. "No matter if he did – I killed him, boy; I'm to blame. If we'd brought him down in the proper way he'd be fine, I'm sure of that. All right, we might have had a few scratches from the old devil, but he'd be alive and well. Now he's gone – and poor old Mrs Chapman has lost her only companion in life. I'm to blame, Tadpole – me, and nobody else. I feel so, so bad about this."

"Come on Darkie – that's the way things go. It's a shame, yes – it would have been better had it not happened, but that's life – and death, of course. Who knows, he might still have died even if we'd brought him down on a ladder. He's an old cat; it could be simply his time had come. Dammit, Darkie, back in the war we saw scores of dead – people, not animals; terrible sights some of them, children amongst them. We took it in our stride, didn't we? Upsetting and dreadful though it was, we just carried on and did our best. So if we can do that in the face of people dying – some, terrible deaths – then we can handle the passing of an old cat, can't we?"

"It's different, boy, don't you see? It's true about the terrible things we saw in the war – the deaths, the suffering, the destruction; but we weren't to blame for it. When it comes to Ernest, we are to blame – no, no not we, but me, I'm to blame. I gave the orders to knock him out of the tree with a hose, so I'm to blame – totally – and I'll. . ." His lament of self condemnation was suddenly interrupted.

"Is everything all right, Mr Dalton? Is Ernest all right?"

All male heads turned instantly at the sound of the elderly female voice. Mrs Chapman was standing immediately behind them, although the sight of her dear stricken pet was hidden from view by assorted leggings and booted legs.

"Is there something wrong with Ernest? I see he's down from the tree, but I don't see him in the garden. He is all right, isn't he?"

The diminutive lady, who had come out of the back door to see what was happening, was most concerned to note a group of firemen who, by their demeanor, gave the impression that not all had gone to plan. For a very few seconds there was silence. It was about to be broken by Darkie Dalton who was going to say – he knew not what. But it was, in fact, broken by Tadpole Drake who handled a desperately fraught situation quite superbly. But then, if anybody could talk them out of what had the real potential of being a development which could bring them all grief – Darkie especially, of course – then Tadpole was the man. Some twenty years older than the sub-officer – thus better versed in the vagaries of life and human nature – he had always been a quick witted man who had honed his skills with fellow human beings thanks to a variety of jobs over the years which had him dealing with folk – door to door salesman, milkman, postman and barman being amongst them. His failure to make great progress in the working world in terms of either finance or status was down largely to the 'Rolling Stone's avoidance of moss' syndrome. Darkie Dalton, though, was to say to his dying day that had it not been for Tadpole's quick wit and articulate tongue that day, his career as a fire brigade officer would have come to an abrupt and dishonourable halt.

Turning abruptly, Tadpole faced the distressed lady, took her gently by the arm, steered her away from the body of her pet, and said in soft, sympathetic tones, "Mrs Chapman, I'm so desperately sorry to tell you that dear Ernest has passed away; we believe he must have suffered a heart attack – probably not an unusual occurrence in a cat of his age. It was such a shock for us all – in fact, I think we're all feeling it greatly. Sub-officer Dalton, who is very good at first aid, did all he could to revive Ernest but it was no good – his heart had stopped and sadly that was the end for him. A terrible blow for you, Mrs Chapman – and for us in a way; we're here to save and preserve life, animal as well as human; we really are very, very sorry and sad about it all."

The firemen listening to Tadpole's brief soliloquy to Mrs Chapman – regular filmgoers all – reckoned that Laurence Oliver could not have delivered the quite eloquent, well chosen words with any greater conviction, solemnity and sincerity.

For several seconds Mrs Chapman stood still, silent, her expression devoid of any emotion. Eventually she looked at Tadpole – "Thank you, Mr Drake," then looking the way of Darkie, "and you Mr Dalton," then at the rest of the crew, "and you other gentlemen, of course; you are always so kind, helpful and understanding." She lapsed briefly, then continued, "I am a deep believer, gentlemen. I taught in Sunday school for many years – as some of you know, because I remember teaching you when you were boys – I certainly taught you Mr Dalton. I retired from that some years ago, of course, but I still go to the chapel most Sundays, unless poorly. I believe totally that matters of life and death are in the hands of the Lord – and I believe that applies to animals as well as to people. He saw that Ernest had run his race – he was very old, you know; older than I am in cat years; so he clearly thought that the time had come to remove him from this world, into the next. And when I really think about it, his time had come; he was a lovely pet at his best, a dear friend to me – and oh, how I will miss him. But he has been a cause of worry these past couple of years in different ways – his habit of getting stuck up in the elm tree and me having to bother you gentlemen to get him down not the least of them. And, I'm sorry to say that though in the past he has always been the cleanest of cats, for a while now he has decided on occasions – especially if the weather was bad – to do his business in the bungalow rather than in the garden, which is most unpleasant. So, the more I think of it, I would have to say it's probably a blessing that he's gone – and in such a painless way; at least, I imagine it was."

Darkie Dalton nodded so fiercely his head was in danger of

falling off – "Oh yes, Mrs Chapman, totally painlessly – instantaneously, in fact, as Tadpole – er, Mr Drake – said, his, his, his, heart just gave out. We are still so very sorry though. If there's anything we can do, in any way, then please say."

It was one of the stock phrases, and though sincerely meant, Darkie did not expect a positive reply. In that he was wrong.

"Well, yes, there is perhaps something you could do, Mr Dalton – you and the other gentlemen; perhaps you would bury Ernest for me. I'd not find it easy to dig the pit – and I know that even if physically I could do so, I would find it most distressing."

The sub-officer, briefly, was a touch nonplussed by such an answer, but rapidly pulled himself together, and responded, aware that thanks to Mrs Chapman's stoicism, courtesy and forbearance he, and to a much lesser extent, his crew, had seemingly avoided any unwelcome (though probably deserved) consequences from their unconventional – and undoubtedly unacceptable – method of removing cats from trees. "Yes, of course, Mrs Chapman," he replied after a pause, "we'll do that right away – though I wish we didn't have to," added he, hastily. "I wish Ernest, was still with us" – not the total truth. "You tell us where to bury him and we'll get on with it."

"I've got a little pet's cemetery down the corner of the garden, just behind a tall, unproductive row of old raspberry canes. You cannot miss it; there are several different graves there – four cats, one dog, and two budgies. They're all marked with wooden stakes stuck in the ground above them, each one bearing the name of the pet buried there. If you would find an empty space down there – and there's quite a bit – and bury poor Ernest, it would be so much appreciated." She stopped talking for a few seconds, gazing ahead into the distance, then she turned to Darkie and said, simply, "Mr Dalton, I would like to see Ernest for one last time if I may."

"Of course, ma'am." The sub-officer quickly moved across to below the elm, picked up the body of the ginger cat and slowly brought it forward for his elderly owner to look at.

Mrs Chapman did not touch Ernest – rather she gazed down upon his corpse, laying in the fireman's hands; she nodded, wiped a few tears from her eyes with a handkerchief that had been stuffed in her apron pocket, thanked Darkie for his kindness, then started to walk slowly towards the back door; she stopped, suddenly, and half turned:

"When you gentlemen have buried Ernest, there will be a cup of tea for you all in the kitchen; and some saffron buns – they're quite fresh, as I only baked them yesterday afternoon."

Her ears filled with enthusiastic expressions of thanks, she again moved off towards the back door to Chapel Bungalow; again she stopped and half turned.

"Oh, Mr Dalton, one other thing – perhaps you would be so kind as to pull off that small branch hanging down, partially broken, from the elm; it looks a touch untidy. I think it's only just happened, so I can only think your colleagues accidentally struck it with their jet of water a little earlier. Still, it's the first time that has happened; you never did any damage with your hoses on the previous occasions you rescued Ernest."

The old lady re-entered her bungalow leaving behind her a group of men stunned, temporarily, into both silence and inaction as the relevance of the words she had just spoken swept over them. Recovering themselves, they continued with their work of clearing up and then packing away, into the appliance, the equipment used in the abortive attempt to rescue, successfully, Ernest Chapman. All were exceedingly subdued.

Everything done, all accounted for, they filed silently and most sheepishly into Mrs Chapman's small abode to receive victuals which, assuredly, they did not deserve. One thing for sure – which had lodged itself in the minds of each man – was that the 'usual drill' had suddenly been consigned to history.

# IX

# Christmas Shopping

Joe Foster pushed away the cleared plate, leant back on the kitchen chair, then picked up the mug of strong, very sweet tea standing before him on the bare table. He drank deeply of it, returned it from whence it had come then sighed mightily – he felt very content. This was a part of the day he always enjoyed, especially on a fresh, late autumn morning such as this. The milking and early feeding having been done, and the laden churns taken out to the rough-hewn platform beside the road to await collection by the lorry from the dairy, he had come into a kitchen well warmed by an elderly Rayburn, had consumed one of his Beryl's magnificent 'fry-ups', was tackling the ample contents of a nearby teapot, and did not need to return to his daily routine in the yard for the best part of half an hour.

Such a benign mind-set was not to last too long, however – due to a pronouncement, then a statement of intent, which was destined to come forth from the lips of his wife of some thirty-five years. Finishing her own cup of tea, she looked intently at her husband.

"They were on about Christmas on the wireless just before you came in, Joe – saying it's not much more than a month away."

"True enough, maid," her husband concurred. "But it's no great secret is it? I mean, Christmas comes the same time every year and seeing as we are now in the second half of November, then, clearly, there's not much more than a month to go. Not the biggest surprise or news item in the world, though, is it?" He snorted as he said the words, grinned broadly, then drank some more tea.

"No, of course it's not," retorted Beryl, a little testily. "I know when Christmas is, Joe, obviously. It's just that time goes so quickly – it'll soon be here. And I feel I'm not ready for it. There's so much to do."

"You say that every year, maid – yet you always are. You always have been. You're a born organiser, a master when it comes to coping with things – again, you always have been. There's been some difficult times come your way over the years – some real crises, in fact – but you've always handled them, sorted them out, and never panicked. So I don't know why you're so concerned now – it's no bigger deal now than it's ever been, surely?"

"No, it's not in one sense. But I've been feeling for some time now that it's time we got back to making it a bit special again – got back to making it like it was before the war. For the past ten years or so it's not been special, in a way. Yes, it's always a nice time. A time, even back in the war, when you felt you could relax just a little bit – just indulge yourself and your family a little. But it was only a modicum, of course – it was a touch better than the everyday hardships and problems, but not a lot. Now, though, at last I feel we can move forward – not just us two, but everybody. The war's been over for more than five years now, so it really is time for folk to move on, to enjoy Christmas again; have a few treats, give proper presents. Yes, I know many things are still rationed – which is shameful in itself. I sometimes wonder what we gained from winning the war, from all the heartache, the sacrifice, the worry, the tragedies that came the way of so many of us. I sometimes wonder it if was ever worthwhile."

"Oh, it was worthwhile, maid. Just think where we'd be now if we hadn't fought and won it – either dead or in some prison or concentration camp or suchlike. Certainly if we were alive, our existence – and it would be miserable, you can be certain of that – our existence, everything we did, would be dominated by the Germans. Dictated by them. Oh, it was worthwhile, all right." Joe Foster said the words softly, but with rare gravity.

His wife acquiesced instantly: "Yes, of course it was; and I know it was. We had to fight the war; and win it. And we did, thank heavens. It's just that in 1945 I don't think anybody would believe we'd have to go short of so many things for so long in the future. But that's the way it's been – and I suppose, it's the way it's been for most folk throughout the country. One thing about living on the land, of course, is that we're not going to go short of basic food. And we've been able at times – certainly at Christmas – to give the odd nice bit of food to family and suchlike, all of which, I know, has been much appreciated."

"Like pork," said Joe. "At least these days we can do it legally – there's nothing to stop us killing the odd pig now. Different back in the war, and for a while after, of course. Could have been locked up for it then, in theory at least." He laughed as he said the words, drained his cup, then reached for teapot, milk and sugar to replenish.

"It's not funny, Joe," retorted his wife, angrily. "I always thought it was very wrong, although I have to admit I was as bad as anybody as I always used the cuts you brought whether it was our own pig or a neighbour's. It was a case of 'when needs must, the Devil drives', I suppose. But I always felt so guilty about it – so ashamed – and still do. The man who really should feel shame, though, is PC Barton. I mean, not only did he turn a blind eye to it, he would always have a piece himself."

"The first cut, as well – and always one of the best." The farmer laughed. "Good old Claude – he always seemed to know if and when one had been killed – and where. The good thing was, mind you, that once he'd had a bit he was implicated. He couldn't take any action against anybody even if he'd wanted to. In fact, he had far more to lose than any of us. If we'd been caught, we'd have probably only been fined – if he'd been caught he'd have lost his job, his house and his pension. That would have been a massive price to pay for a piece of pork – no matter how big. Still, I know for a fact that on occasions he would buy insurance by passing on part of his share of the meat to the Inspector in Tavistock. Clever move. No fool, old Claude. Many think he is to a certain extent, but they're wrong. He's always had it worked out."

"It was shameful, Joe – corruption, that's the only word for it. And I feel ashamed of myself for my involvement – I always will. Too late now, of course, but if I had my time over again, I'd have no part in it. I'd rather go hungry."

"No great harm to it, maid – just country life, nothing more than that really," stated her husband, urbanely. He did, though, avoid her eye for whilst he felt no great guilt about it, he was aware she was right. He also knew that she did, indeed, feel shame that she cooked, and ate, pork which came her way in such nefarious circumstances. A lady of much conscience and rectitude was Beryl Foster – an aspect of her character her husband respected, indeed, admired.

"Still, as I said just now, I've been thinking about Christmas, Joe – and not just since they mentioned how quickly it's coming upon us on the wireless earlier. No, I've been thinking for a while that it's time for us all to make a greater effort to make Christmas really special again, like it was before the war. Obviously it was impossible during the war years – there was so much else to worry about, to occupy our time and our minds. And you could get precious little of anything and I don't just mean food and drinks. Toys for the children were so hard to get hold of. You often had to settle for second hand, or buy something somebody local had made – and not always made well either. And for the first few years after, things weren't much better. Now, though, I feel that at last we might well have turned the corner – not just us, personally, but everybody, this whole country. Things are still not easy, mind you, but there are goods about now that weren't there just, say, six months ago. So I think we should give real thought to Christmas this year – to getting quality presents for Jane and Arnie and for the grandchildren, of course. At the WI a couple of weeks ago they were saying how one or two more shops have opened up in Plymouth, along with the ones that opened about six months ago. They've still a long way to go before they finish re-building the shopping centre, of course. It'll take them years yet. But that it's beginning to take place the way it is, is good – certainly it's well ahead of what was predicted just after the war. They said then it would take probably fifteen years to get

212

Plymouth back in decent shape – which was understandable when you consider the pounding it took from Hitler."

"Worst bombed city in Britain," her husband interjected. "Folk forget that – they talk about Coventry, London, Hull and suchlike, but for its size, it was the worst bombed place in the land. They even bombed Home Park." He spoke the last five words in bitter tones – demolishing a large part of the home of his beloved Plymouth Argyle was truly an act beyond forgiveness.

"Yes – yes, I know Joe – you make that comment just about every time the name of Plymouth is mentioned." – Which was not without some truth (though exaggerated). The farmer had long been aggrieved that the great dockyard city which had made such sacrifices towards the war effort had never had them fully acknowledged, or appreciated, by Government – or the nation as a whole. And not just the last one either. The immense contribution of the ancient port towards the security and prosperity of the nation went back to before the routing of the Spanish Armada by Sir Francis Drake. "And what you say is true – I'll not argue with that. But the Government clearly has made quite a bit of money available for re-building, and that's what they're doing – which is good. I've not been to Plymouth for about three months now; even though new shops had opened there was not a lot in them the last time I was there. But again they were saying at the WI that a lot of new goods have come into them in recent weeks. At last there are clothes and – and – so much more to buy. In two or three years time, of course, there'll be far more than there is now, but the important thing at present is that there could be some nice things to buy for people. I'd like to get some clothes for Jane – and for little Peggy and Louise. And some new toys for Arnie's James. Something different for Arnie himself too, something better than a bottle of drink."

"Better than a bottle of drink?" Joe Foster spoke the words in tones of incredulity. "Better than a bottle of drink?" He repeated, still finding it difficult to believe he'd heard his spouse speak such words. "What, Beryl, could be better than that at Christmas? We gave Arnie a bottle of Scotch last year – a bottle of Scotch, maid. Just think about it. What a present. To a man who likes his

k

whisky – and Arnie's like me, he loves a drop of Scotch – there could be no better present. And think of the trouble I had getting it. Whisky was virtually unobtainable during the war, and whilst it's been a touch easier to get these past couple of years, you still have to ask around a bit – and hope. Billy Baldwin at the Tamar View got hold of a bottle, as you know – it was expensive too. Broke my heart to give it to Arnie to tell the truth – I've not had my fair share of Scotch for years. You talk about something being better than a bottle of drink – nothing, Beryl, nothing in this world is better than the gift of a bottle of Scotch; nothing we can afford, anyway." He added the final few words somewhat hastily, aware that there were better gifts – but all would be infinitely more expensive.

"Yes, true Joe, whisky was a nice present for Arnie – he enjoying the occasional tipple." She was aware as she said the words that the use of 'occasional' was none too accurate; her son, like her husband, being a keen and regular imbiber of many different alcoholic drinks (though none to excess). Indeed, the bar of the Tamar View Inn would host both of them for periods of three or four evenings most weeks, their son who was an agricultural engineer, living in the village with his wife and their grandson. "But to me it never seems a proper present. Somehow, nothing you can eat or drink seems really appropriate as a gift, either at Christmas or for a birthday. True, in recent times with everything being so short – so rare – good drink and rich foods have been good gifts. They've been good things to receive on their own account, and also filled the void in that there has been so little about in terms of clothes, cosmetics, shoes, toiletries, even books – and, of course, toys for the children. Now, though, as I said just a moment ago, things are beginning to change for the better, with there being nice things coming into the shops. Nothing like there was before the War, mind you, but a vast amount more than there's been in the past ten, eleven years. Not that we bought much of what was available back in the thirties – we never had the money then. Not many people did when you look back. Perhaps that was why there always seemed to be plenty about – few could afford to actually buy it! These days it's the opposite. Many folk, like ourselves – though not well off – have a few pounds in our pockets at last, and can afford to buy something nice, something a bit different for special times like Christmas, but there's been so little to buy. Now it's changing, and I feel we should take advantage. Look around, see what's about, and buy if we fancy it – and it's not too expensive, of course. I keep an eye on the shops in Tavistock, regularly – had a good look around when I went in with you last Wednesday week when you took that heifer to market. I saw one or two new lines there which had just come in – things to keep in mind. But before I buy anything there, I want to have a look around Plymouth and see what they've got to offer – for Jane, Arnie, the grandchildren; and for myself too, for that matter. I've had no decent new clothes for years – I deserve some after all this time. But I don't want to do it all on my own. I want your help, Joe, both with ideas and being there – being there when I actually buy things. I want you to see things, give your opinion – I don't want to do it all myself. So I reckon we should go shopping in Plymouth, say, this Saturday – you and me. We could go down by train if you didn't want to take the car in. We could get in there late morning, have a bit of dinner, then have a look around the shops. Then, if we went by train, we could come home on the one that goes about four o'clock, and you'd still be home in time to help Tiddler Tom with the milking."

"What – what – go to Plymouth; Shopping?" The words were spoken in broken, almost strangulated tones so great was the farmer's shock over such a suggestion. "I mean – I mean – I've not been shopping in Plymouth for years; since before the war. I wouldn't know what I was doing – I wouldn't have the slightest idea what to look for or suggest for anybody. I'd be more trouble than I'm worth. If you fancy a day in Plymouth, then why not. And if there's some clothes you fancy for yourself, then buy them. Like you say, it's a long time since you had anything new. Take Jane with you – she'd enjoy a day out, I'm sure. And a woman needs another woman's advice when buying clothes, not a man's. No, get hold of Jane – she'd be delighted, I'm sure. What with the kids and all the work she does with Sid on their smallholding, she doesn't get out much at all. And things are a bit tight with them as well – their soft fruit's been hammered by the weather these past couple of years, so they've not made much. No, she'd enjoy a day out, I'm sure."

"Yes, I'm sure she would, Joe – but I'm not going to ask her to come for the simple reason she's one of the ones I want us to buy for. I want to get her some clothes – a pretty young woman like her, only just turned thirty, it will lift her no end to have something new, something stylish and fashionable. And I don't want to buy just for her, or for myself. There are the grandchildren, as I said earlier; and my sister Pauline in Tavistock and her husband Bas. And others, too, when I think about it. Rollo and Tiddler Tom come to mind."

"What – Rollo and Tiddler Tom? What do you mean, maid – we've never bought for them. Rather we've always seen they get plenty of Christmassing from here, from off the farm."

Indeed, the Fosters' long-serving duo of workers had long since had much of their Christmas fare provided by their employers. Rollo had worked continuously for them for over twenty years, whilst Tiddler Tom (so named because of his diminutive stature – five feet two inches tall and just eight stone in weight) worked there from school for about eight years right up to the war then, unlike most who worked the land, eschewed his right to be classified as working in a reserved occupation, preferring to sign up for the Devonshire Regiment. Despite his lack of size, he had spent most of his very honourable war service (being mentioned in despatches) driving a tank for Montgomery's legendary Eighth Army in North Africa and Italy. A tough, resilient and valiant man was Tiddler Tom; Joe and Beryl's delight at welcoming him back to the farm after his demobilisation in early 1946 was matched only by his pleasure in returning.

"Even when Tiddler Tom was away through the war we always made sure that his family and their two children still got their Christmas fare – appreciated it was too, though it was the least we could do, him away fighting for King and Country – even though he could so easily have got out of it. They look forward to their Christmassing, maid – it suits them down to the ground. They don't want a present as such – they want something they can eat and drink, and we certainly provide that. A nice capon – and they're coming on well this year – a hundred weight of spuds that'll keep them going for weeks, swedes, brussels, a few eggs and to wash it down, a flagon or two of scrumpy, made here on the farm. A powerful brew it is, too this year. I'll be going round with it Christmas Eve – that's been the routine for years. There's so much of it, it almost fills up the van."

"Yes, I know all that, Joe, and I'm sure it's very much appreciated. And I'm not saying we shouldn't continue to give them spuds, veg and suchlike. But a proper present would be nice – something that's still around in a week or two, not eaten. I feel we've all of us got to move away from this wartime attitude and mindset, where everything was geared towards food and survival. We've got to move on, and I'm determined to do so."

Clearly she was, and when she made her mind up to do something, Beryl Foster was not easily dissuaded, a fact her husband knew very, very well indeed.

"So this Saturday, Joe, I want to go to Plymouth – and I expect you to come with me. And in the meantime, I want you to think of presents for family and friends, and think beyond what can be eaten."

The farmer sat upright, suddenly, as if high voltage electricity had passed through him.

"Saturday? Saturday? I can't go shopping on Saturday," he cried. "Argyle are home – playing Nottingham Forest. Big game, Saturday."

"So what? Every match played at Home Park is a big game according to you, Joe," came the uncompromising response.

"So what? Why, they're top of the league – it really is a big game. Good side, Forest."

"And Argyle are a poor one who are nearly bottom – which means they'll almost certainly lose so I would have thought it would be a relief to have an excuse to miss it." Beryl in this vein was more than a match for her husband.

"No reason why they should lose, though they'll be up against it, true. It's always good to see one of the better sides, though –

and – and – and Argyle often play better against the top sides."
He really was now marshalling ever weaker arguments.

"Nonsense, Joe," retorted his wife. "It seems to me that lately
no matter where a team are in the league, Argyle usually play
badly – and even more regularly, manage to lose."

"There's something in that, true. Certainly they've had no luck
this season – none at all. With a bit of decent luck – a decent run
on the ball, they'd be half way up the table; even higher, possibly.
Nothing seems to go for them, though – and the referees they get
at Home Park. . . Well, I fancy half of them must travel with the
away team."

"You said much the same last year, Joe, when, I think I'm right
in saying, they finished fourth from bottom and only narrowly
missed being relegated. And the year before that, wasn't it only
fifth from bottom they ended? Didn't they avoid the third division
by just two or three points?" Beryl was taking no hostages; She
was very well aware of her husband's remarkable myopia, short
memory, forgiveness, optimism, sentimentality and sheer
illogicality when it came to the fortunes (or, more usually,
misfortunes) of Plymouth Argyle Football Club.

"Well, yes – true. The past few seasons haven't been too good,
I have to say." Momentarily he lapsed into silence, but before
Beryl could launch another verbal assault, he returned to his
defence – "It's at times like these, though, they need the
support. Anybody can follow a side when they're winning –
when they're losing, though, that's when they need people
behind them. A lot of folk have turned their back on Argyle in
the past two or three years, just 'cause they've not had the sort
of success they had back in the thirties. I'm not one of those,
maid, as you well know – I've followed them ever since I was a
young lad when my father first took me, and there's no way I'll
stop now. It's a bit like marriage – through thick and thin, for
better for worse."

His wife looked aghast. "Like marriage? You cannot really
mean that, Joe – this is a football team, not a partner for life. You
did not go to church and pledge yourself before God to lifelong
devotion and loyalty to – in fact, love of – Plymouth Argyle. Like

218

marriage, indeed – you should be ashamed of yourself for saying such a thing, really you should."

As soon as the words had left his lips, the farmer had realised they were, at best, way beyond rationality, at worst offensive. He wasted no time in apologising.

"Sorry, maid, that was a daft thing to say, it really was – and I really am sorry. I got carried away a bit. Of course, it's not like marriage – I know that. But it's important nonetheless, I feel that folk who follow the club should remain loyal to them, especially when things aren't going well. It's – it's – well, it's like being loyal to an old friend, isn't it?" The final words were posed more as a plea than a question, and his wife responded with a modicum of sympathy – or so her tone implied.

"Yes, that's so to some extent, Joe – I can fully see that. But it's not your supreme loyalty in life – and from what you said just now, you know it. Nor should it be your priority. That, this Saturday, will be a visit to Plymouth to help me select, buy and carry Christmas presents – and that's what we're going to do." It was a statement which had about it a finality that would allow no argument or deviation.

Joe Foster, though, whilst very aware he was down and very nearly out, fired off one final, desperate salvo in the hope of sinking his wife's iron clad resistance to his reluctance to accompany her on the shopping expedition to the big city.

"But what about Arnie, maid? What's he going to do? I mean, we always go to football together. I can't let him down like this. We always go together and stand together – have done for years, of course. I can't suddenly let him down, can I? It's not as if I'm ill, or anything, or there's an emergency or some such thing. No, I can't let him down can I – you surely see that?"

The final words were spoken in a tone he felt would appeal to her, basically, compassionate, sympathetic nature – words and intonation he felt could yet induce in her a change of heart. He was to be disappointed.

"I'm sure Arnie can find his own way to Home Park," she retorted. "He's been going there long enough."

"Well, yes – yes, of course, Beryl, but that's not the point. We go together. I mean, there cannot be more than a couple of occasions these past three seasons we've not been there together."

"Well, now there's going to be a third," came the blunt reply.

The farmer was on the very brink of defeat, and about to concede as much – when he had one final flash of inspiration and attempted, with desperation, to grasp the ultimate lifeline. "But I'm driving – I'm picking up Arnie on Saturday. His car, as you know, is out of action – needs a new gearbox and probably clutch as well. It could be out of action for a week or two – you know that, Beryl. So he's no way of getting to Argyle if I don't take him. I can't let him down, maid, can I? He certainly wouldn't let me down – nor you for that matter."

"But he will have a way of getting to Argyle, Joe, won't he," stated his wife, instantly. "He can get to Plymouth the same way as we'll be going there on Saturday – by train. That, after all, is how most folk get there including, I don't doubt, those going to Home Park. If he gets out at North Road Station, he's less than half a mile from the ground. There's no problem at all that I can see; and knowing Arnie, I cannot think he'll see any problem either. He can catch the one o'clock train – or it's around that time anyway – and he'll be in Plymouth by half past one, so in ample time for the match. We can catch the one that goes just after eleven, and be in there for an early dinner then a look around the shops. If we come back on the four-fifteen, we'll be home in time for you to help with the milking as I said earlier. I don't think, Joe, there's much more to be said about it, do you?"

She was right, there was little more which could be said so he decided that the only wise way now was to cut his losses, shrug his shoulders and manfully accept his fate. Saturday, instead of him standing on Home Park's bleak, probably rainswept terraces, would find him treading Plymouth's likewise rainswept streets – avoiding the bomb-sites which remained numerous – in the wake of a single minded spouse determined to banish the wartime habits and mentality from their lives by pursuing the kind of Christmas they had known before the great conflict.

Fate, though, was in mischievous mood – and he was destined to nudge it in his direction (something for which he did feel a

220

modicum of guilt). His salvation started to manifest itself the following morning, in the village Post Office. He'd gone to the village to get the newspapers, then, those collected, had joined the short queue next door to buy half a dozen stamps. The lady at the head of the queue was served quickly, then turned away from the counter and was in the process of walking past him, briskly, towards the door when she noticed him awaiting his turn.

"Mr Foster – oh, that's strange I should see you. I'm on my way home and when I get there I intend to phone Beryl; Will she be at home, do you know?"

The tall, spare form of Mrs Celia Maxwell, the rector's wife – and chairman of the local Women's Institute – stood before him. "Well, yes, Mrs Maxwell – as far as I know. She was there when I left about twenty minutes ago and, unless she's nipped out to do something in the yard or the outhouses, she'll be there, almost certainly."

"Good. As soon as I get to the Rectory, I'll phone her. It's just that a small emergency has arisen on the WI front – though emergency's not really the word; More that something unexpected has come up and we need to mobilise forces to tackle it." (Mrs Maxwell clearly had been considerably influenced by the constant flow of military jargon which had spewed forth from the wireless during the long, dark years of conflict.)

"You see, it's the Annual Christmas Bazaar in the Parish Hall this Saturday, organised by the Football and Cricket Clubs. It's usually quite successful – even in the war it was well patronised. We in the WI though, have not taken part for some years because in early December we've always run our own seasonal sale which has proved very, very popular for a long time. So reluctantly we decided many years ago not to take part in this bazaar, very good and well run though it is. Beryl, of course, will be well aware of this, being a member for many years. Last night, though, I had a phone call from Mr Armitage of the Football Club to tell me that suddenly they had had a withdrawal and subsequently have a stall going begging on Saturday – most unusual, as it generally is a most popular event." She shook her head in a mixture of disapproval and exasperation. "Apparently he had been told only an hour before he contacted me that the Young Wives' Group had disbanded just yesterday afternoon and so, of course, would not be taking the stall they've had there over the years. That they've disbanded doesn't surprise me in the slightest – they're down to just six members I'm told, and they're all over fifty, which hardly fits the description."

She snorted, laughed in her somewhat brisk fashion, then continued.

"It was ridiculous and thoughtless, though, to do this only three days before the bazaar. Either they should have disbanded weeks ago or carried on until after the weekend. Whatever, that's the situation – there is a stall available in the Parish Hall on Saturday and Mr Armitage has offered it to us, the WI. The bazaar is in the afternoon from one-thirty to five. I immediately made a chairman's decision and said we'd take it – it's an important event, and they have been badly let down, so I thought that being the responsible organisation we are, the least we could do would be to fill the void. Now normally we would probably have a cake and general food sale, jam and preserves as well, but there's not nearly enough time to organise that. So I thought instead we'll have jumble, bric-a-brac, white elephant – that type of thing; which is why I need to contact Beryl with some urgency, because as you know, most of all the items that have come our way over the years are stored in your farmhouse. We had that little lock up store at the back of the Parish Hall for some time, but we had to pay rent for it and, worse, it proved to be quite damp. Then you and Beryl so very kindly allowed us to store it in your house – where it all remains."

"Yes, yes, of course – I'd forgotten that. Though I'm not sure how I forgot it, as it's all in the old scullery area at the back of the kitchen – or in part of it at least. I go in there often for other things, so I should be aware of it. A good place for it – plenty of room, and because on the opposite side of one wall lies the Rayburn, that wall is always warm, so keeps the scullery warm – and damp free as well."

"Indeed it does, Mr Foster. And it really is appreciated that you have it there cluttering up the place – and charge no rent. Still, the situation now is that we need to raid the store to select items for the stall on Saturday. I mean, it's Thursday today so we've only forty-eight hours. A few of us need to come along tomorrow to pick through it – that's if it's convenient to Beryl and yourself, of course – ready for Saturday morning. Seeing as it's stored in your house I thought that Beryl would probably want to be involved in everything – and not just in picking over the items, but in manning the stall on Saturday as well. She's always a hard worker, anyway, is Beryl, and does like taking part in things. So that's why I need to contact her – to find out when it would be convenient for us to come out to the farm, and also to see if she will be able to help out in the Parish Hall on Saturday. You don't happen to know, Mr Foster, if she has anything special arranged for Saturday, do you?"

Joe Foster paused before answering. For this, potentially, was a moment to savour. Salvation, like the cavalry, could well be galloping to his rescue, sweeping down from the hilltop to put to the sword the fiery dragon of Christmas shopping which threatened to incinerate him just two days hence. He decided the way forward would be to avoid giving any information – that way he'd not tell a lie.

"Well, as I said just now Mrs Maxwell, you'll find her at home. Only she can say whether or not she'll be available tomorrow and Saturday, so it's best you phone her as soon as possible, so that you can both make plans. There's no time to be lost as you so rightly say."

"Quite so," she agreed. "I've done all my shopping so I'll be off home right away and phone Beryl the instant I get there. Thank you, Mr Foster, and good morning to you."

With that she was gone – never a lady to tarry, the rector's wife, unlike her husband, a genial, gentle, exceedingly likeable Christian gentleman who, whilst he was an excellent preacher – able, when in the mood, to threaten sinners with 'Hellfire and Damnation', which delighted his substantial congregation – was quite an indolent man, lacking ambition in terms of furthering his career, and, at times, ministering to his flock with a touch less zeal than some country parsons.

The farmer, his stamps purchased, dropped into Lol Parnell's fusty barbershop for a much needed haircut, so it was the best part of an hour before he arrived back at the farm. No sooner had he entered the kitchen in search of a cup of tea to alleviate the raw late autumn weather, than his wife, just putting pasties into the oven, updated him with the latest news.

"I've just had Celia Maxwell on the phone Joe. She said she saw you in the queue at the Post Office a bit earlier. I don't know if she told you about the bazaar on Saturday?"

"Well, no, not really – I mean she rattles on at such a rate it's not always easy to follow exactly what she's on about. I know it's something about the jumble we've got stored here and so forth." He answered her question with masterly vagueness, then awaited the report of her conversation with the WI chairman. It came, instantly.

She spoke of everything the rector's wife had told him, then said that she felt obliged to help with the sorting of the motley goods and – the glorious tidings as far as he was concerned – with the stall on the Saturday. "So, we'll not be able to go shopping in Plymouth – we'll have to put it off to the following weekend."

He accepted the news with a masterly show of disinterest. "Fair enough, maid – it's up to you, of course. I'll grab a quick cup of tea a minute, then go out and give Tiddler Tom a help feeding round. Stock need full bellies this time of year."

The big iron kettle perpetually being either boiled, or near to it, on one of the large hotplates, he was soon swallowing the hot, sweet beverage – plus consuming a couple of Rich Tea biscuits – before heading out to pursue his business, a spring in his step, his heart lightened considerably thanks to the phone call from the rector's spouse.

Fate, 'fickle jade' that it was, certainly favoured him, for he was destined to avoid Christmas shopping in Plymouth entirely. For Beryl went to Tavistock the following Wednesday, when he went to the Cattle Market. She took herself around the shops and – to her surprise and his delight – found a couple with totally fresh stock; clothes, toys and other items which fulfilled her requirements, so she bought them. A pre-festive shopping journey to Plymouth became unnecessary – though she did promise herself a good look around the city in the early New Year when there would be a few sales on. There was also good news for Tiddler Tom and Rollo; for Beryl saw nothing in the shops which she thought would be suitable for them, so they ended up with what assuredly they desired – a goodly quantity of Christmas fare and scrumpy, not a shirt, tie or even worse.

As Arnie and he negotiated the tortuous roads leading to the Peninsula on that Saturday afternoon, however, at about the same time Beryl would have been helping to pack up the WI stall at the Christmas Bazaar, Joe was by no means certain that Dame Fortune had smiled upon him to the extent he had anticipated. For he realised that he had avoided a pleasant, leisurely dinner with his wife in a decent restaurant, followed by a none too stressful perusal of the contents of well warmed shops, to spend the afternoon at Home Park, standing on barren terraces being watered, incessantly, by an icy drizzle, all in the cause of witnessing his beloved Plymouth Argyle playing like a fourth class pub team, getting battered by Nottingham Forest to the tune of five goals to nil. Oh well, it could only get better – but when, nobody knew.